This one's for Taffy…
You've always believed in me.
My sister. My best friend.

Special Thanks to everyone who made this book possible:

As always, my biggest thanks must go to my loving husband who supports me sacrificially and without question or complaint. He's my in-house specialist in all things guns, police, and military related.
I love you.

Thanks to my best friend, Megan, who's the best beta reader anyone could ask for.

Thanks to EVERYONE who read and loved The Soul Summoner. This journey is going to keep getting better.

MY AWESOME LAUNCH TEAM
THE BOOK SUMMONERS
I would be nowhere without you! (Alphabetically):
Nikki Allen, Elsbeth Balas, Karla Barker, Tracie Bechard, Connor J. Bedell, Lilia Bingham, Betty Bowers, Cindy Brown, Gabriela Cabezut, Tiffany Cagle, Marsha Carmichael, Shweta Chopra, RK Close, Céleste Couture, Lisa Cowens, May Freighter, Sarah Gillaspie, Venice Gilmore, Rick Gottinger, Melody Hall, Lina Hanson, Bridget Hickey, Kira Hodge, Wendy Howell, Paula Hurdle, Misi Hurst, Susan Huttinger, Ashley Huttinger, Kristin Jacques, Ara James, Deborah Jay, Tango Jordan, John K. Park, Erani Kole, Debra L. Rutschman, Erica Laurie, Linda Levine, Rena Lott, Juliet Lyons, Lori Mahan, Chuck Mason, Sal Mason, Kellie Milon, Michel Moore, Susan Oates, Tammy Oja, Teresa Partridge, Wendy Pyatt, Jenny Quinn, Lucy Rhodes, Megan Robinson,, Marsha Sanderlin, Lisa Shaw, Vandi Shelton, Ana Simons, Sherry Skiles, Stephanie Smith, Rata Stevens-Robinette, Heather Grace Stewart, Ann Stewart-Akers, Debbie Stout, Leigh W. Stuart, Angela Tinkham, Nina van Vlierden, Ana Victoria Lopez, Ronnie Waldrop, Susie Waldrop, Lennie Warren, Shanna Whitten, Russ Williams, Stephanie Williams, K. Williams, Bridgett Wilson, Natalie Wolicki, Terrilynne Work, Ann Writes

Book 1 - The Soul Summoner
Book 2 - The Siren

Standalone Novella - The Detective
FREE at www.EliciaHyder.com

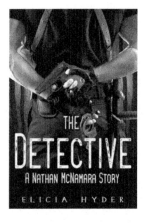

1.

WHOMP WHOMP WHOMP WHOMP WHOMP.
CLACK, CLACK. EEEENG! EEEENG! EEEENG!

"This is a test. This is only a test of the Emergency Broadcast System." I was practicing my best radio announcer's voice.

"Sloan, stop talking," my father said through his microphone. "And please, lie still."

Lying still was becoming increasingly more difficult with each second that passed. I had been trapped inside the deafening MRI machine for more than twenty minutes. My father had insisted on the test after my last hemiplegic migraine, but I knew its results would be as useless as the last two CT scans he had ordered. There was nothing wrong with my brain, and there was nothing wrong with me...except it seemed I had the power to read and control people's souls. That, however, had nothing to do with my migraines that I was aware of.

The trigger for my latest headache was the same as the others: Warren Parish had left town. He and I seemed to be bound together by an electrifying force, and when we were apart, paralyzing migraines were the penalty.

The MRI was going to be inconclusive.

When the machine stopped whirring and knocking like the inside of a drag racer's engine, I wiggled my feet from side to side. "Are we done yet?"

"All done," Dad said. The MRI table slid slowly out of the electronic cave I had been confined to.

My father was fascinated and terribly worried by my new development of headaches, but I knew telling him the truth wouldn't help. My adoptive parents were incredibly loving and supportive, but they were also medical professionals who believed everything had a scientific explanation. Being that my father was a geriatric physician who specialized in dementia, I knew what his diagnosis would be—mental instability.

Dad walked into the room as I sat up on the table and adjusted my twisted gown. Even in his fifties, he was still movie-star handsome with the brightest blue eyes I'd ever seen. He was looking down at a sheet of paper in his hand. "You can get dressed."

I held the back of my gown closed while I stood up. "What did the test show? Is it all sawdust and rocks up there?"

Dad rolled his eyes. "Nothing stood out to me, but I'm going to have a friend of mine in neurology look over it to be sure."

I put my hand on his arm and looked up at him. "Dad, I'm fine."

He kissed my forehead. "I can't be too careful with you. You're the only Sloan I've got." He started toward the door. "Do you want to grab lunch before you head to work? I have another hour or so before my first patient of the afternoon."

I looked at the clock on the wall. I had told my boss

that I would be in around noon, and it was already after eleven. "Will you be terribly heartbroken if I skip lunch this time? I want to pop in and check on Adrianne before I go to the office, if that's OK."

He smiled. "Of course. Give her my love, and tell her I'll drop in to see her sometime this week," he said. "I'll see you at dinner tonight?"

I nodded. "I'll be there."

"Will Warren be joining us?" he called as I shuffled toward the door in my socks.

I looked back and shrugged. "I'm not sure. He's flying back in from D.C. sometime today, but I can't remember when his flight lands. I'll let Mom know if he gets back in time."

"All right, sweetheart. We'll see you later," he said.

Adrianne Marx, my best friend, had been a resident of the hospital for almost three weeks since the guy she was dating decided to drive drunk and flip his Jeep into a highway guard rail. I had knocked out his front teeth in return and none of us had seen him since.

When I got to her room, she was reading a trashy tabloid magazine and munching on potato chips. Her hair was finally starting to grow back from where they had to shave it, and aside from the pink scars left by the stitches, her face looked almost back to normal.

I rapped my knuckles against the open door. "Knock, knock."

She looked up and smiled. "Hey, weirdo." She shifted against her mound of pillows as I crossed in front of her feet and plopped down in the chair by her bed. "What are you doing here?"

"I just had an MRI upstairs. I thought I would swing by and say hello before I went to work."

She sat up in her bed. "An MRI? I thought you just

had a few broken bones and some stitches?"

Barely two weeks before, Warren and I had helped Detective Nathan McNamara take down a serial killer who had been murdering women across the state of North Carolina for over a decade. Billy Stewart had drugged me, beaten me, and then dragged me to his Bundy-style, secret body-stashing spot where he planned on raping and burying me in the woods. Thanks to Warren's ability to track down dead bodies and Nathan's protective instincts, I walked away with only a few broken ribs, nerve damage in my hands, and enough gashes on my arms and legs to potentially keep me in pants for the rest of my life.

I shook my head. "Dad wanted the MRI because he's worried about my migraines. I had another really bad one on Sunday."

Her head tilted to the side. "So Warren is gone?"

"Yeah. He had to go to Washington for a meeting at the Pentagon."

She folded the open end of her bag of chips and laid it on the bedside table. "That sounds alarming. What do they want with him?"

I shrugged. "I'm sure they want to know how he tracked down all those missing girls."

Her eyes widened. "I wonder how he's going to explain that."

I laughed, though I was more worried than amused. "I don't know, but I don't think telling them he can *feel death* is going to cut it."

"Probably not," she agreed. "When he left, did you puke all over the detective again?"

Heat rose in my cheeks at either the embarrassing memory of my last migraine or at just the simple thought of Nathan McNamara. I wasn't sure which. My endocrine system had been thoroughly confused since Warren and Nathan came to town. "No. I was with my parents, and I didn't puke on anyone this time."

"How is Nathan?" she asked.

I leaned against the armrest. "I guess he's doing OK. I haven't seen him in a few days. This week he's in Greensboro looking for Billy's last victim on our list who hasn't been found."

"Which one is she?" she asked.

"Rachel Smith. She was reported missing by her co-workers in 2008. She didn't have any known relatives, so her case went cold pretty fast. She was a social worker," I said.

Adrianne shook her head. "That's so sad."

"Let's talk about something else, please." I was desperate to change the subject. Talking about the whole case still made me feel squeamish.

She nodded. "OK. How's the boy drama?"

"Oh, it's still drama." I sighed. "Warren finished moving all his stuff into my house this week. He put his furniture in storage over in West Asheville, but all his clothes and his many weapons are at my house. My guest room looks like a freaking armory."

She looked at me sideways. "Are you planning on living together, like long term?"

I laughed and shrugged my shoulders. "I haven't planned anything with Warren up until this point, and life hasn't exactly allowed for a lot of forethought and decision-making. I don't know what we're doing."

She raised an eyebrow. "What does Nathan think about it?"

I sat back in my seat. "I have no idea. It's not like we have heart-to-heart discussions on the subject. He still comes by the house and my office all the time, so I guess it hasn't fazed him too much."

"Is he still dating Shannon?" she asked.

ELICIA HYDER

The muscles tensed in my jaw at the mention of Nathan's girlfriend because if I had a nemesis, Shannon Green would be it. But that bitterness was rooted a lot deeper than in just her relationship with Nathan. His presence only added fuel to embers that had been smoldering for over a decade.

I rolled my eyes. "I guess they're still together, but you would never know it. He's always around, and she's never with him. And he doesn't talk about her at all."

Adrianne held out her hands. "Why is he with her?"

My brow lifted in question. "I've been asking the same thing for a while now."

"What does Warren say about Nathan showing up all the time?" she asked.

"He doesn't say much. They actually spend more time together than Nathan and I do these days. Warren's been helping recover the missing victims, and aside from their constant ping-ponging of insults back and forth, they've actually become pretty good friends. They love to hate each other."

"I've noticed," she said. "To be honest, I kind of feel bad for Nate. He's crazy about you, and then Warren showed up and it was over with you guys before it even got started."

I nodded. "I know. Warren came into town like a hurricane." I chewed on my pinky nail. "Wanna hear a secret?"

She scooted forward in her bed. "Of course."

I pointed a warning finger at her. "And you promise to take it to the grave?"

She crossed her heart. "I swear."

I lowered my voice. "I keep thinking about that night in the woods when Nathan dove in front of that bullet for me. He could have died trying to save me. That's love on a whole different level."

"Are you having second thoughts about you and Warren?" she asked.

I shook my head. "No. That's what makes it so hard. I genuinely care about them both, but it's too different with Warren for there to even be a competition. He's like gravity or oxygen. I can't *not* be with him."

"You guys are really intense," she said.

I tapped my finger against my forehead. "Intense enough for migraines." I laughed. "Enough about my supernatural soap opera. How are you doing?"

"I'm doing OK. I started physical therapy yesterday which sucked more than you could ever imagine," she said with a groan. "But they are talking like I'll be able to go home maybe tomorrow or the next day."

"That's awesome," I said.

She nodded. "Yeah. They are all pretty shocked at how fast I've recovered. Most of them didn't think I would live, much less be walking out of here anytime soon." She eyed me suspiciously from the bed. "I'm pretty sure I have you to thank for that."

I shrugged. "Who knows?"

"Sloan, you're the only one I remember being here during the beginning of all this. I remember you being in my room when I still couldn't even talk," she said. "It was like I could feel you right here next to me."

"Really?" I asked, surprised.

She smiled. "Yeah. I think Warren is on to something. I think you healed me."

"Well, I wouldn't say 'healed' necessarily." I laughed. "Have you seen your hair today?"

She threw a pillow at me. "Shut up."

"So, what are you going to do when you get out of here? Go back to your apartment?" I asked.

She shook her head. "Not for a while. I can't get up and down the stairs yet. I'll probably stay with my parents till I'm fully recuperated."

ELICIA HYDER

"And what about work?" I asked.

She shrugged. "They're holding my booth at the salon, but it will probably be a while before I can be on my feet all day again."

I leaned forward and put my hand on her broken leg.

"Are you putting your voodoo on me?" she asked with a smile.

I winked at her. "It can't hurt."

* * *

It was noon when I got to my office at the county building downtown. Most everyone was gone to lunch, leaving the halls unnervingly quiet. As I hurried to my office, I kept a careful watch back over my shoulder. My father would call it PTSD from my recent attack. I would call it common sense after all I'd been through. In my rush to unlock the door, I almost missed the yellow sticky note attached just above eye-level. *Call me when you get in. -Sheriff Davis.*

I pulled the note down as I walked into my office. "That's odd."

After tucking my briefcase under my desk and turning on my computer, I dialed the direct line to the sheriff's office at the jail. I prayed he wasn't going to ask me to come by. My gift never felt more like a curse than when I was in that building. The jail, with all the dark souls locked inside it, was a panic incubator for a girl like me.

"Sheriff Davis." His gruff voice was more like a bark than a greeting.

I sat back in my office chair. "Hey, Sheriff. It's Sloan. I just got the sticky note you left on my door."

"Hello, Sloan. How are you feeling?" he asked.

I smiled. "I'm healing up pretty well. I still have a few itchy scars on my legs, and I haven't gotten all the feeling back in my hands, but it could be a lot worse." Billy Stewart, the serial killer, had dragged me by a pair of steel handcuffs through the woods, causing extensive nerve damage in my hands. The doctors said the numbness and tingling could last for up to a year.

"Well, I'm glad to hear you're on the mend. Listen, I've been trying to get in touch with Detective McNamara all morning. You seem to always know where he's at, even though *I'm* his boss. Got any idea where I can find him?" he asked.

I thought for a second. "I talked to him yesterday, and he said he would be up in the woods all day in Greensboro. He probably doesn't have cell phone service."

"Yeah, that's what I figured," he said. "I thought you might both want to know a report came across my desk this morning that they found a third body on Billy Stewart's property in Stephens County, Georgia. They believe it's a twenty-three-year-old female who disappeared from a camping trip last year."

My mouth fell open. "You're joking?"

"This isn't really a joking subject, Sloan."

"I know it isn't. That just means we were wrong about the last victim—the one who is still missing on our list." I thought of Nathan and his team who were still trudging through the forest looking for a body that wasn't there.

"Either that or there are more victims than we initially thought," he said.

I knew for a fact there were only twelve victims. It was part of Warren's gift. Of course, I couldn't explain that to Sheriff Davis without sounding like a lunatic.

"Perhaps you're right, Sheriff."

"Tell McNamara to call me," he said.

"I will." He hung up his phone before I could say goodbye.

I yanked my cell phone out of my purse and dialed Nathan's number. It went straight to voicemail, so I left a message. "Hey, it's Sloan. You can come home. You're not going to find a body in Greensboro. The sheriff called and said they recovered a third body on Billy Stewart's property in Georgia, so she must be victim number twelve, not Rachel Smith. Call your boss. Bye."

I ended the call and dialed Warren's number. He answered on the first ring. "Perfect timing. I just got off the plane," he said by way of a greeting.

"In Asheville?" I asked.

"Charlotte. I have an hour layover, and then I'll be home."

Home. It was strange to hear him say it out loud.

"How are you?" he asked. "Did you sleep better last night?"

"I'll sleep better once you're back." That was the truth. I'd had nightmares about my abduction almost every night Warren had been gone.

"I'll be there tonight," he said. "Are you at work?"

"Yep. I just got here," I said. "I had that stupid MRI this morning."

"How did that go?"

"Oh, it was long and very boring. Dad said he didn't see anything wrong, but he's going to have some more doctors look at it."

"Are you ever going to tell him the truth?" he asked.

"I don't know. Dad believes so much in modern medicine he would never accept this is beyond explanation. He would probably have me committed to the psych ward."

Warren laughed. "That's highly unlikely. He loves you and he's worried. I think you should tell him."

I scrunched up my nose at the idea. He was right and I knew it, but just the thought of that conversation was daunting, no matter how loving I knew my parents were. "I'll think about it." I drummed my nails on my desk. "So, what time will you be back here?"

"My flight lands sometime around three, so I should be back before you get off work at five," he said.

I smiled. "Great! We're having dinner at my parents' house tonight."

He groaned. "Do we have to? I was planning on us staying at home. We've got a lot to talk about."

The tone of his voice was alarming. I didn't like it at all. "We do?"

"This wasn't a leisure trip, babe," he said.

My blood pressure jumped up a few points. I decided avoidance was the best course of action. "Well, it's gonna have to wait. I promised my parents I would come because I haven't been at all since you moved in. And they keep badgering me about when you're coming to see them again."

He sighed. "OK. I'll go to the house and change when I get back in town. You can pick me up on your way."

"All right," I said. "Guess what."

"What?"

"Rachel Smith wasn't Billy's victim. They found a third body in Georgia."

"Interesting," he said. "So that's all of them, then?"

Leaning back in my chair, I stared at the halogen light above my desk. "That's all of them."

"Did you let Nate know?"

"I tried, but the call went to voicemail. Have you talked to him?" I asked.

He chuckled. "Sure. He called earlier to ask how my trip was going and what the weather was like in Washington and if I'd gotten a good night's sleep…"

I rolled my eyes. "Oh, shut up."

"I'll see you in a few hours, Sloan."

"Bye." I disconnected the call.

On the desktop of my computer, I clicked open the missing persons file Nathan had sent me. It contained all the victims we had originally believed had been murdered by Billy Stewart. I found Rachel Smith's folder and opened it. I printed off her picture and her missing report which had been filed in 2008. She was twenty-four when she disappeared, beautiful with long, dark hair and light brown eyes. Her co-workers at Child Protective Services in Greensboro, North Carolina reported her missing. There was a note that no family had been found or notified of her disappearance.

For a moment, I stared out the window behind my desk and wondered what had become of her. The upper side of downtown Asheville was poised against the colorful fall backdrop of the North Carolina mountain range. The forest in the distance was popping with gold, orange, and bright red trees.

It reminded me I had work to do.

The fall tourist season was in full swing in Asheville, and the Buncombe County event calendar needed to be updated. I tucked Rachel's sheets into my briefcase and turned toward my keyboard to attempt to type with the few fingers I still had control over.

* * *

Warren was waiting on my front porch when I pulled up to the curb after work. He had showered, and his shoulder-length black hair was still wet and tied back in a ponytail. He was six-foot-three with oh-point-no body fat, and he had a chiseled tan face and killer black eyes—literally. He shared a lot of my strange abilities, but his gift was more specific, practiced, and frightening than mine. I could summon the living; he could find the dead. I had the ability to heal people, and he could kill them with a glance.

Warren was like antifreeze: effective, delicious, and absolutely deadly.

I felt a little dizzy just watching him come down my

stairs.

When he opened the passenger side door and angled inside, my eyes nearly rolled back in my head as his ice cool cologne filled my car. "Gah, you smell good."

He leaned over and gave me a welcoming kiss on the lips. The familiar buzz of his touch zinged through me. "I've missed you," he said, smiling when he pulled away.

I savored the taste of his kiss. "I don't wanna go see my parents now."

He laughed and moved his seat back as far as it would go to accommodate his long legs. "You said we had to."

I dropped my head back against the headrest. "We do have to, or I'll never hear the end of it." I put the car in drive and pulled away from the curb before I could talk myself out of going. "What did they want with you in Washington?"

He didn't look at me. "Too much to tell for a short car ride. We'll talk about it later."

I frowned. "Should I be worried?"

Reaching across the car, he squeezed my shoulder. "Of course not, babe. How was work today?"

I relaxed back in my seat. "Boring. After hunting down missing people and serial killers, I'm not sure how I'll ever be satisfied with county newsletters and press releases again."

With his long arm still draped across the back of my neck, he began twisting strands of my long brown hair around his fingers. "Maybe we should go into private investigating," he suggested. "We could work together."

I raised my eyebrows. "The only problem is none of our tactics would ever be explainable in court," I said. "I would love to see the look on a judge's face when I say 'my boyfriend is sort of like a human cadaver dog.' That's totally plausible, right?"

He stopped twisting my hair and grinned at me.

"What?"

He shrugged. "I just like it when you call me your boyfriend."

Rolling my eyes, I shook my head. "You know, for you being such a badass, you're more of a girl than I am sometimes."

He laughed, but he withdrew his arm and shoved me playfully in the shoulder. "So, what's on the agenda at your folks' house tonight?" he asked.

I shook my head as I turned onto the main highway. "Nothing special. Just Monday night dinner."

His head whipped toward me. "But it's Tuesday."

I grinned. "I think Mom moved it on purpose because she knew you'd be gone."

The house smelled like roast beef and Mom's secret-ingredient mashed potatoes when Warren and I walked through the front door. It smelled so good I could have licked the air. Mom had once promised to divulge the secret if I ever took the time to learn how to cook. My cooking skill set extended to being able to burn toast and make coffee. Someday I knew I would make time, but until then I would have Monday night dinners at their house, and I had Warren at home. He was almost as good of a cook as my mother.

"Hello! Hello!" I called from the foyer.

Mom's gray head peeked around the corner of the kitchen. "Hey! Come on in! Hi, Warren!"

Warren wiped his shoes on the welcome mat. "Hello, Mrs. Jordan."

She put a hand on her hip and shot him a teasing smirk. "How many times do I have to tell you to call me Audrey?"

He laughed. "A few more, Mrs. Jordan."

Tugging on Warren's hand, I led him to the kitchen. Dad stood up from the table where he was reading a thick book. I walked over and gave him a kiss on the cheek. "Hi,

Daddy."

"Hey, sweetheart." He shook Warren's hand. "It's good to see you again, Warren."

"Thank you, sir. It's good to see you as well." Warren smiled politely. "Thanks for letting me crash dinner."

"Nonsense. You're always welcome here," Dad said. "How was your trip?"

I couldn't discern Warren's face. The man could make a killing at poker.

He cleared his throat. "It's cold in Washington."

Mom laughed. "I'm sure it is." She stepped over to give him a side-arm hug. My tiny mother fit neatly under the hook of Warren's strong arm. It made me smile.

"Whatcha readin', Dad?" I asked as I pulled out a chair next to his.

He held up the book so I could see the cover. "Hemiplegic Migraine Symptoms, Pathogenesis, and Treatments," he read aloud.

Warren caught my eye and cocked an eyebrow.

My shoulders slumped. "Dad, we need to talk."

He took off his reading glasses. "About what, sweetheart?"

I reached over and closed the book. "You're not going to find the answer to my headaches in here."

"How can you be so sure?" he asked.

My mother put the roast on the table. "Come and sit down. You two can talk while we eat. I don't want dinner to get cold."

When our places were set and our plates were full, my father looked to me for an explanation. "Now, back to the headaches. What did you want to tell me?"

Warren reached over and gave my hand a reassuring squeeze.

My mother noticed his show of support, and she put

her fork down. "Is everything OK?"

I nodded before drawing in a deep breath. I carefully looked at both my parents. "It's not a tumor. It's not weak blood vessels that are going to rupture. And it's not an injury. You're not going to find the answer in a book or on a CT scan or on an MRI image."

My parents exchanged confused glances.

"Then what is it?" Dad asked.

"It's something supernatural."

2.

Certain memories will always be crystal clear in my mind. Watching the jets crash into the World Trade Center is one. Seeing Warren for the first time and wondering if he was actually dead is another. But even international terrorism and an animated corpse could never compare to seeing the look on my father's face when I chose the word *supernatural* to explain my migraines. I was pretty certain I would've gotten the same reaction had I told him I could burp rainbows and spit out golden coins.

Beside me, Warren snickered.

"Supernatural?" my mother repeated, to be sure she had heard me correctly.

I looked to Warren for help, but he put his hands up in resignation and chuckled. "You're on your own here."

Dad leaned forward on his elbows and pushed his untouched dinner plate out of the way. "Please explain, dear."

My palms were starting to sweat. "You guys love me, right?"

"Of course we do," Mom said.

"And I'm not prone to lying or hallucinations or being dramatic, right?"

Dad shook his head. "No."

I looked at both of them. "Do you remember why we left Florida when I was eight?"

Simultaneously, their expressions melted.

My eyebrows rose. "I think it's time we talk about it."

Mom's mouth was smiling, but her eyes were not. "We moved because your father got a job here."

I leveled my gaze at her. "We moved because I was attacked on the playground." I rubbed the scar over my eyebrow. "We moved because people were figuring out I was different."

Dad held up his hand. "Sloan, you were having problems at school, but let's not dramatize it. We did believe a change of setting would be beneficial for you, but we didn't move here just because the other kids were giving you a hard time."

I cut my eyes toward him and held both hands up in question. "You never sent me back to that school, and we packed up and moved a week later."

He shook his head. "It's still not the whole reason we moved." He folded his arms on top of the table. "Don't you think we love you enough to at least talk to you about it if we were *that* worried?"

For that, I didn't have an answer. "Didn't you ever wonder what was wrong with me?"

His brow scrunched together, and his lips bent in a deep frown. "Sweetheart, there's nothing wrong with you. But I do have some good friends at the hospital if you want to talk to—"

Cutting Dad off, I pointed at him and looked at Warren. "See? I told you he'd try to have me committed."

Warren covered his face with his hands, his shoulders

shaking with silent laughter.

Dad pushed his chair back a few inches, clearly not as amused as we were. "I'm not trying to have you committed."

I smiled. "I know." I leaned on my elbow. "Do you want to hear what I have to say or are we going to pretend that this, too, never happened?"

He looked like he wanted to argue or berate me for the snide remark, but he didn't. He gave a slight nod instead. "Please continue. Tell me all about your supernatural headaches."

Here goes nothing...

I sucked in a deep breath. "I have some sort of sixth sense. I *know* people before I meet them. It's kind of like when you see someone at the grocery store who looks familiar, but you can't remember their name or how you met them. You know what I'm talking about?"

My mother nodded hesitantly.

"Well, I'm like that with everyone. I don't meet strangers. It's like I can already see a person for who they really are on the inside before I ever even speak to them." I turned my palms up on the table. "I think I have the ability to see people's souls."

All the blood drained from my father's handsome face, and I'm pretty sure Mom almost fainted.

I shifted uneasily on my chair. "Anyway, it's how I found that little girl, Kayleigh Neeland, and it's how I helped find that serial killer and those missing girls. I knew they were dead as soon as Detective McNamara showed me their pictures."

Neither of them spoke.

"I know this all sounds crazy, but the headaches aren't explainable, except it has something to do with Warren and I being separated. Every time he's left town, it has happened to both of us," I said.

They turned their puzzled eyes on Warren who, in turn, scooted his chair back a few inches. He cautiously raised his hands in defense. "She's right, but I'm not causing it."

My mother rolled her eyes. "That's preposterous."

"It happens every single time, Mom. I swear."

Her mouth was still gaping. "That's highly coincidental then."

"Mom, it's not a coincidence," I said. "Tell her, Warren."

Warren shook his head. "I'm staying out of this."

My dad looked like *he* was getting a migraine. "So, Warren, do you have this sixth sense as well?"

Warren hesitated. "Yes, sir." I doubted he would be willing to elaborate on the differences between his gift and mine. I was right. Warren didn't say another word.

My mother was staring at her plate like it might get up and walk right off the table. Dad took off his glasses and pinched the bridge of his nose, pressing his eyes shut. Warren, whose mouth was clamped closed so tight that his lips turned white, appeared to be counting the number of steps to the closest exit.

I put my hands in my lap. "I know this is a lot to take in. I just don't want you worrying that I'm going to have an aneurysm and die or anything. It's not normal, but I don't think it's life-threatening." I looked at my father. "Dad, I'm not crazy."

He slowly opened his eyes and focused on me. His expression was inscrutable, but he reached out and squeezed my shoulder. "I know." He sat back in his seat and looked at my mother. "This is just a little hard to…" His voice faded as he searched for the right word.

"Believe," I said, filling in the blank.

He shook his head adamantly. "No. It's a lot to process, Sloan, but I'll never doubt you." He nodded toward Mom.

"We've always known you were special."

Mom's shoulders seemed to relax a bit. She nodded in agreement but didn't elaborate.

For several moments, the table was quiet. It wasn't awkward or tense, but I was desperate to know what my parents were thinking about.

Finally, Mom's gentle laugh broke the silence. "You terrified me as a child," she said. "We would go to the grocery store or the mall, and you would just take off and start talking to people."

Dad chuckled. "I remember that. The stranger-danger talk with you was completely pointless."

Mom put her hand on Dad's arm. "Robert, do you remember Mean Santa?"

Laughing, Dad dropped his face into his hands. "How could I forget?"

I had no idea what they were talking about. "Mean Santa?"

Mom leaned forward. "You were maybe four or five, I guess, and we took you to the annual Christmas party with the hospital staff. Every year, they had a Santa there for the kids to have their picture taken with. Naturally, we waited in line with you so you could sit on Santa's lap. When it was your turn, your dad lifted you up and put you on Santa's knee." She paused and covered her mouth to stifle a giggle. "You looked right at the man and said, 'You're not Santa.' When he tried to argue, you fired right back, wagging a finger in his face and everything. You told him, 'Santa is jolly and you are not jolly. You're a mean Santa.'"

I laughed. "Really?"

Dad nodded. "And you were right. I had to work with that Santa for a few years, and he's one of the most hateful men I've ever met."

I shook my head. "I don't remember that at all."

Mom's laughter slowly subsided, and she reached across the table to take my hand. "Like your dad said, we've always known you were special, in the very best way."

Tears prickled the corners of my eyes. "Thank you."

Dad held up a finger. "And while we did not leave Florida just over the incident at your school, we did believe you'd be better off growing up in a smaller town." His eyes softened. "We probably should have tried harder to talk to you about all this, but you must understand that we really didn't know what we were dealing with. To us, you were simply very outgoing and intuitive. Your behavior was different but not alarming, so we agreed to not press the issue as long as you seemed healthy and happy. I hope we weren't wrong in that decision."

I shook my head. "Honestly, I'm kind of glad you didn't make a bigger deal out of it. I already felt like enough of a freak."

Warren's arm slid across my shoulders. "And I, for one, think she turned out just fine."

We exchanged smiles and a quick kiss.

Mom's eyes widened and she pointed at us. "This is why you had the blood test done! This is why you wondered if you were related."

I nodded.

Dad's eyes narrowed. "I know how you met, but how did you ever find each other?"

Warren leaned into me. "I saw her on the news when she saved that little girl. Like she said, we have a sense about people just by looking at them. I couldn't read her at all."

I looked at him. "And I thought Warren was a zombie when he first showed up in town."

My mother ran her hand down her face.

I smiled. "It's not as creepy as it sounds."

"So, who all knows about this?" Dad asked.

I looked around the table. "Well, us. And Adrianne and Nathan."

Mom's eyes widened. "The detective knows?"

I nodded. "Yeah. I sort of let it slip when we first met."

"That's a hell of a slip, isn't it?" Dad asked.

"A life-changing one," I agreed.

Dad's expression softened. "Maybe it was time."

Warren squeezed my hand.

I smiled. "Maybe it was."

* * *

"Well, that went better than I expected," Warren said when we walked out of the house after dinner. As we walked to the driveway, he wrapped his arm around my waist, hooking his thumb into one of my belt loops. "Not nearly as bad as you have feared all these years, correct?"

I shook my head. "Not at all."

He glanced back toward the house. "They're pretty great, you know?"

A warm tingle of gratitude rippled through me. "*Great* doesn't do them justice."

He looked down at me. "What exactly happened when you got that scar? It seems odd to me that other kids wouldn't like you."

I nodded. "I know. I've always thought it was weird. But there was this one kid, Ivan Moots, who always picked on me. I'll never forget him. He's the one who threw the rock and split my face open."

"Why?"

I shrugged my shoulders. "Don't know, really. I kind of had a meltdown one day at school because of this horrible substitute teacher who was put in my classroom." Looking up at him, I widened my eyes. "She was so scary my parents had to come and get me. The next day on the playground, Ivan was worse than ever, teasing me, calling me names...He and a couple of his friends started throwing rocks at me while I was on the swings." I touched my brow. "He hit his target."

"Seriously?" We reached the car, and he turned to face me. "That's horrible."

"Yep. Knocked me off backward." My body shuddered. "It was awful."

"Want me to hunt the bastard down?" He was grinning as he looked down at me.

I relaxed and smiled. "No, but thank you anyway."

He pulled me close and pressed a kiss into my hair. "I say we go home, open a bottle of wine, and take a bubble bath."

I rested my head against his chest. "That sounds like heaven."

He held out his hand. "Give me the keys. I drive faster than you."

Laughing, I kissed his perfect lips.

When he turned onto my street, a familiar tan SUV was parked in front of my house. Completely against my will, butterflies took flight in my stomach.

I looked at Warren. "Did you know he was coming?"

Warren laughed. "Do I ever?"

We parked in the driveway, and when we walked back around front, Nathan McNamara was waiting on the sidewalk. He wore camouflage pants and a black fitted shirt. On his blond head, was an olive green ball cap that had a space on the front for interchangeable embroidered patches to suit his mood. That day, the patch was a grayscale American flag signaling he was on duty.

"What are you doing here?" I asked as we approached.

He spread out his arms. "I haven't seen you all week and that's the kind of greeting I get?"

I nodded and walked past him up the stairs. "Yes, when you show up uninvited and unannounced."

"Sloan, you know you've missed me." He followed Warren and me up the stairs. "Warren, I'm a little surprised to see you back from Washington so soon. I figured they would have found you a nice warm bed in Area 51 by now."

"Sorry. You're not that lucky." Warren handed me my keychain and added some dramatic flair while pulling out his own keys from his pocket. "I've got the door, babe."

Nathan noticed. "Do you have a quota of times per day you need to remind me you live here now?"

I huffed. "Not this again. Don't even start, Nathan." Warren was smiling, and I pointed at him. "And you quit trying to stir up crap!"

Warren laughed and pushed the door open.

There was a fine line between admiration and loathing between Warren and Nathan. They secretly liked each other, but with me in the middle, they would never admit it. Warren and I were together, but there was a very gray area with Nathan McNamara. And everyone knew it.

After kicking off my shoes at the front door, I walked around to my white sofa. I plopped down and put my socked feet up on the coffee table. "What's up, Nathan?"

Warren went to the kitchen, and Nathan sat down next to me. He leaned forward and rested his elbows on his knees, locking his fingers in front of him. "I got your message today about Rachel Smith."

I frowned. "You could have told me that in a text message."

He smiled. "I thought you should know I'm going to continue to investigate her disappearance."

"Good for you," I said and closed my eyes.

He nudged my leg with his knee. "You know you want to help me."

I shook my head but refused to look at him. "No, I don't. I'm done with police work and missing people and murderers—"

He cut me off. "You want to sit behind a desk and exchange emails with reporters and government officials all day? Keep working on the county online cookbook?"

I rolled my eyes toward him. "I have to eat and pay the bills around here. You've used up all my personal and sick time for the next ten years."

He opened the folder in his hand and passed me the same picture of Rachel Smith I had printed in my office earlier that day.

I passed it right back to him. "Not to sound harsh or anything, but why do you want to go chase down another dead girl? She's not even in your jurisdiction."

He cocked an eyebrow in question, a curious smile playing on his lips. "What if she's not dead?"

I glared at him. "I've been looking at this photograph for months. She's dead."

He pulled another piece of paper from the folder and put it on my lap. It was a still image from the video surveillance system of a convenience store. The image was date-stamped just two days before. The exact same girl was looking directly into the camera.

"Are you sure she's dead?" Nathan asked with a smile.

3.

Warren walked behind the couch and looked over my shoulder as I sat up and examined every detail about the woman's appearance. As if reading my mind, Nathan handed me the photo from her missing report again, and I compared them side by side. "This is impossible," I finally said, knowing exactly how wrong I was.

Nathan tapped the picture with his finger. "Is she alive or dead?"

"Dead," Warren and I answered at the same time.

One side of Nathan's mouth tipped up in a half-cocked smile. "This was taken two days ago. Didn't you think she was dead before then?"

"This must be someone who just looks like Rachel Smith," I reasoned.

Nathan frowned. "You know it's the same woman."

"I hate to say it, Sloan"—Warren shook his head —"but I think Nathan's right. They're the same."

Nathan laughed and turned back to look at him. "How did those words taste coming out of your mouth?"

"Don't get used to it," Warren said.

Nathan leaned against the armrest of the sofa and angled his head to look at me sideways. "Do you remember saying you felt like Warren was dead when you first saw him?" Nathan jabbed his thumb toward Warren behind me. "And here he is, alive and irritating and—"

"And living here with Sloan," Warren interrupted with an evil grin.

I gave them both dirty looks. "Stop it." I turned my attention back to the two photos of Rachel Smith in my hands. Finally, I looked up at Warren. "Do you really think this is possible?"

Nathan laughed. "No offense, but how can the two of you be possible?"

Warren walked around the couch and sat on the coffee table in front of us. "I guess we aren't alone," he said. "I've always wondered if there might be more people like us out there."

I held up the new picture and looked at Nathan. "How did you get this?"

Nathan sat back with an annoying amount of satisfaction. "The FBI sent it over while I was gone to Greensboro. Rachel Smith—or whoever this woman really is —isn't dead."

I handed the photos back to him. "Good. Case closed."

Warren and Nathan both stared at me, and as if on cue, they crossed their arms over their chests in unison.

I blew out a deep sigh and looked between them. "You seriously want to go and hunt this woman down?" They both smiled. I groaned and dropped my face into my hands. "The two of you are going to end up getting me fired."

Nathan clapped his hands together with excitement.

Warren winked at me.

I pointed at them both. "If we do this, I'm laying down some ground rules. I'm not refereeing the two of you the whole time, and I'm not doing any more hiking trips searching for dead bodies."

They both laughed.

Warren reached toward Nathan for the photograph. "Where was this picture taken?"

Nathan passed it to him. "San Antonio, Texas."

I thought it over. "I like San Antonio. Good food, good shopping…"

Warren smiled at me. "Road trip?"

I shook my head. "I don't drive anywhere over six hours. That's why God created airplanes."

"Is that a yes?" he asked.

I put up my hand. "Hold up." I looked over at Nathan. "This isn't related to your work. Why are you so interested in this?"

He shrugged and flashed me one of his tantalizing grins. "I guess since you helped me solve my big mystery, it's time for me to return the favor and help solve yours."

"But this isn't exactly police work. How will you get the time off?" I asked.

"Vacation time?" he suggested.

Frowning, I scrunched my eyebrows together. "You've been at the department for two months. You don't have vacation time."

He pulled a half-eaten bag of Skittles out of his pocket. "I just solved the biggest case in North Carolina's history. I don't think the Sheriff's going to object."

I cleared my throat. "Correction: *we*"—I pointed between Warren and myself—"just solved the biggest case in North Carolina's history."

Nathan popped a handful of candy into his mouth. "You helped," he said with a wink.

Warren rubbed his palms together and looked at us both. "So, we're doing this?"

"I'm in," Nathan said. "Sloan?"

They were watching me expectantly.

With a huff, I dropped my shoulders in resignation. "Let's go to Texas."

* * *

The next morning, as I brushed my teeth in front of the mirror, Warren came into the bathroom and wrapped his arms around my waist from behind. A dizzying current of electricity flowed through me as he dragged his warm lips down the side of my neck. For a second, my eyes rolled backward. Only Warren Parish could turn dental hygiene into foreplay.

I spat out my toothpaste because moaning is much less seductive when foaming at the mouth. "Mmm...Good morning."

"Good morning." His voice was low and rough. "How did you sleep?"

I squirmed against him. "When you *let me* sleep, it was peaceful." I leaned over to rinse my mouth out with water, and I could almost feel his blood pressure rise. I straightened and smiled at him in the mirror. "This is nice. You being here when I wake up."

He slipped the strap of my tank-top down and kissed my shoulder. "You just like that I make coffee," he said, smiling against my skin.

"And you can cook," I added as I wiped my mouth with the hand towel.

His hands slid across my hip bones. "Stay home today."

"You're seriously going to get me fired," I said, laughing.

He rested his head on my shoulder. "That's OK. I'll

take care of you."

I looked over at him. "You don't have a job, remember?"

He grinned. "Good point."

I put my toothbrush in its holder and turned around in his arms. "I tell you what. I'm going to go to the office and turn in my vacation paperwork. Then I'm going to work really hard and try to get done early today. And tonight, we can stay at home. Just us. No parents. No Nathan. No interruptions."

He smiled. "I like that idea, but I like the idea of carrying you back to bed right now even more." He leaned in to kiss me, but I blocked his lips with my hand. His eyes popped open and then narrowed in frustration.

I shook my head. "Don't even go there," I said. "I can't walk into work late and then ask for paid time off."

He growled and bit the palm of my hand. "Well, you'd better hurry up and get out of here before I decide to not let you leave." He tightened his arms around me. "We didn't get to have our talk last night."

I held up my hands. "That was Nathan's fault. Not mine." After successfully wrenching myself free from his grip, I walked to my closet. "Do you want to talk about it now while I get ready?"

Shaking his head, he went back to the bedroom. "No. We'll talk about it tonight."

"What are you going to do today?" I asked over my shoulder.

The bedsprings squeaked under his weight. "I guess I'll look into flights and hotels for our trip."

I pulled a white blouse and a pencil-line black skirt down off their hangers. "Do you want me to leave my credit card so you can book them?"

He laughed. "I may be out of a job, but that doesn't mean I need your credit card."

I picked up a pair of black high heels off the floor. "I have \$172 in my bank account to last me till payday. I wouldn't be able to eat without a job."

I carried the day's wardrobe back to my room and stumbled a bit taking in the sight of the shirtless mercenary who was reclined back against my fluffy pillows.

He was oblivious to my stupor. "I have a tad bit more than that in savings. I banked all of my combat pay over the years just in case I ever needed it." He winked at me, almost recovering my full attention to what he was saying. "I think we'll be OK."

A part of me—the shallow part that liked to buy shoes —wanted to ask how much money we were talking about, but I didn't dare. And the other part of me was so distracted by the Adonis stretched across my comforter that I dropped my clothes onto the floor when I meant to put them on the bed.

He chuckled. "You missed."

"Shut up." I bent and gathered them back up.

Refusing to look at my boyfriend—or his perfect set of abs—I spread my outfit across the foot of the bed before turning toward my dresser. Inside the top drawer, where I stashed my mostly-fake jewelry, I found the silver angel pin Kayleigh Neeland had given me after Nathan and I rescued her. Like a talisman to keep me safe, I fixed it to my blouse, as I did every morning.

When my clothes were in order, I retrieved some clean underwear from the dresser before returning to the bathroom and turning on the shower. I stuck my head back into the bedroom and looked at Warren. "I'm locking this door."

He grinned. "You don't trust me?"

I laughed. "Not even a little bit."

* * *

My brain was everywhere but on my work that day,

and the minutes seemed to be ticking backward each time I glanced at the clock. I thought about Rachel Smith. I thought about Texas with Nathan and Warren. And, most of all, I thought about whatever big talk Warren was planning for that evening. I worked through lunch in hopes of leaving early, and despite all my mental wandering, I had everything completed by four. As I packed up my things, my boss stepped into my office.

Mary Travers was waving a sheet of paper in her tiny hand like a surrender flag. "Vacation request, huh?"

I smiled from behind my desk. "Yeah. I'm heading to Texas for a little break."

She handed me the paper that was stamped APPROVED in bright red letters. "You should be aware, there's a rumor going around Human Resources that Detective McNamara asked for next week off as well. There's speculation that it may be more than just a coincidence." She was grinning as she peered at me over her brown, plastic rimmed glasses.

I laughed and put the paper on top of the stack in my inbox. "Detective McNamara is going with me, but I can assure you it's nothing to gossip about. We're just friends."

She put a hand on her hip. "I may be old enough to be your mother, but I'm not senile or blind. You've had a thing for that boy since the first day he started work here."

I folded my hands on my desk. "My boyfriend, Warren, is going with us," I said. "Do you remember him? I introduced you at the Mexican restaurant a while back."

"Tall, dark, and handsome?" she asked.

I nodded. "That's Warren."

"I heard my name," Warren said, walking into my office behind Mary.

She spun around so fast I thought she might fall down. She clasped her hands over her heart. "You startled me!"

I laughed and covered my mouth with my hand.

Warren smiled and squeezed her shoulder. "I apologize," he said. "It's good to see you again, Ms. Travers."

"And the same to you, Warren." She looked back over her shoulder. "Have a good night, Sloan."

I waved. "You too," I called out as she left.

Warren leaned over my desk and pressed his lips to mine. My heart fluttered. "Hey gorgeous," he said when he pulled away.

"What are you doing here?" I asked.

He sat down in one of the chairs opposite my desk and relaxed back with his arms on the armrests. "Can I not come see you at work?"

I tilted my head to the side. "Of course you can, but you never do. What's up?"

He looked down at his watch. "I was in the neighborhood, so I thought I would come by and pressure you to leave early."

I smiled. "Well, you're in luck. I was just getting ready to head out of here."

"Great minds think alike then," he said.

I pushed my chair back. "Do you want to go out?"

He shook his head. "No. I want to go home." He was looking out the window.

"Are you OK?" I asked.

His eyes snapped to mine. "Yeah. I'm OK." He stood up. "You ready now?"

I nodded. "Yes, sir." I stood and picked up my laptop case and purse. "What about dinner?"

He took my bag from me and winked. "I'll worry about dinner."

I kissed his lips again. "Best roommate ever."

When we got home, I changed into sweats while he started cooking. In the few minutes it took me to swap out my clothes, the first floor of my house had been flooded with the savory aroma of curry mixed with cinnamon. I shuffled barefoot into the kitchen and slipped my arms around Warren's waist. I stretched on my tip-toes to peek over his shoulder. "Want some help?"

He was chopping up vegetables. "You can get me a beer out of the fridge."

"I can do that." I released him and walked to the refrigerator. "Oh, you got the good stuff." I pulled out two Green Man IPAs.

He looked over at me. "I love this city."

I smiled and reached for the bottle opener. "Beer capital of the US." I opened one and handed it to him.

"Thank you," he said, tipping it up to his lips.

I opened my beer and hopped on top of the counter, a safe distance away from the cutting board. "What did you do today?"

He didn't look up from the plump potato he was butchering.

I nudged him with my toe. "Earth to Warren."

"Huh?" His head whipped toward me, and he blinked like he was trying to reset his thoughts.

I laughed and took a sip of my beer. "What's with you?"

He put the knife down and took a deep breath, nervously knocking his knuckles against the counter. "I'm being reactivated with the Marines."

I almost fell onto the floor. "What?"

He crossed his arms over his chest and cut his eyes up at me. "That's what the whole trip to Washington was about."

My pulse began to pick up speed. "But you're out. You're not in the Marines anymore."

He dropped his head back and looked at the ceiling. "I screwed up when I signed my contract seven years ago. They offered me more money to take four more years of active duty and then four years on IRR if I chose to get out."

"IRR?" I asked, confused.

"Inactive Ready Reserve," he said. "It means I'm out, but for four years they can call me back for any reason they want. I have one year left before I'm completely free and clear of the military."

I put my beer down. "What does this mean?"

"It means I have to report to MEPS in Charlotte in thirty days—well, twenty-nine days now."

I shook my head. "So many acronyms. What's MEPS?"

"Military Entrance Processing Station," he said. "I'll do a lot of paperwork, have a bunch of medical tests and shots, and then they'll ship me out."

"Ship you where?"

He shrugged. "The Middle East most likely, but they haven't told me."

Tears began tickling the corners of my eyes, and he must have noticed because he closed the space between us before the tears hit my cheeks. Sandwiching his torso between my legs, he ran his strong hands down my arms. "I'm so sorry," he said. "This is all my fault."

I sniffed. "It's not your fault. It's *my* fault."

He laughed with surprise. "How do you figure?"

"I pulled you into the case with the missing girls. I put you on the government's radar when we landed on the news," I said.

He tucked my hair behind my ears. "No you didn't. I should never have agreed to that many years on IRR. I got greedy, I guess. And at the time I didn't have any good reason to turn the money down for a shorter term. Now I do." He tipped my chin up to look in my eyes.

"How long will you be gone?"

He shrugged. "I don't know. It could be up to a year."

A boulder dropped into my stomach. "A year?"

He moved his head from side to side. "It will probably be more like nine months. Maybe shorter if it's just a mission they want me on. It won't be longer than a year though."

I put my head on his shoulder. "A week is too long."

He stroked my hair. "We'll get through this, I promise. I'll always come back for you."

His words gave me chills rather than comfort. Statements like that were more ominous than anything, but I didn't ruin the sentiment with my fears. I pulled back and looked at him. "What about our trip to Texas?"

He smiled. "We can still go. I've got a whole month. In fact, I booked our tickets before I left the house, and I got us a nice suite at the Hyatt Regency right on the River Walk. The room overlooks the river and everything."

"What about Nathan?" I asked.

He dropped his head and cut his eyes up at me. "I will do anything in this world for you, but I draw the line at sharing our hotel room with another man."

I laughed and wiped my eyes with the back of my sleeve, smearing mascara on the cuff. "That's not what I meant."

"God, I hope not." He tugged on the strings of my hoodie. "I texted Nate and told him where we're staying. He can stay where he wants. Our flight is Saturday at 7:45."

"In the morning?"

He chuckled. "Yes. In the morning. And you're going to be pleasant and grateful."

Frowning, I looked up at him. "You're asking a lot."

He gathered my hair back behind my head and looked at me seriously again. "I am really sorry, Sloan."

I laced my hands together behind his neck, and he rested his forehead against mine. "Warren, I don't want you to leave." I teared up again.

"Shh." He kissed my eyes. "We're not going to worry about that till we have to. You never know, they could call it off between now and then."

Deep down, I knew our luck wasn't that good, but I nodded like I believed him. I looked up into his deep, black eyes that had faint halos around the pupils. After a lifetime of seeing into the souls of everyone around me, it was still a refreshing surprise that this man was so much a mystery.

"I love you," I blurted out.

He pulled back, his eyes wide with shock.

I covered my mouth with my hands and laughed with embarrassment. "I've never said that to anyone other than family or Adrianne before."

He smiled. "Really?"

I bit my lip. "Never."

Warren closed his eyes and shook his head.

Panic washed over me. *Oh no. It's too soon. What have I done?*

"Sloan." His voice was barely above a whisper. When he looked at me again, tears sparkled in his eyes. "No one has ever said that to me *at all.*"

The magnitude of his statement could have been calculated on the Richter scale. Tightening my arms around him, I pulled him close. "I love you, Warren," I said again.

And quietly in my ear he replied, "I love you, too."

4.

"No." In protest, I pulled the covers up over my head and rolled to cocoon myself in the blankets of my warm bed.

"Sloan, it's 4:30. I let you sleep an extra half hour." Warren kicked the side of the bed frame with his boot.

"I don't want to go to Texas anymore," I whined into my pillow.

"Don't make me get mean," he warned.

I ignored him.

A moment later, I was hurled across the bed, unwinding from my swirl of covers like a spinning top being flung across the mattress. Stunned, I landed on my back against Warren's pillows. He was holding my comforter in both hands.

He pointed at me. "If you go back to sleep I'm going to break out ice water and fog horns."

I frowned. "I love you a little less in moments like this."

He was still pointing at me. "We're about to have our first fight, woman." He walked to the door and flipped on the light to add insult to injury. It scalded my eyeballs. "We're leaving in twenty minutes if you want to stop at your parents' house on the way to the airport." He turned before I could object, and I heard his heavy footfalls on the steps downstairs.

Apparently, I was wrong to believe that once I became a fully-functioning adult, somehow my internal alarm clock would awaken and, like my mother, I would begin bounding happily out of bed at sunrise. Perhaps my hatred of mornings was further proof I was adopted.

Warren was probably right that our first fight would likely happen over our morning schedules. He was always awake at four like clockwork, and I believed it was ungodly to be up before the sun. On the rare occasions when I was forced to wake up with his alarm, he was so dang perky before coffee that I wanted to slap him till he felt as terrible as I did. I groaned and pushed myself off the bed.

Thankfully, I had showered and packed the night before, so there wasn't much to do besides brush my teeth and pile my hair onto the top of my head in a messy bun. Twenty minutes later, I trudged to the car in my sweats, dragging my bags behind me. The October chill of the North Carolina mountains nipped at my face, but it still wasn't enough to jar me from my sleepy stupor.

Warren shook his head with grief from where he waited at the trunk of his black Dodge Challenger.

I held up a finger in warning. "Not one word." I rubbed my eyes, blindly handing him my toiletries bag and my makeup case that I hadn't opened that morning.

"Here," he said as he handed me a travel mug full of coffee.

"Bless you," I whispered. I walked to the passenger side door, wrenched it open, and climbed into the already-warm car.

When he got in and fastened his seatbelt, he looked

over at me before putting the car in drive. "We'll have about fifteen minutes to spend at your Mom's. We need to be at the airport pretty soon."

I looked at the clock. It was five minutes till five. "Our flight isn't for almost three hours."

He pulled away from the curb. "Yes, but we've got to park, check our bags, get through security, and get to the gate on time."

I pulled my knees up to my chest and sipped my coffee. "It's the Asheville Regional Airport, Warren. Not Chicago/O'Hare. They have one terminal and only seven gates. I think we can manage."

He reached over and pushed my feet off his black leather seat. "Has anyone ever told you that you're kind of a bitch before nine a.m.?"

I nodded. "Yes."

He laughed and shook his head.

We drove to my parents' house in blessed silence. I envied the houses that were dark and untouched by the cruelty of morning, their undisturbed inhabitants still dreaming in bed. Such was not the case at the Jordan homestead, however. Every light in my parents' house was on. Knowing my mother, I was certain the coffee was fresh, breakfast was on the stove, and that she'd already been for a morning jog around the neighborhood.

Yes. There was no doubt I was adopted.

My mother met us at the door. "You look terrible," she said, stepping aside as we entered.

I smirked as I slipped off my winter coat. "Love you too, Mom."

Mom squeezed Warren's arm. "You're an angel, dear boy."

He laughed. "Has she always been like this?"

Mom nodded. "Since the day I brought her home."

She put her arm around my shoulders. "Do you need some more coffee, sweetie?"

I shook my head. "I'm good."

A familiar, uncomfortable sensation came over me that I was noticing more and more only around my mother. It was like something unseen was pulling at my attention, but I couldn't figure out what it was. I turned and studied her face. "What's wrong with you?" I asked, not meaning for the words to come out the way they did.

Her eyebrows lifted. "She's pleasant, isn't she?" Mom asked, looking up at Warren and shaking her head.

Warren pinched my side so hard I flinched. "What's the matter with you?"

I held up my hands in defense as we followed her to the kitchen. "I didn't mean it like that."

Dad came down the stairs already dressed for the day. He looked me up and down. "Is it Christmas morning and I forgot? You're never here this early without the promise of presents and food." He walked over to give me a hug. Over my shoulder, he spoke to Warren. "You're a brave man, son."

"Or a very stupid one," Warren said.

Dad laughed and stepped back. "To what do we owe the pleasure of your company this morning?"

"We're going to Texas for a vacation, so I wanted to tell you goodbye before we left," I said.

Dad crossed his arms over his chest. "What's in Texas?"

"Sand," I answered as I plopped down on a stool at the bar.

Warren leaned against the counter. "We're going to San Antonio for a little while. We found another woman who might be like us."

Dad's eyes widened. "Someone with your same gifts?"

"Maybe. That's what we want to find out," Warren said. "And hopefully it will be a little bit of a vacation as well. I just found I'll be getting deployed next month."

"Deployed?" Mom asked.

Warren nodded. "The Marines are recalling me. I'm not sure why, but I assume they will be sending me back to Iraq or Afghanistan."

My dad shook his head. A sincere frown was on his face. "I'm sorry to hear it. We were just getting used to having you around."

Warren sighed and rolled his eyes. "Trust me. You aren't as sorry as I am."

"So, will it just be the two of you in Texas?" Mom asked. "That sounds very romantic."

"And Nathan," I added over the rim of my coffee cup.

My mother cocked her head to the side. "Really?"

I was sure my mother's mind was spinning with confusion and excitement. She really liked Warren, and she was truly happy for me, but Audrey Jordan had picked out Nathan McNamara as her new son-in-law the very first time she laid eyes on him.

"We've all become really good friends," Warren said.

I raised an eyebrow. "Liar."

He chuckled.

My mother put a bowl of fruit down in front of me along with a fresh, steaming blueberry muffin from the oven. "Eat something, dear. It will raise your blood sugar and possibly make you a little more tolerable."

I fished a green grape from the bowl. "Thanks," I grumbled, popping it into my mouth.

"Warren, would you like some breakfast?" Mom asked, holding up the basket of muffins.

He shook his head. "No thank you, ma'am. I ate at the house before we left."

I rolled my eyes, pointing in his direction. "Warren eats healthy crap that tastes like horse feed and grass in the mornings."

Mom gently shook my shoulder. "Maybe you should follow his lead. I like this man more and more as I get to know him."

I did too, but I was too grumpy to agree with her or make Warren feel good about himself.

"I will take some more coffee, if you don't mind, Mrs. Jordan," Warren said.

"Certainly, Mr. Parish." My mother's tone was mocking as she took his travel mug.

My father leaned against the counter with his coffee cup. "Parish? Like the church?" he asked.

Warren nodded. "Exactly like the church. When I was a baby, I was found outside of St. Peter's Parish in Chicago. No one knew my name, or even if I ever had one, so the caseworker who came and got me named me Warren after her father, I believe, and Parish after the church."

I looked up. "I didn't know that."

My mother handed him the refilled mug. "That's fascinating."

Warren shrugged and screwed the lid back on his cup. "And pretty sad."

My mother patted Warren's cheek. "Not sad at all. I think it's very remarkable how you have lived your life despite such a mysterious beginning."

He smiled at her. "Thank you."

She squeezed his hand. "And no matter how heinous our daughter can be in the mornings, I hope you know you have a family now."

"I'm not heinous," I protested.

Warren slipped his arm around my shoulders from behind and kissed the top of my head. "Yes, you are, but it's OK. I love you anyway. Are you about ready to go? We need to get to the airport."

I groaned and stood up. "Can I have alcohol on the plane?"

My mother shook her head and sighed.

I gave her another hug. "I love you, Mom. I'll see you when we get back."

"Have a wonderful time. Tell the detective we said hello," she said.

"I will."

I hugged my dad. "I love you, Dad. Maybe I'll bring you back a cactus or a ten-gallon hat."

He winked at me. "I'll wear it with pride. I'm sure my patients would love it." He grabbed my hand as I turned to leave. "Did you remember to pack your meds? Your headache prescription and your Xanax?"

I nodded. "Yeah, don't worry. I've got them. And Warren's going to be with me the whole time, so I'm sure I'll be fine."

Dad shook Warren's hand. "Have fun. Take care of my little girl and enjoy your downtime."

"I will. Thank you, sir," Warren said.

We walked out of the house, and on the way to the car, Warren looked at me. "You take Xanax? For anxiety or what?"

I nodded. "Usually only when I know I'm going to be around really bad people. Like, the jail causes me to go into hysterics."

"That's interesting."

"Why?"

He shrugged. "I tend to be sharper, more focused around bad people. Not anxious."

I looked up at him. "That is interesting."

When we reached the car, he opened my door. "I like your parents a lot."

"Yeah, they're great," I said without emotion, still hugging my coffee.

He shook his head. "Maybe you need Prozac in the morning."

I got in the car and looked up at him. "Maybe you shouldn't talk so much."

He laughed and shut my door.

As we pulled out of the driveway, I turned in my seat to look at him. "Does my mom give off anything weird to you?"

"What do you mean?" he asked.

I shrugged. "I don't know. For the past few months I've gotten this really strange feeling around her."

He laughed. "Is that why you snapped at her back there?"

"Yeah, but I didn't mean it as hateful as it sounded," I said.

He shook his head. "I haven't picked up on anything. What's it feel like?"

I thought for a moment. "Do you know that fairytale called the Princess and the Pea?"

His head turned in my direction. "Really? Do I look like a fairytale kind of guy to you?"

I laughed. "It's about this princess who can feel a pea at the bottom of twenty mattresses."

"What the hell?" he asked, laughing as he turned onto the highway.

"There's this girl who claims she's a princess, and this old woman hides a pea under twenty mattresses that the girl is going to sleep on—"

He interrupted me. "Who the hell sleeps on twenty mattresses?"

"Pay attention!" I snapped. "In the morning, they asked the princess how she slept, and she said she slept terribly because there was a pea under her mattress," I explained. "They knew she was a real princess because she could feel the pea hidden at the bottom."

"Fairytales are stupid. That makes no sense." He glowered over at me. "I'll bet you couldn't feel a pea. You're definitely not a princess."

"You're missing the point, Warren."

"What's the point?" he asked.

I was getting frustrated, and he was grinning because he knew it. "That's what it feels like with my mom. There's something there that's hidden, but I can still feel it." I held up my hands in question. "You don't sense anything strange around her?"

"Peas?" He shook his head. "No peas."

I rolled my eyes. "You're impossible."

He reached over and put his hand on my knee. "I'm sorry. I'll pay more attention when we see her again."

I sighed. "Thank you."

The airport was almost empty when we arrived. We checked our bags, declared the arsenal Warren had brought along with us, and made it through security with well over an hour to spare. I wanted to say *I told you so*, but I kept my mouth shut. I stretched out on the sandpaper-esq carpet near the gate and used my carryon bag as a pillow. Warren sat in a chair with a newspaper.

"Did Nathan book the same flight?" I asked.

"I thought so, but he should be here by now," he said.

I closed my eyes and felt the rumble of planes on the tarmac outside. "He's probably still in bed asleep like a normal person," I mumbled.

"What?" Warren asked.

"Nothing."

I woke up sometime later with the toe of Warren's boot nudging me in the ribs. I opened my eyes.

"Feel better?" he asked.

I yawned. "A little." I struggled to my feet while

Warren picked up my bag. I looked around to see that Nathan still hadn't shown up. "Do you think I have time to get more coffee?"

"They'll have coffee on the plane," he said.

To my surprise, the flight was almost full. In our row of three seats, I took the middle so Warren could wedge his six-foot-three frame into the aisle seat.

I rested my head against his shoulder. "How long is the flight?"

He looked down at the large tactical watch encircling his wrist. "We should be there by noon. We have to change planes in Atlanta."

I nodded and closed my eyes again, this time enjoying the scent of Warren's cologne. It was strong and masculine, but it reminded me of the ocean breeze and moonlight. The peaceful hum of electricity between us was almost enough to lull me to sleep again despite the chatter and fumbling of luggage all around me.

"Uh oh," I heard him say just as I began to feel sleepy again.

I sat up and looked at him. "Uh oh, what?" I followed the direction of his gaze.

Nathan was shoving a large red carry-on into an overhead compartment six rows ahead of ours. He waved when he saw us. I smiled and returned the gesture. But when he stepped out of the narrow aisle, my smile quickly faded and my stomach did a backflip.

Shannon Green was standing right behind him.

5.

"You have got to be freaking kidding me!" I shouted, causing the older gentleman in front of us to turn around in his seat and look at me.

Warren gripped my hand and squeezed. "Keep your voice down."

"Did you know he was bringing her?" My voice was a squealing whisper, like an emphysemic banshee.

He shook his head. "No, I didn't."

I sat back hard in my seat. "What was he thinking?"

Warren turned toward me. "He was probably thinking he didn't want to be the third wheel here with us," he said. "Would you want to be tagging along with another couple by yourself?"

Yanking my hand from his, I folded my arms over my chest. "I would be by myself for all of eternity before I would even go to the grocery store with that woman. I'm certainly not going to Texas with her." I furiously shook my head. "No. No. No."

He angled his shoulders to face me. "So, what are you

going to do? Get off the plane?" It was obvious Warren's patience was wearing very thin.

"Do you have any idea how much I can't stand her?" I jabbed my thumb into the center of my chest. "Do you know how hard this is for me?"

He narrowed his eyes, and for the first time ever, he almost looked angry with me. "Let's think about that for a second." He pointed over the top of the seats toward Nathan. "That guy up there more than obviously has a thing for you. You work together, you hang out together, and he's even stayed the night at your house—in your bed—at least once. I don't think you've slept with him, but he's kissed you before, and if he had half a chance he would edge me out of the picture without a moment's pause." He was fighting to maintain control of the volume of his voice. "Still, you don't see me yelling on the plane because he's here."

"That's not the same."

He blinked with surprise. "How's it different?"

"Nathan only thinks he has a thing for me. You know, people fear you and they love me." I gestured between us. "It's part of...whatever *this* is."

"Right, Sloan! Because a dude falling for his hot co-worker is so out of the ordinary!"

I pressed my lips together and shrank back into my seat. "But I—"

He held up his index finger, daring me to continue my protest. "Enough."

I stared at the blue seat back in front of me and picked at a loose thread from the fabric. "I can't promise I'm going to be nice to her."

He didn't say anything more. He just opened up the SkyMall magazine and began thumbing through the pages, not pausing long enough to read any of it. He was definitely mad.

I needed to get a grip. Fast. I had chosen to be with Warren which forfeited any right I had to a temper tantrum over Nathan being with someone else. But damn it was hard. And of all people...Shannon? Talk about salt in an open wound.

Still, it didn't change the fact that I was wrong.

"I'm sorry." And I was.

Warren didn't even flinch in acknowledgement.

After a moment of being ignored, I leaned into him. "How did you know Nathan kissed me?"

He didn't look up from his book as he continued to flip through the pages. "I was there."

My brain scrambled. "You were there?"

"At your house, the first night I met you. He kissed you at the door and stormed out." His eyes slowly rolled toward me. "Why? What kiss are you thinking about?"

Crap.

My shoulders sank, and I tried to squelch the guilt churning in my stomach even though, technically, I hadn't done anything wrong. "It was before you and I got serious."

"When?"

Every muscle in my body tensed. "The last time, it was —"

He cut me off and closed the magazine. "The *last* time? How many times have there been?"

I cringed. "Three." He didn't respond, so I continued. "The last time was the night after we found his sister's body in Raleigh. The night I got our DNA test results."

His teeth were audibly grinding, and he turned his gaze back toward the seat. I half-expected it to start smoking. "That was the last time?"

I put my hand on his arm. "I swear it was."

He nodded, but still didn't look at me. "I already knew about that."

My head snapped back in surprise. "You did?"

"Nathan told me when we were out looking for bodies a couple of weeks back." He seemed to relax a bit.

My jaw went slack. "Why didn't you say something?"

"There was nothing to say. You were right. It was before we got serious."

His leniency and patience creeped me out. Rather than coming across as being a bit of a doormat, his steel resolve to be objective and understanding was unnerving. It was scary to think what would happen if Warren was pushed past his limit. I certainly didn't want to find out.

"I haven't slept with him ever," I added, quickly and with conviction.

"OK." He turned his attention back to the magazine.

I shuddered.

My cell phone buzzed on my lap. It was a text message from Nathan. *Good morning, sunshine. Surprise.*

I tapped out a reply with my thumbs. *I hate you.*

A moment later, another message came. *I know.*

It was a short flight to Atlanta, and we didn't have much of a layover. Nathan and Shannon exited the plane before us, but waited for us in the terminal. I tried to look pleasant as I watched Shannon examining her fingernails as we approached. Her blond hair was neatly framed around her face, she was wearing a black pants suit, and—unlike me—she had opened her makeup bag that morning. She was ready for the six o'clock news; I was ready for a cardboard box under a bridge.

Shannon was looking at me with an equal amount of disgust.

I forced a smile. "Good morning."

"Don't you look lovely?" Nathan laughed as his eyes scanned me up and down. He nodded toward my head. "Your hair looks like a bird's nest."

I cut my eyes at him and looped my arm through Warren's. "Well, your face is stupid."

Nathan just laughed.

"You guys barely made it this morning, didn't you?" Warren asked.

Shannon flipped her hair over her shoulder. "I had to do the news at five this morning." She giggled and put her hand on Nathan's arm. "We had to, literally, run down the terminal!"

I glanced down at her four-inch high heels. "In those shoes? And you didn't break your neck?"

Warren nudged me with his arm.

I looked back at Nathan. The patch on his ball cap read *Shitstarter*. I pointed to it and smirked. "That's appropriate. I didn't know you were bringing a friend."

Shannon laughed. "I certainly wouldn't classify me as a friend."

I shook my head. "I wouldn't either."

Her mouth twisted into a deep frown.

Warren cut his eyes down at me, but the corners of his mouth were twitching as he tried to suppress a smile. He looked back at her and extended his hand. "You must be Shannon. I've heard a lot about you. I'm Warren Parish."

She blinked her bright green eyes up at him and smiled so big I wondered if her face might crack. "I've heard a lot about you too." She was still holding onto his hand. "It's nice to finally put a face with your name."

I pulled his hand away from her. "That's enough of the pleasantries. We've got a plane to catch."

I pushed my way past them, and Warren did a double-step to catch up with me. "Did I just detect a hint of jealousy back there, Ms. Jordan?" He was smiling wildly down at me.

"No," I answered.

He laughed and hooked his arm around my waist. "I

think you were just a tiny bit possessive for a moment."

I bumped him with my hip. "Don't let it go to your head, Mr. Parish."

He kissed my cheek as we walked. "I like it when you get territorial."

"Do you want me to pee on your leg or something?" I asked.

He laughed. "Nah. Dirty looks and snide remarks are enough."

When we finally landed in San Antonio and walked outside to get our rental car, the heat almost reduced me to a puddle on the sidewalk. It had been forty-two degrees when we left Asheville that morning, and even before noon in Texas, it was already pushing ninety. All four of us were severely overdressed. On the curb outside the airport, I stripped off my coat. Unfortunately, I was still wearing a hooded sweatshirt.

Shannon, in her black pants and suit jacket, looked like she was seriously rethinking her decision to tag along on our trip. "We have got to find some air conditioning." She panted as she fanned herself with what appeared to be an unused barf bag from the plane.

Nathan slipped on his sunglasses. "Let's get the car and go to the hotel. We'll figure out the rest of the day after that."

A bead of sweat drizzled down my spine. "I'm going to need a shower."

Warren was looking at the rental car signs. "Which way are we headed, Nate?"

"Budget," Nathan answered, pointing to the left.

I looked up at Warren. "We're sharing a rental car?"

He nodded as we followed Nathan and Shannon. "Yeah. Is that a problem?"

Cautiously, I lowered my voice and slowed my pace to put some distance between us and them. "I promise I'm not just trying to be whiney or difficult, but have you considered how we are going to go searching for Rachel Smith with Shannon tagging along?" I asked. "You don't think Nathan told her about us, do you?"

He shook his head. "I doubt it. Maybe he just plans on letting her play at the spa all day while we are combing the city. She seems like a spa kind of girl."

I giggled.

He laughed, looking down at me. "I'm so glad you're not high maintenance. I would honestly prefer your hot mess over that nonsense any day."

"What? You don't want to see me in four inch heels?" I asked, smiling.

He flashed me a devilish grin and lowered his face toward mine. "I don't know. Would you be wearing anything else?"

I poked him in the ribs. He wrapped his hand around mine as we walked. In front of us, Shannon was throwing her hips from side to side as she navigated the sidewalk. I sighed. "This is going to be an interesting trip."

He laughed. "Just think of it as a personal growth opportunity for you."

I groaned.

* * *

The Hyatt Regency, right on the River Walk in downtown San Antonio, was undoubtedly the nicest hotel I had ever been in. The grand lobby stretched high above our heads with balconies lining the walls looking over the sparkling reflecting pool in front of us. Even Shannon looked impressed as we walked to the check-in desk.

While Warren got our keys, I walked over to the small bridge that stretched across the water and looked out of the massive window that framed the view of the San Antonio River Walk. A gondola full of tourists was floating by, and there were bistro tables covered with colorful umbrellas that stretched along the water's edge. The tables were full of smiling patrons nibbling pretentious looking edibles.

A moment later, Warren was at my side. "You like it?" he asked with a raised eyebrow.

I laughed and leaned against the railing. "I feel like total white trash right now. Why did you let me show up at this nice hotel looking like a hobo?"

His jaw dropped. "Like you would have listened to me!"

I couldn't really argue.

Nodding toward the floors above, he offered me his arm. "You ready to go upstairs?"

I hooked my arm around his elbow. "Heck yeah, I am!"

We rode the glass elevator to the seventh floor, and I followed him down the hallway to our room. He opened the door to a spacious suite with a fluffy, white, king-sized bed centered between a leather couch and a massive window that overlooked the city. The flat-panel television hanging on the wall dwarfed the one I had at home. I stepped inside and inhaled the scent of green apples and Clorox.

"This is ridiculous." I laughed and dropped my bag on the bed. I walked to the window and pulled the curtains the rest of the way open, displaying the peaceful San Antonio River and restaurants below.

He walked up behind me and encircled me with his arms. "Did I do well?"

"You did crazy well. This is gorgeous." I was buzzing from his energy and from excitement. "I may not want to ever go home."

He kissed the side of my neck and let me go. "I'm going to change into something lighter. Are you going to take a shower?"

"Yeah." I walked back toward the bed and unzipped

my suitcase. "What's the plan for today?"

Warren pulled his shirt over his head, and I forgot what I was doing. It was like his torso had been sculpted out of cream cheese. A large talon shaped tattoo stretched over the right half of his body, both front and back, with hooked claws like that of an eagle snatching him away from above. He had the word *Azrael*, meaning the Angel of Death, inked in script just below where his right side holster normally rested on his hip.

I bit my lower lip.

"I told Nate we would meet them for lunch in an hour." He stopped rifling through his bag when he noticed me staring at him. "What?"

I felt my cheeks flush red. "You're just very distracting."

He smiled. "I'm glad I'm not the only one who gets distracted in this relationship."

I walked over and pushed his suitcase back and sat down in front of where he stood. I ran my fingers across the tattoo peeking out from the waistband of his jeans. "Why Azrael?" I asked. "You've never told me."

His chest expanded with a deep breath. "When I was in Iraq about five years ago, we had to clear a section of Baghdad around an Islamic mosque. We entered into this building where, I guess, some Shiite leaders were meeting. This one guy with a long white beard looked at me and freaked out. I mean, we were all dressed in our cammies, carrying M-4s and everyone was pretty nervous, but this guy was looking just at me. I thought he might jump out the window."

"Really?" I asked.

He nodded. "He had these crazy eyes, and he pointed at me and said the word *Azrael*. I didn't know what it meant at the time, but I asked our translator. He said it is the name some Islamics use to refer to the angel of death or the angel of retribution."

"And you had it tattooed on your hip?" I asked.

He shrugged. "If the shoe fits."

"Do you think that guy knew who you were—or *what* you were?" I traced my finger over the word again.

He sighed and shook his head. "If not, it's one hell of a coincidence."

The angel pin little Kayleigh had given to me was attached to the front of the pocket on my jeans. I ran my finger across it. "I don't believe in coincidences anymore." I looked up at him. "Do you think whatever we are could be linked to angels?"

He sat down next to me and laughed. "No." He turned his palms up. "But then again, who knows? I certainly haven't come up with any other reasonable explanations."

"Do you believe in angels? Or God for that matter?" I asked.

He blew out a deep sigh. "I don't know. It's hard for me to wrap my brain around the notion of some loving, all-powerful being with all the hell I've seen over the years. But I believe there is more out there than just what everyone thinks. You and I are proof of that."

I nodded. "Yeah. I agree."

He pushed himself up and leaned on his arms over me. His perfect face was inches from mine. "I do know one thing for sure."

I grinned. "What's that?"

He shook his head. "You are no angel before nine in the morning." He laughed and kissed the tip of my nose.

* * *

Nathan and Shannon were waiting at a table at Paesano's restaurant on the River Walk, just down from our hotel, when Warren and I caught up with them. Warren, Nathan, and I were all dressed in jeans and t-shirts. Shannon had changed into a green sundress and a hat that was almost as big as the umbrella over our table.

I adjusted my sunglasses and looked up at Warren as we walked toward them. "I'll play nice, but there are no guarantees I won't push her into the river."

He laughed and tucked his fingers into my back pocket.

Warren pulled out my chair, and I sat down between him and Shannon at the square table. Nathan was across from me, sipping on a beer, wearing aviator sunglasses underneath his Shitstarter ball cap.

"What are you drinking?" I asked him.

"Peroni." He held the glass toward me. "Wanna try it?"

I shook my head. "I've had it before. I think I'll order one too." I picked up a menu. "This place is delicious. I ate here when I came for a conference last year."

Shannon was fanning herself with the wine list. "I don't know why anyone would come here. It's too hot," she griped. "We should have gotten a table indoors where there's air conditioning."

I blinked my eyes in question at Nathan, wondering what he was thinking in bringing her along. He just grinned back at me.

Shitstarter is right, I thought.

After we'd ordered and our beers were delivered, Warren split a glance between me and Nathan. "So, what's our game plan while we're here?"

Nathan sat up in his chair. "Well, we can't do a whole lot of work until Monday, but I was able to get my hands on some records for caseworkers in the city, females with the last name of Smith."

I tipped my beer up to my lips. "What if she's not a caseworker now? And what if she's not going by Smith anymore?"

"Who?" Shannon asked.

"The woman we are here looking for." I turned my attention back to Nathan. "What if her name never was Rachel Smith?"

He shrugged his shoulders. "We've got to start somewhere. I also got the information for the convenience store where she was last seen. That should help narrow the list down a bit."

"How far is it from here?" Warren asked.

"Just a few miles east," Nathan said, nodding in the direction away from where the sun was sinking lower in the sky. "We can cruise over that way this afternoon and look around if you want."

I shook my head. "Let's just have some downtime for the weekend. We can work on Monday."

Shannon laughed. "Sloan and I actually agree on something."

I leaned my elbows on the table and glared at Nathan. "What's Shannon going to do while we're working?"

"I'll come along, of course," she answered.

I cut my eyes across the table. "Nathan?"

"I can answer for myself, thank you very much," Shannon snipped.

I blinked at Nathan again.

He put his hand on hers. "It might be best if you stay at the hotel while we're gone. The case we're working on is classified."

She laughed and turned her nose up in my direction. "Classified? I don't think Sloan has any kind of secret clearance."

He pulled down his sunglasses enough to make direct eye-contact with her. "Shannon, we talked about this. I told you if you wanted to come, you were going to have to be on your own some." He leaned toward her. "What we're doing might be dangerous."

"Then why does she get to go?" Shannon was pointing her finger at me, and for a moment I considered reaching out and breaking it off.

I held my hands up and pushed back from the table. "OK. We need to get a few things straight here." I looked her square in the face. "We're not just here for some kind of double-date vacation. Nathan is helping me and Warren with finding someone we need to talk to. This is business. So don't think you and I are going to be part of some kind of wives' club that gets our nails done while the boys go to work."

Shannon's mouth fell open. I was becoming accustomed to that expression from her.

Nathan reached over and took her hand. "I'm sorry, but I told you all of this when you asked me to come along. Sloan's right. You've got to sit this one out."

She pushed her chair back and stood, tossing her hair dramatically over her shoulder. "Well, maybe I should just sit lunch out too then!"

"Don't leave." Nathan sat back hard in his seat and folded his arms over his head in frustration.

She turned on her stiletto and stalked down the sidewalk, her heels click-clacking as she marched. He started to get up, but I held out my hand to stop him. "No, let me," I insisted.

Warren caught my arm. "You play nice."

I rolled my eyes and yanked my arm free from his grip. I jogged to catch up with her. "Shannon, wait!"

She spun around with her finger in my face. "You know, everything was perfect before you showed up!"

I reared my head back in surprise. "Me?"

"Yes, you! It's like I haven't even had a boyfriend since he met you!" She stamped her foot on the brick sidewalk.

The river just behind her looked terribly tempting. *Just*

one little shove…

I took a deep breath, to calm my temper. "Shannon, listen. I don't know what's going on with you and Nathan, but it's not about me."

"Don't lie to me, Sloan! You may have your hunk of a boyfriend over there, but that doesn't mean there's nothing between you and Nathan." Her voice cracked with emotion.

My jaw was clenched so tight I thought my teeth might break. "Did you come here just to babysit us?"

She didn't respond.

I shook my head. "Look, I honestly don't know what Nathan sees in you, but you are going to lose him if you keep acting like a jealous, self-centered wench. I'm sorry if your relationship is on the rocks, but I can promise you if it is, you're probably the problem. Maybe you should stop worrying so much about me and start taking a little better care of him. God knows, you don't deserve him."

"Why do you hate me so much?" She yanked off her oversized sunglasses. "Because I hooked up with Jason Ward in high school? That was a million years ago!"

I took a step toward her and kept my hands at my sides so I didn't punch her in the face. "No, Shannon. It's because I trusted you! I thought you were my friend, and you betrayed me!"

She threw her hands into the air. "You told the entire school I had syphilis!"

I laughed. "Yes. I did! But only because you hurt me. There, I said it. You were my friend and you hurt me."

Her eyes widened, but she didn't respond.

I let out a deep sigh. "Now, I'm not going to pretend I like you because you know I don't, but I'm willing to try and get along since I don't have much of a choice. So, will you please stop acting like the drama queen you are and come back and sit down at the damn table for lunch?"

She pressed her lips together and shifted her weight from one foot to the other.

I offered her my hand. "Truce?"

She eyed it, and then looked at me. Her shoulders sank, and she huffed as she shook my hand. "Truce."

6.

After lunch, the four of us walked along the river, visiting the shops and acting almost like a group of normal friends. Shannon insisted we go on a gondola ride, so we did. I settled under Warren's arm at the back of the boat. The sun was dipping lower and lower on the horizon, and the heat was finally starting to taper off for the day. The gondola driver was giving a detailed history of the area, and Shannon was listening intently with Nathan a few rows ahead of us. I stared up at the deep blue sky and enjoyed the feeling of my head against Warren's shoulder.

He nodded toward Shannon up ahead. "So, did the two of you kiss and make up?"

I shrugged. "I called a truce. You're right. I don't want to be miserable the whole time we're here. I can go back to hating her with full force when we get back to North Carolina."

He laughed. "That's my girl."

"Sorry I was so bitchy this morning," I added.

He pulled off his black sunglasses and hooked them on

the front collar of his shirt. "I'm getting more used to it, but I don't think we're ever going to get along in the mornings."

I scraped my fingernails down his thigh. "We get along just fine when I wake up with you still in my bed."

He chuckled. "How many times has that happened? Maybe twice?"

I dragged my nails back up. "Maybe, but wasn't it very well worth it on both occasions?"

He tightened his arm around my shoulders. "You start talking like that and I'm going to make him turn this boat around."

I settled against him. "It wouldn't be the worst thing."

He looked down at me. "Can you believe we've only known each other for six weeks?"

My head fell to the side. "Six weeks? Are you sure that's all?"

"Crazy isn't it?" He motioned down to his watch. "I've been counting. This is the longest relationship I've ever been in."

I laughed. "Seriously?"

He nodded. "Yeah. I guess it's a by-product of emanating fear to everyone you meet. I mean, the bad-boy thing kinda works for me for a while, but it doesn't last." He smiled. "It's nice to be treated almost like a normal person when I'm with you."

"What is normal?" I laughed as we passed under an arched, stone bridge.

"True." He leaned his head against mine. "Can we talk seriously for a sec?"

I rolled my head back to look at him. "Sure, I guess. Talk about what?"

"If it's all right with you, I'm going to leave my stuff at your place when I leave next month," he said.

I frowned. "I don't want to talk about that."

He was drawing circles on my shoulder with his finger. "We have to talk about it sooner or later. I'd rather just get it over with."

"Of course you can leave your stuff at my house. You know that." I perked up a bit. "Wait, even the car?"

He nodded. "Even the car. Just please don't wreck it."

"I promise I won't." I crossed my heart.

"And before I leave I'll have to update all of my paperwork with the government. I'm going to make you my power of attorney, and if something were to happen to me while I'm gone, everything will be left to you."

My heart felt like it forgot to beat for a second. "I *really* don't want to talk about *that*," I said, poking out my lower lip.

"Sloan, they wouldn't be calling me back if this wasn't for something major. This is probably going to be really dangerous, and I want you to be prepared for worst case scenario."

"You're going to make me cry again," I warned.

He shook his head. "No more crying." He squeezed my shoulder. "I also want you to know, if something does happen to me, you should stick close to Nathan. He knows about what you can do and the weight it brings. He'll take care of you."

My mouth fell open. "Are you seriously giving me your blessing to be with Nathan if you die?"

"Hell no." He laughed. "If you end up with him after I'm dead, I'm going to haunt the shit out of both of you."

"You promised you're going to come home to me," I reminded him.

He pressed a kiss to my temple. "Always."

I crumpled a little in my seat at the thought of a world without Warren in it. Even in such a short amount of time, I realized how completely dependent on him I had become.

Being with Warren was like needing to breathe oxygen. Considering the migraines, I was beginning to wonder if it was even physically possible for me to go on without him.

I reached over the side of the boat and cupped a handful of cool water. I splashed it on my face and laughed. "Geez, I'm going to need to get off this boat and do some serious drinking." I flicked the rest of the droplets onto his face.

"I could get on board with that plan." He sat up straight and craned his neck to see over the people in front of us. "Hey, Nate!"

Nathan turned to look at us.

"We did your girl's boat ride. After this, my girl wants to go to a bar!" Warren called out.

Nathan smiled and gave us a thumbs-up.

* * *

An hour later, we were at Durty Nelly's Irish Pub. Nathan and I were drinking beer, Warren was drinking straight whiskey, and Shannon was sipping a cosmopolitan that seemed to offend the bartender to make. Thank god she had, at least, taken off her ridiculous hat because it might not have fit in the crowded room. We were huddled around a small wooden table near the bar that backed up to a piano where a man was singing Irish drinking songs.

"Anybody else think it's weird to have a bar this Irish next to the Alamo?" Nathan asked, holding up a napkin with a bright green shamrock on it.

Warren laughed, and I looked around at them confused. "Who fought at the Alamo?"

Nathan's eyes rolled toward the ceiling like he was searching his memory.

Warren pressed his lips together as he stared at the back of the piano.

Shannon's head fell to the side. "The British?"

I shook my head as I finished the last of my second beer. "That's definitely not it."

"You want another one?" Warren asked, nodding to my empty glass.

"Please," I said and gave him a peck on the lips.

He stood up and walked to the bar.

Nathan was still thinking. "Davy Crockett was there. But I'll admit I only know that because of the Disney movies."

"Maybe we should tour the Alamo tomorrow and find out!" Shannon shouted over the music.

I leaned back in my chair. "I was thinking about going to that really pretty Catholic church we passed down the street on our way to the hotel."

Nathan's head tilted in surprise. "Are you serious? I didn't know you went to church."

"And you're not Catholic," Shannon said.

I shrugged. "I have a theory I want to explore."

"What kind of theory?" he asked.

I drummed my hands on the table. It was sticky. "I want to see what someone there can tell me about angels."

Nathan's eyes widened, and he straightened in his seat. "Really?"

"Angels? Why?" Shannon asked.

"I'm just curious." It wasn't a lie. "I have some questions."

Warren placed another frosty mug of amber beer in front of me. "Questions about what?" he asked.

I looked over at him as he sat down with another tumbler of Jameson. "I was just telling them I think I might go by that cathedral we passed earlier today and see if I can talk to a priest or something about angels."

"A priest." He nodded his head. "That could be interesting."

"What do you want to know?" Shannon asked. "I'm

not Catholic, but I am Baptist, and I've heard about angels almost all my life."

I was surprised at her willingness to talk to me and actually try to be helpful. Perhaps it was the vodka. "What do you know about them?" I asked.

She shrugged. "Well, the Bible says they are beautiful and they sing and they announced Jesus's birth."

I looked at Warren. "Well, that theory is out. Your singing sucks."

"Amen to that," Nathan said, raising his beer.

Warren laughed and sipped from his glass.

Shannon finished off the last of her drink. "The angels in the Bible are like messengers. They told Mary she was going to have Jesus. They told the shepherds in the field when Jesus was born. And they told Mary Magdalene that Jesus had risen from the dead."

"How did they tell them?" I asked.

Shannon pushed her chair back and used her hands for wide gesturing. "They came down from the sky, all dressed in white and shining like the sun, and they said 'Fear not! I have come with good news for all people!'"

The people in the bar were staring at her.

"Fear not," I repeated. I looked curiously up at Warren before turning back to Shannon. "Were they scary?"

She shrugged. "I dunno. A man walking out of the sky would scare the bejeezus outta me."

I leaned into Warren and lowered my voice. "Fear seems to fit with you."

"But not with you," he added.

She started counting on her fingers. "There were angels who guarded the Garden of Eden when Adam and Eve got kicked out. There was also the Passover angel who killed the first-born sons in Egypt. And there were angels who protected Daniel in the lion's den."

"So, angels have different jobs?" I asked.

She tossed her hands up. "Beats me. That's all I know."

"Thanks, Shannon." The words felt strange as they left my mouth.

She smiled. "Sure."

Nathan leaned toward Warren and pointed his finger between me and Shannon. "Did a pleasant exchange just really happen here or am I drunk?"

Warren laughed. "The world might be coming to an end, man."

I elbowed my boyfriend. "Shut up."

Nathan waved to our waitress. "I think this is cause for celebration." The waitress stepped over to our table. "Can we get four Irish Car Bombs?" He held up four fingers.

"Oh no." I shook my head as she walked away. "Liquor and I are not friends."

Nathan shook his head. "You and Shannon aren't friends either, but obviously anything is possible."

I laughed. "Yes, anything is possible. Me dancing on tables and picking fights with strangers is certainly possible." I tipped my beer up to my lips again.

Shannon shoved Nathan in the shoulder a little harder than she obviously intended and sloshed his beer onto his lap. "Did you tell them your good news?"

He sighed as he sopped up his lap with a napkin.

I glanced at Warren who seemed just as clueless as I was. I looked back at Nathan. "Good news?"

He shifted uncomfortably in his seat and wadded up the napkin. He drummed his fingers on the sides of his glass. "Yeah. The FBI officially offered me a job."

"Really?" Warren asked, sitting back. "That's awesome, man."

"Where is it?" I asked.

He looked down at his beer. "I'll do training in

Virginia, and then I'll probably be working out of Charlotte."

My heart sank a few inches. "You're moving again?"

He shrugged his shoulders. "Well, I don't know yet. I haven't given them a definite answer."

My lower lip protruded. "Everybody's leaving me."

Warren squeezed the back of my neck.

Nathan looked at Warren and pointed at him. "Are you leaving?"

It was Warren's turn to appear uncomfortable. He nodded. "Yeah. In a few weeks. I'm being involuntarily recalled to the Marines."

"You're joking?" Nathan said, pushing his beer away from him.

Warren shook his head. "Unfortunately not."

"What do they want you for?" Nathan asked.

Warren turned his palm up. "Who knows? I'm pretty sure they are sending me back to a combat zone for something. They hinted they're looking for someone specific, but I'm not certain who that is."

"Have you checked the most wanted list? Even if it's global terrorism, the FBI might have them listed," Nathan said.

Warren shrugged. "No, I haven't checked. All I know is they want me back and I don't have a choice in the matter."

Nathan leaned against the back of his seat. "I hate to hear that."

I wasn't so sure that was true.

Unable to think any longer about Warren leaving, I looked at Shannon. "What will you do if Nathan takes the job in Charlotte?"

She shrugged and smiled at Nathan. "We haven't decided yet." She reached over and squeezed his hand. "I might be able to transfer to a station out there, but we haven't seriously talked it over."

Nathan looked grateful when the waitress reappeared with a tray of four dark beers and four milky shot glasses. She passed them around. I looked at the drinks in front of me. "You've all been warned that I might get belligerent. And Warren, I hope you're prepared to carry me back to the hotel."

He smiled and leaned down to kiss me. "Gladly."

* * *

Forty-five minutes and another round of shots later, the bar was beginning to swirl in and out of focus. The music sounded *fantastic*. Shannon had convinced Nathan to dance, and I had decided to sit in Warren's lap instead of on my chair. I looped my arms around his neck. "I'm dizzy."

He smiled up at me. "I can tell. I'm wondering if I might actually have to carry you out of here."

I narrowed my eyes. "I'm not that drunk."

"That's what all drunks say."

I tugged on his nose. "You're pretty cute, you know?" I said. "In a cute and scary kind of way."

He laughed. "Cute and scary, huh?"

I held my thumb and index finger millimeters apart. "A little bit scary."

Warren pointed at Nathan who was twirling Shannon around a non-existent dance floor. "How much has he had to drink? He doesn't strike me as a dancing kind of guy."

I laughed. "Nathan, you look ridiculous!" I cupped my hands around my mouth as I shouted, and I tipped a little off-balance and almost fell in the floor.

Warren's capable hands steadied me.

Upon hearing his name, Nathan stopped dancing and came over and grabbed my hand. "Can I borrow her for a second, Warren?"

"Bring her back in one piece," Warren said. "And watch where you put your hands. I've got my eye on you."

Nathan pulled me to my feet and spun me under his

arm toward the piano.

Shannon sat down at the table obviously drunk because she wasn't even mad she had been jilted for me.

"You think I look ridiculous, huh?" Nathan asked.

I laughed as he twirled me around. "You can't dance."

"Maybe not, but you can't either!" He dipped me back so far that I almost toppled over, taking him down with me. He straightened up and rested his forehead against mine laughing.

Warren was snapping his fingers in our direction. "Hey! Leave room for the Holy Spirit there, McNamara."

Nathan laughed and took a step back from me. He started hopping from one foot to the other like a drunken leprechaun.

I laughed and grabbed his forearms. "Let's go get more drinks. I'm thirsty."

He stopped hopping. "OK. Hey, Warren! Shannon!" he called out. "Want another round?"

"Yes!" Shannon squealed.

Warren held up his half-full glass. "No thanks. I'm good."

Arm in arm, Nathan and I supported each other as we pushed our way across the room. His eyes were still dancing, and he had sweat trickling out from under his cap. He laughed as he tried to catch his breath.

We leaned against the glossy, wooden bar, and he looked around for the bartender.

I bumped him with my hip. "I'm pretty mad at you, you know."

He laughed. "I know."

"I'm serious."

He looked over at me and his laughter faded. "What was I supposed to do though? Not bring a date and hang out with you sitting on his lap all weekend? That's not me."

I looked back to the table where Shannon was giggling something to Warren and sitting a little closer to him than I was comfortable with. My raging hypocrisy surprised even me as I realized I was still clutching Nathan's arm. I released him. "Are you serious about her?"

He shook his head. "No."

"So, you're not going to move her to Charlotte if you take the job?"

He frowned and raised an eyebrow at me.

I laughed. "I didn't think so. You should probably tell her though. It's not fair. Not fair even for Shannon Green."

He nudged me with his elbow. "I think you're starting to like her."

I smirked. "Hardly."

The bartender stopped in front of us with an expectant stare.

Nathan leaned forward. "Two Smithwick's and another damn Cosmopolitan, please."

I laughed when the bartender rolled his eyes.

We turned around as we waited. Shannon was talking to Warren with dramatic and flailing arms like she was cheating at a game of charades. He looked at us with wide, pleading eyes, begging for our quick return.

Nathan looked over at me. "What are you going to do when he leaves?"

My face fell. "I've been asking myself that since the minute he told me. Survive, I guess."

He shook his head. "I can't imagine the migraine that will come as a result of him leaving the country. I might as well book your hospital room now."

Nathan had been there the first time Warren left and I developed my first hemiplegic migraine. He had actually broken through my back door and carried me to the ambulance. Then he slept in a chair all night beside me at the hospital. The second time it happened, I was with him again. That night, I puked all down the front of his pants and ruined his tactical boots.

"I don't know what I'm going to do. Especially if you're in Charlotte and not there to let me throw up all over you." I smiled at him.

He grimaced. "That was the most disgusting night of my life. I don't even want to think about it."

I laughed and felt my cheeks flush. "Well, you've repaid me by letting Shannon crash my vacation."

He shook his head. "Not even remotely close."

The bartender brought us our drinks. I picked up my beer and Nathan followed me back to our table. Warren looked bewildered as I leaned down in front of him. "You OK?" I asked.

"I don't think she has an off button." He jerked his thumb toward her. "Getting her drunk was a very bad, bad idea."

I laughed and kissed him. "I'm going to run to the bathroom."

"Sloan, wait!" Shannon called as I walked toward the bathroom. I stopped and she nearly plowed into me.

She hooked her arm through mine, and I turned around in time to see Warren and Nathan sharing a laugh at my expense. I stuck out my tongue at both of them.

After using the restroom, I washed my hands while Shannon slathered on a new layer of lipstick like a fat-fingered kindergartner using a red crayon for the first time. To keep from laughing, I bit the insides of my lips.

The water ran cold over my hands, and a chill zinged down my spine. I shuddered. The room looked brighter. The music seemed louder. For a second, I felt lightheaded. *No more booze for me.* I shut off the water and reached for a paper towel.

"Your boyfriend is hot, Sloan." Her speech was slurred, and she staggered as she stepped back and smacked her red lips together.

"I know he is." I pointed at her. "You stay away from him."

She laughed. "That was a long time ago. I was just jealous of you."

"Jealous?"

She waved her arm toward me and nearly fell into the sink. "Yeah. You won homecoming and you were the captain of the cheerleading squad, even though you're uncoordinated as shit," she confessed. "I secretly hated you."

I smirked. "That's good to know."

"I am really sorry though. I was a bitch." She was making a serious attempt at a pouty face.

I nodded. "You've got that right."

She grabbed me by the shoulders. "I mean it, Sloan. I'm really sorry."

Rolling my eyes, I took her by the wrist. "Come on, blondie."

When I hauled her out of the bathroom and turned toward our table, I slammed face-first into the blackest soul I'd ever seen.

7.

"Oh, excuse me." The man's moist breath hit my face, reeking of bad scotch and stale cigarettes.

I would have screamed had I been able to breathe.

He ran a calloused hand over his oily black hair and brushed against my arm as he walked past. I thought my skin might peel away from the bone.

The room began spinning out of control. My legs crumpled under me, my knees landing with a thud on the scuffed and sticky hardwood floor.

"Sloan? You all right?" Shannon's voice sounded far away.

The only response I could muster was shaking my head.

A calming wave washed over me as Warren's strong arms closed around my waist. He hoisted me back up to my feet, and for the first time in almost a full minute, I inhaled. My hands were shaking, and sweat was prickling my forehead.

"Sloan, what is it?" He turned me around and studied my eyes.

"Men's room" was all I could choke out.

Warren spun his head around. "Nate!" he shouted and pointed at me.

Shannon grabbed my hand when Warren stepped away, and Nathan caught me in his arms just before my knees buckled again.

"Outside." I was beginning to hyperventilate. "Take me out."

He hooked his arm around me. "Shannon, tell the waitress we'll be right back. I'm going to take her out for some air."

"What's wrong?" The panic in her voice was evident to everyone who could hear. Other patrons were looking around with alarm.

"Outside," I said again, digging my nails into his arm.

"Just go!" Nathan shouted at Shannon.

I put my arm around his shoulders as he helped me across the crowded room toward the front door.

When we were outside in the warm night air, I gasped, sucking deep into my lungs every molecule of oxygen I could. It was too much, and I puked in the planter on the sidewalk.

Once again, Nathan held back my hair.

When I was finished, he steered me away from the door to a park bench nearby. I collapsed onto it the second we were close enough.

He dropped to a knee in front of me, but he wobbled a bit and had to catch himself before falling over. "What happened?"

Shaking my head, I continued to focus on breathing. To be honest, I wasn't exactly sure what had just happened inside the bar. "There was a guy." I was still panting, but I could finally speak. "Oh God, he's bad. He's done something really horrific."

"Where?"

"He went into the bathroom," I said.

He started to get up, but I grabbed his hand. "No. Please stay with me. Warren went to check it out."

Nathan nodded and sat down next to me. He rubbed my back. "I don't think I've ever seen you freak out quite like that."

I took another deep breath and blew it out with forced control. I held up my hand so he could see it violently shaking in the air. "Now you know why I take Xanax when I go to your office."

He clasped his hands over mine and held them still.

A moment later, Shannon came outside with a glass of water. "Here." She spilled a little as she offered it to me.

For the first time maybe ever, I was sincerely grateful for Shannon Green. "Thank you."

She pointed back toward the building, but the motion threw her off balance and she stumbled a bit. "I'm assuming the party's over and it's time to go home," she said. "I'll just go in and settle our tab."

I nodded and drank the water. I wanted to get as far away from Durty Nelly's as humanly possible.

On her way back inside, she knocked shoulders with Warren as they passed in the doorway. He didn't even notice. His eyes were dark and dangerous. There was a quickness to his step that he hadn't had all day.

"What *was* that?" I asked.

He shook his head. "I haven't had that feeling since I was eight." He flashed a loaded glance in my direction.

When Warren was just eight years old, he and another girl were placed in the home of a child molester who had somehow made it into the foster system. It was the first time Warren had ever used his power to kill someone.

I had only seen him do it once to end Billy Stewart, and at that moment, I wanted him to do it again.

"I felt"—I swallowed hard—"I felt weird in the bathroom. I thought it was the alcohol. Then I came out and he was right there."

Warren's face was set like stone. The muscles in his forearms were rigid as he clenched his fists at his sides. "I felt it too. Then I saw you hit the floor."

The door to the bar opened and the man came outside. I put my head between my knees and willed myself to not start throwing up again. Alcohol plus a panic attack was a bad combination.

Warren knelt down in front of me. "I'm going to follow him and see where he goes." He looked at Nathan. "Are you sober enough to get her back to the hotel?"

Nathan nodded. "Yeah, I'll be fine. But are you sure you don't want me to come with you?"

Warren shook his head as he stood. "No. Some things need to be done in the absence of the law." He kissed the top of my head. "Breathe. I'll be back as soon as I can. You stay with Nathan."

We watched until Warren disappear out of sight down the River Walk. Beside me, Nathan was gently slapping his cheeks to sober up. I handed him what was left of my water.

"Thank you," he said before draining the glass.

Shannon came out a few minutes later with my purse and hers. "We're all settled up. Where's Warren?" she asked, looking around.

"He's going to meet us at the hotel. Sloan, can you walk?" Nathan asked, offering me his hand.

I nodded and he helped me to my feet.

"What was all that about?" Shannon teetered on her heels as we turned in the direction of the Hyatt.

I patted my chest over where my heart was slowly beginning to settle down. "It's a long story."

Nathan didn't let go of my hand until we crossed the

bridge and I realized it was awkward. I pulled my hand away. He was still watching me like I might keel over at any second. I was a little worried it was with good reason.

When we reached the elevator inside our hotel, he pressed the number five button for their floor. I reached over and pushed the number seven.

"Just come with us," he said. "Even Warren said for you to stick with me."

I shook my head as the doors closed and we began to ascend. "No thanks. I'm just going to go to my room and lie down."

He frowned. "You don't look so good. I don't think you being by yourself is a good idea. We'll stay with you till Warren gets back."

I put my hand on his arm. "I'm OK. Seriously."

The doors opened on the fifth floor and they stepped out. Nathan blocked the doors with his arm and leaned in. His eyes were slightly bloodshot. "I'm worried about you," he said, lowering his voice.

"Don't be," I said. "I'll be fine."

He pointed at me as the doors began to close. "Call me."

"I will. Goodnight, guys. Shannon, we'll pay you back," I called to her.

"No worries. Goodnight, Sloan!" She bumped into a planter in the hallway.

The doors shut, and I sank back against the glass. I took a few more deep breaths and closed my eyes. When I got to my room, it felt much smaller than before. I tried to open the window, but it was sealed closed. I thought about taking my medicine, but I worried about it mixing with the alcohol.

My cell phone beeped. It was a text message from Warren. *Jumped in a cab to see where he goes. Be back soon. Don't worry.*

I put my purse on the bed and tapped out a response. *I may go to the pool to try and clear my head. Please be safe. I love you.*

Love you, he replied a moment later.

I flipped through the concierge book and found out the pool was located on the roof, and it was open till midnight. I sighed with relief. The open air of a rooftop sounded like paradise. I changed into the black bathing suit I had thrown into my suitcase and put on one of Warren's t-shirts and my flip-flops.

As I walked toward the door, I caught sight of myself in the full-length mirror. I stopped and examined my arms and legs, quickly remembering the night I was dragged through the woods by Billy Stewart. My right leg looked like I had been mauled by a tiger. Silvery pink scars stretched up the side of my calf and up my thigh. The rest of my limbs hadn't fared much better.

It occurred to me, I was about to go out of my room at night alone. If the walls hadn't felt like they might suffocate me, I might have just crawled into—or under—the bed. Instead, I slung a towel over my shoulder and walked out the door before I could change my mind.

On the elevator ride to the roof, I sent Nathan a message telling him not to worry and that I was going to the pool. For a moment, I considered asking him to join me, but decided that was in no one's best interest.

When I opened the door to the rooftop, the long, rectangular swimming pool was sparkling in the moonlight. Tension began to leave my neck and shoulders just at the sight. There was a couple curled up together on a lounge chair, but the pool was empty. Jazz music floated up from the streets below along with the distant hum of the San Antonio nightlife.

I placed my phone, room key, and towel on a lounge

chair and stripped off Warren's shirt. After kicking off my shoes, I walked to the edge of the deep end. Looking at the still water, I sucked in a calming breath before diving in headfirst. The cool water flowed over my body as I dolphin kicked to the surface. I rolled to my back and kicked my feet up in front of me, till I was completely horizontal and floating.

There were more stars than I should have been able to see in the city.

When Kayleigh Neeland was kidnapped, Adrianne had convinced me that my ability must have been given to me to serve some kind of purpose, but as I floated on top of the water, feeling the adrenaline diffusing in my bloodstream, my powers felt like a curse. It was commonplace to encounter bad people, but every once in a while, I encountered someone who was truly evil. I shuddered at the mere thought of that man's eyes.

I swam to the edge and pushed off the side and began swimming slow laps across the pool to push the sickening thoughts out of my mind. As I finished lap eight and opened my eyes under water to look for the wall, I saw a pair of perfect calves and bare feet dangling in front of me. I stopped swimming and picked up my head to wipe my eyes.

Nathan was at the edge of the pool wearing only a pair of red and black swimming trunks.

I reached for the ledge of the concrete beside him and looked around. "Where's your girlfriend?"

He laughed. "Passed the hell out. She didn't even take off her clothes or makeup before she collapsed onto the bed. I've never seen her drink that much."

"I think we were all headed in the same direction before the evening took a nosedive," I said.

He laughed. "Probably so. Hell, I'm still a little buzzed."

"Wonder what Shannon would think about you being

up here?" I asked, raising a skeptical eyebrow.

He eased down into the water. "At this point, I'm sure she wouldn't be surprised."

A bright pink circular scar was gleaming on his chest. That hole had been put there to save my life. I gently pushed on his shoulder. "Turn around and let me see your back."

He turned so I could see the entry wound scar. Nathan had been shot in the back as he dove between me and Billy Stewart's Smith & Wesson. His lung had collapsed when the bullet tore through both sides of his ribcage.

"At least you got some cool scars out of it," I said, smiling as I gently ran my finger across the smooth scar tissue.

He laughed as he turned back around to face me. "Heck yeah. Chicks dig scars."

I held up my forearms and slowly turned them over to display the spots where the nurses had to dig gravel and splinters out of my skin. "Do guys dig scars too?" I scrunched up my nose with disgust.

He winked at me. "You could be missing your arms completely and you'd still be hot."

A half-hearted smile crept across my face. "Thanks."

I turned around and rested my back against the side of the pool, sinking down till the cool water touched my chin.

Nathan leaned back on his elbows and looked over at me. "Are you feeling better now?"

I blew out a deep breath and shuddered. "That was bad. That guy was terrifying."

He looked up at the stars. "I wish I knew what it felt like."

I shook my head. "No you don't."

"Who do you think he was?" he asked.

I shrugged my shoulders. "I have absolutely no idea. Warren sent me a text and said he was taking a cab to follow him and see where the guy goes."

Nathan nudged my leg with his foot under the water and grinned with the soft rippled light from the pool reflecting off his face. "It must be bad for him to leave you at a hotel with me."

I laughed for the first time since we left the Irish pub.

"Other than the ending, did you have a good time tonight?" he asked.

"Yeah. I have to admit that even hanging out with your obnoxious and belligerent girlfriend was even a little fun. She actually apologized to me in the bathroom for what she did in high school."

"No shit?"

"No shit."

"Are you going to let it go?"

I shook my head. "Not a chance."

He chuckled.

"Did you enjoy yourself?" I asked.

He nodded. "Yeah, I haven't had that much fun in quite a while." He sank down to my level in the pool. "What's new with you these days? We don't talk much since Warren moved in."

I smirked at him. "I talk to you more than I talk to my own mother, even with Warren around."

He looked sad. "It's not like it was before though."

He was right. Before Warren moved to Asheville, I spent so much time at Nathan's house that he had bought a leather loveseat to put in his home office just for me to have a comfortable place to sit. Much of that time was dedicated to pouring over the investigation of missing girls across the state, but we did enjoy our time enough that it made Shannon extremely jealous.

I thought about those days in stark contrast to my new life with Warren. "There's not much to tell. I'm pretty boring, Nathan."

He laughed. "Aside from the superpowers and all."

"Aside from that." I laughed. "Oh, I did finally tell my parents about it."

"Really?"

I dropped my head back and pressed my eyes closed. "It was kind of hilarious. I just sort of blurted it out. We were talking about headaches, and I told them my headaches were supernaturally related to Warren's absence."

He cracked up laughing. "Supernaturally related? And you're not locked in the looney bin? I'm shocked!"

I smiled. "They actually handled it spectacularly well."

He shook his head. "I'm not surprised. Your parents are great."

"Oh, that reminds me, my mother said to tell you hello."

"Your mom loves me, you know," he said.

I nodded. "Oh, I know."

He smiled. "When she came to visit me in the hospital after my chest surgery, she asked me to dump Shannon and marry you."

I gasped. "No, she didn't!"

"Wanna bet?" He sank under the water to soak his blond head. Then he came back up and raked his fingers back through his hair, leaving it spiked in different directions.

"Well, my mom loves Warren now too," I said.

He looked over at me. "Do you?"

I was stunned by his candor. "Do I love Warren?"

He nodded.

"Yes. I love him very much."

He looked back up at the sky. I felt like I wanted to apologize, but I knew it would only make everything worse. I stared at the water droplets drizzling down the side of his face until he looked at me with questioning eyes.

"What are you thinking about?" he asked quietly.

"You, me, Warren," I admitted.

He turned toward me. "What do you think would have happened if he had never shown up?"

I had asked that same question a lot since the Friday afternoon when Nathan cornered me in my office and confessed he wanted to be with me. But there, face-to-face in the pool with him while Warren was gone, was not the time to be daydreaming about what might have been. It felt wrong to even be entertaining the question.

I sucked in a deep breath and blew it out nervously as I searched for the right words to say.

"Sloan."

While I had been lost in thought, Nathan had closed some of the distance between us. The moonlight bounced off his dangerously tempting gray eyes that were fixed on my lips. The jazz music from the streets below was nearly drowned out by my pounding heart, and every nerve ending in my body began to tingle. His face was inches from my own.

And then the moment was gone.

The door to the building opened, and Warren walked outside. His step faltered as if he could sense the tension on the rooftop.

I snapped out of my daze as he slowly walked over. "Hey," I said.

Nathan rolled his shoulders back and exhaled before turning around.

Warren looked down at us both. It was obvious he wanted to ask what was going on, but he didn't.

"What did you find out?" Nathan asked, avoiding direct eye contact with either of us.

Warren knelt down at the edge of the pool. "Well, I followed him to a house on the West side of town, not too far from here. I got the address." He tapped his chest pocket and looked down at Nathan. "Do you think you can work some magic and figure out who he is?"

Nathan nodded. "Yeah. I can make some calls in the morning and see if I can find a name and some information."

"What did you get off of him?" I asked.

"Well, he hasn't killed anyone." He turned his palms up. "Not in the literal sense anyway. I'm sure he's ended plenty of lives though."

I reached up for his hand. "Are you all right?"

He kissed my knuckles. "Yeah. Not exactly how I wanted to end such a fun night, though. Are you feeling OK now?"

"Yeah," I said. "Swimming and the night air helps. Nathan's been a good nursemaid like always."

Nathan laughed and then looked back at Warren. He rested his arms on the side of the pool. "So, do you want to go after this guy?"

"Oh, I'm going to go after this guy." Warren's response had no hesitation. "There's no question about it."

"You realize there is zero probable cause here," Nathan pointed out.

A thin smile spread across Warren's lips, and he cut his eyes down at Nathan. "You realize I'm not a cop, right? That I have all the probable cause I need?"

Nathan laughed. "All right, man. Just leave my name out of it."

Warren looked at me. "You ready to get out?"

I nodded. "Yes."

He tightened his hand around mine and pulled me up onto the deck. Nathan got out behind me.

Warren looked around the roof. "Where's Shannon?"

"The girl can't handle her alcohol." Nathan laughed and dried off with the towel he had deposited next to my flip-flops. "I told Sloan she passed out as soon as I opened the door to the hotel room."

Warren laughed as I retrieved my things off the lounge chair. "She's so loud when she's drunk, and she doesn't shut up."

I wrapped the towel around me as we walked inside. "Does she shut up when she's sober?"

Nathan laughed, but hung his head and shook it sadly.

When the elevator stopped at our floor, I looked back at Nathan. "Are you coming to mass with us in the morning?"

His head snapped back with surprise. "You're really going?"

"Yeah," I said.

He shook his head. "No. Probably not. I'm pretty sure I'm going to have to babysit someone with a really severe hangover."

"Probably," I agreed. "I don't envy either of you."

"We'll catch up with you after," he said. "Maybe we can grab lunch. I wouldn't mind going back to the pool in the sunshine."

"That sounds good to me. Goodnight, Nathan," I told him.

"Night, guys," he said as the doors closed behind us.

Warren and I walked to our room. He looked down at the black bundle in my arms. "Is that my shirt?"

"Maybe," I answered as he slipped the room key into the slot.

We went inside and he locked the door behind us. I turned around to look at him. "Tell me the truth. Did you kill that guy?"

He shook his head. "No, but I thought about it."

"Why didn't you?"

He emptied his pockets onto the desk. "I've learned it's best to have all the facts before making a decision like that. What if he's got hostages or something stashed somewhere?"

He was right, but I didn't like it. I touched his arm.

"Are you sure you're OK? I know how badly he got to me tonight, and it seemed to hit really close to home for you."

He tugged on my towel and pulled me close. "Yeah. I'm just sorry he screwed up a pretty fun night." He pushed my wet hair back off my shoulders. "Who would've ever thought we would enjoy a night out with Nathan McNamara and the syphilis princess."

I laughed. "I know."

"So, church in the morning?" he asked with questioning eyes.

"Yes," I said. "You don't have to go, but I'm going to stop in and see if I can find someone to talk to."

He shrugged. "I'll go. God knows I've got a lot of repenting to do."

I giggled. "Are you going to go to confession?"

His fingers found the knot in my bathing suit ties at the back of my neck. He worked the strings loose and smiled as the straps came down. "Maybe. And I might have a few more things to add to the list before morning."

8.

In all my life, I had attended church exactly three times. It was an impressive, or sad, record considering I grew up in a town with a steeple on just about every street corner. I went once with my mom's sister around Christmas, once for Easter because the Presbyterians were having an egg hunt, and once because a distant cousin was being baptized. None of those churches were Catholic. All I knew about Catholicism was what I learned from television: they had a Pope, they liked Mother Mary, they were allowed to drink alcohol, and priests wore white collars and black suits.

The nicest outfit I had packed was a floral sundress with spaghetti straps. I guessed it was hardly appropriate for church, but I was certain it was better than blue jeans. I was slipping on my flip-flops when Warren walked out of the bathroom. A cloud of steam rolled through the door with him, like his own personal stage production. I half-expected spotlights and the sound of angels singing.

"You look great," I said. And it was true. He was in dark jeans that clung to all the right muscle groups and a simple, black button-up shirt. I scrunched up my nose. "But I'm afraid you're going to burn up in the sun."

"It's Texas. I'm going to burn up regardless." He walked over and tugged on the hem of my dress. "You look cute."

"Thanks. Are you ready to go?"

He looked a little nervous. "As ready as I'll ever be."

Outside the hotel, directly across the busy street, was the stone face of the Alamo. I pointed to it as Warren took my hand. "You know, it still doesn't seem right that the Alamo is in the middle of the city. You think Alamo, you think desert."

He laughed, squinting his eyes against the sun as he slipped on his black sunglasses. "I think Alamo and I think of rental cars and steak houses."

It was going to be another hot day in Texas. I thought of the swimming pool on our roof. "What do you want to do this afternoon?"

He didn't miss a beat with his answer. "Go disembowel that guy we saw last night."

"Well, that's gruesome." I shuddered at the thought of the night before. "That was such an awful feeling. I wonder who he is."

"I don't know who he is, but I have an idea of what he's up to," he said.

I shook my head. "I don't want to know. Let's talk about something else. We could go look for Rachel Smith this afternoon. At least cruise through the area around the convenience store and see if anything looks interesting."

"We can if you want," he said. "I wonder how long the service will last."

"I have no clue," I said. "I've never attended mass before."

"I've never been inside of any church that I can remember," he admitted.

I looked up at him with wide eyes. "I wonder if you might burst into flames."

He laughed. "I wouldn't be surprised."

The San Fernando Cathedral was a sight to behold. Two high, Gothic-style stone pillars were adorned with crosses on each side and weathered by almost three hundred years of Texas sunshine. In the middle, there were three arched, heavy wooden doorways that sat below circular windows framed in peaks that resembled royal crowns. There was certainly nothing architecturally comparable to it in the mountains of Asheville. It looked like it belonged on a hill in Italy, not at the corner of Main and South Floures in downtown San Antonio, Texas. A sign out front stated the church had been founded in 1738, and it was the oldest church in the state.

We followed a group of people inside. Mass was already in progress. A choir was singing with a piano at the front of the elaborate sanctuary. One soprano was slightly off-key and singing just a little bit louder than the rest. The song was in Spanish, or maybe it was Latin. I wasn't enough of an expert in either language to be sure.

There were no seats left in the pews, so Warren and I stood with the other latecomers in the back of the room. The inside of the church was long and narrow with a high arched ceiling and massive arched columns dividing the room in thirds with the main section straight down the middle. The middle section ended at the far end of the sanctuary with a podium in front of the largest crucifix I had ever seen. Jesus was crucified between enough elaborate stained glass and gold leaflet to pay off my mortgage at least twice over.

Warren leaned down close to my ear. "There's a dead body in here. Maybe more than one."

My breath caught in my chest. "Are you sure?"

"Positive," he replied.

I looked around the room. Behind a group standing in

the corner was a large marble box on the wall. I tugged on his hand, and we inched our way over to it. I read the bronze plaque on the side: *Here lie the remains of Travis, Crockett, Bowie, and other Alamo heroes.*

"You're really weird," I whispered up at Warren.

He winked. "So are you."

When the music ended, a man in a long green robe stepped behind the podium and began to read, in what I was sure was Spanish. He was swinging an elaborate steel pot from a chain which was pouring smoke in every direction. I looked at Warren. He just shrugged his shoulders. I scanned the entrance way, hoping to find a Catholic Mass for Dummies booklet. The next person who got up to speak was also speaking Spanish.

I leaned over to him. "I think we've come to the wrong service. I can't understand a word," I whispered. "This is pointless."

He motioned toward the door we had just come in. "You wanna go?"

I nodded.

Once we were outside, I slipped on my sunglasses and shook my head. "That's not the way the Presbyterians do church."

He laughed and followed me across the stone courtyard. I sat down at a small metal bistro table, and he pulled a chair over next to mine. On either side of us were water fountains shooting up out of the ground like the splash pad at the Buncombe County water park. Somehow I knew these weren't frequented by toddlers in swimming diapers.

He scanned the courtyard. "Well, what do you want to do now?"

I looked up at the elaborate building. "This was a complete bust. I really wanted to talk to a priest or something." I also felt a little defeated that I didn't last more than five minutes in church.

"Do you want to wait till the service is over and try to find someone? Maybe they have people you can talk to when it's all over with."

I shrugged and slumped my shoulders. "I don't know. That's a long time to just sit here and wait in the hot sun."

A large shadow crept over our table. "May I help you?" a man asked behind us.

I turned to see an old man with thick glasses and a dentured smile that was as welcoming as it was contagious. His bald head was covered in sunspots, several of which came together to perfectly form the outline of South America. He was wearing a black suit with a white collar, and a gold cross dangled around his wrinkled neck.

I smiled and jerked my thumb back toward the cathedral. "Do you work here?"

"I have been here for many more years than I can count. May I be of some assistance? You seem a little lost." He was supporting himself on the back of an empty chair.

"I don't want to trouble you if you're busy." I squinted up at him against the sunlight which seemed to form a halo around him. "I just had some questions."

He nodded to the table. "May I join you?"

"Please." I slid my chair back from the table a few inches.

Warren rose from his seat and pulled out a chair for the priest. The old man grimaced as he eased down into the chair like every joint between his head and his toes ached with age and arthritis. He had to be pushing ninety. Warren sat back down next to me and leaned his elbows on the table.

Behind the priest's coke-bottle-thick lenses, his eyes were fascinating. They were brown, but the right eye seemed to be split down the middle. Half of it was brown, the other half green.

I offered him my hand and he shook it. "My name is Sloan. This is my boyfriend, Warren. We are down here visiting from North Carolina."

He smiled. "North Carolina is a beautiful state. I love the mountains there. I haven't been in some time, but it is a spectacular piece of God's handy work, particularly this time of year." He chuckled a bit like Santa Claus. "Not to mention it's a lot cooler there than here."

I laughed and nodded my head. "That's for sure. Can I ask your name?"

"Father John Michaels, but I am old and nontraditional with no need for formalities. You can call me John if you'd like." He had lowered his voice like he was telling us a great secret.

"Father John, can you tell me anything about angels?" I asked.

He studied my face for a moment and then suddenly broke into laughter. "Most questions I get are about mass or Jesus or Mary."

I laughed. "Well, I have lots of questions about mass as well. They really need a cheat sheet in there."

He smiled. "I agree. What would you like to know about angels?"

"Do you think they are real?" I asked.

"Of course I do." He chuckled again and folded his hands over his belly.

"Are they here on Earth? Like, could they be walking around here with us?" I asked, gesturing with my hand toward the courtyard.

He nodded. "Absolutely. The Bible makes that very clear. The book of Hebrews, chapter thirteen verse two, reminds us to 'not neglect hospitality, for through it some have unknowingly entertained angels.'"

"Really?" I looked over at Warren and then back at the

priest. "Here's a weird question." I hesitated for a moment. "Do you know if they can have children? Or maybe reproduce with humans?"

He considered my query. "I believe so, though some others in the church do not. The Old Testament, the book of Genesis specifically, speaks of the Nephilim which were the children born to the sons of God and the daughters of men. However, it has been greatly debated that they were the actual offspring of angels."

Warren leaned toward him. "Do you know anything about Azrael?"

The priest's eyes widened. "Azrael is not mentioned in the Christian Bible, but in other texts, Azrael is said to be an angel of death. The Bible does speak of an angel of death, but he is not named. I believe Azrael is derived from the teachings of Judaism and, perhaps, Islam."

Warren nodded and looked off into the distance.

"You've studied up on this quite a lot, haven't you?" I asked.

He smiled and spread his hands on the table. "I admit I've always had a touch of fascination with the angelic." He looked between us. "May I ask what has stirred your curiosity on the subject?"

Warren and I exchanged glances. I scrambled for an answer. "We have a friend who we believe could have some kind of supernatural gifts. We were curious as to where those gifts might have come from. Does that sound crazy?"

He smiled and shook his head. "No, dear. It doesn't sound crazy at all. God puts us all here with different gifts and abilities to further His kingdom."

I was skeptical. "But what if our friend doesn't share your beliefs about God's kingdom?" I was almost afraid of his answer. "What if she's not sure God even exists at all?"

He smiled and lowered his voice again. "God is still

God, despite what we believe about him."

Warren chuckled.

I reached for the old man's wrinkled hand. "Thank you, Father John. You don't know how helpful you've been."

He squeezed my fingers. "It is my pleasure. I will pray you find the answers you seek." He smiled warmly and sunlight glistened off his glasses. "And remember, even if you don't believe in God, he still believes in you. Ask and you shall receive. Seek and you shall find. Knock and the door will be opened unto you."

I had no idea what he meant, but I smiled like I did and stood up.

"Thank you," Warren said. He shook the priest's hand and then helped him to his feet.

I smiled at Father John. "I'm glad we stopped by, even if we didn't understand a thing about mass. I hope you have a good rest of your day."

Warren put his hand on my back as we turned to leave. Church bells rang out from the cathedral tower, disturbing a flock of black birds.

"Sloan." The priest grabbed my arm, pulling us to a stop.

We turned back toward him.

"I feel like I should give you a word of caution," he said. "Not all angels are good. The fallen angels of Heaven were banished here to Earth when they rebelled against God. If you are on a quest seeking angels, take great care. Even Satan himself masquerades as an angel of the light."

9.

"Well, that was terrifying." I was laughing as we crossed the street but didn't exactly think it was funny. "I've got my hands full worrying about murderers and child molesters. Now I've got to worry about Satan himself?"

Warren laced his fingers with mine. "A lot of what he said seems to fit with your theory."

"Yeah. Maybe it's true then," I said.

"How do we know for sure though?" he asked.

"I think finding Rachel Smith would be a good start," I answered.

He laughed. "Unless she's just as clueless as we are."

"True."

He patted his flat stomach. "I'm getting hungry."

I nodded. "Me too. I wonder what Nathan and Shannon are doing."

My cell phone buzzed in my hand. I looked at the screen. Of course, it was a message from Nathan.

Warren looked down at my phone and shook his head. "That's still pretty creepy."

"I know." I read Nathan's message aloud. "Having lunch at the pool. Where are you guys? Did Warren get struck by lightning when he walked into church?" I laughed.

"Jerk," Warren grumbled.

I looked up and tugged on his hand. "Do you want to have lunch at the pool and cool off for a bit in this heat? I know you must be sweltering in that black shirt."

He smiled down at me. "You gonna wear that bathing suit again?"

"Maybe," I answered. "Do you think it looks bad with all my hideous scars?"

He stopped walking so suddenly that I stumbled backward when his hand jerked mine to a stop. "Are you serious?" he asked.

I turned and looked at him. "Of course I'm serious." I held out my arms and then pulled up the hem of my skirt to show him my leg. "I promise I'm not feigning modesty here. I look like I lost a death match with a cheese grater."

He pulled me close to him. "Sloan, you looked so hot last night, I was a little pissed off you were in the pool with Nate." He tucked my hair behind my ear. "You have absolutely nothing to be embarrassed or ashamed about."

I blushed. "OK. I'll wear it then. Thank you."

He smiled and draped his arm across my shoulders. "We will definitely go to the pool."

Later at the hotel, when Warren and I left our room, I realized worrying about what I looked like really didn't matter. Warren didn't wear a shirt to the pool, so no one was looking at me anyway. On our walk through the building, he caused an old lady to drop her purse and a cleaning woman to run her cart into a wall. When we reached the top floor, every head on the rooftop turned in our direction.

I noted two college-age girls pointing and giggling near the bar. I shook my head and looked up at him. "I'm about to make you cover up."

He laughed and smacked me on the butt.

Nathan waved from a table between the water and the bar. He was shirtless again, a detail I refused to focus on, and Shannon was wearing her enormous hat and sunglasses. Her face was pale, and she was leaning on her elbow for support.

"Is someone having a rough day?" I teased as I put my towel down on the chair next to her.

"I feel like I was run over by a bus." She groaned. "All I wanna do is sleep, and Nathan dragged me up here."

Nathan pointed at Warren's chest. "Nice ink, man. What is it?"

Warren turned to show the rest on his back. "It's a dragon's claw."

I laughed. "I always thought it was a bird."

Warren sat down and shook his head. "Nope. It's a dragon. Why the hell would I get a bird?"

Shannon looked over the top of her glasses with bloodshot eyes. "Why would you get a dragon?" she mumbled.

Warren smiled and wiggled his fingers in front of my face. "Maybe it's a demon trying to carry me away."

I slapped his hand down. "Ugh. Given our present circumstance, that's not very funny."

"How was church?" Nathan asked Warren.

Warren shook his head. "Confusing."

"Did you find out anything?" Nathan asked.

I nodded and stripped off Warren's t-shirt that I had worn again. "Yeah. We found this adorable old priest outside, and he talked to us for a little while."

"And?" Nathan asked.

"And we still don't know anything for sure, but a lot of what he said made sense," I answered.

Warren looked around toward the bar. "I'm going to go up there and order some food. What do you want?"

I looked at Nathan's grilled sandwich. "Bring me something like that," I said. "But I'd like kettle chips instead of fries if they have them. Thanks, babe."

Warren nodded and walked off toward the bar.

There was a file folder on the table in front of Nathan. I tapped my finger on it. "What's this?"

"Oh, it's that list I told you about. Female child protective services case workers in San Antonio named Smith," he said. "It has the addresses where they work."

I shook my head. "The government is a scary beast."

He laughed. "No kidding. You should see what pops up when I run your name through the computer."

Rolling my eyes, I opened the folder. Quickly, I skimmed down the list. It was a total of two pages long. "This isn't as bad as I feared it would be."

He stuck a french fry in his mouth. "It's not too bad *if* she's still going by Smith." He pointed at me. "And if she's still a case worker."

I groaned. "Good point. Well, there are two Rachel Smiths on this list, so I guess that's our starting point."

"Why would a social worker do anything under a fake name?" Shannon asked.

She'd been so quiet, I had almost forgotten she was still at the table. "That's actually a good question."

Nathan shrugged. "She's hiding."

"From what?" I asked.

"Could be anything. An abusive spouse, criminal charges, the IRS. Who knows?" he said.

I pulled off my sunglasses and chewed on the tip. "How would you get a job, multiple jobs for that matter, in the government with a fake name? That seems like it would be a hard thing to do."

He nodded. "It's impossible to do. I'm sure they fingerprint and do background searches and everything for those kinds of positions."

"So how could she be getting away with it?" I asked. "You can change your name, but you can't change your fingerprints."

He shrugged again. "That's a good question. My guess is she doesn't work for the government anymore. Maybe she's working for a private company or a non-profit. Hell, she could be working at McDonalds for all we know."

I looked at the list. "There has to be a better way of doing this."

"Can't you find her?" Nathan asked.

I looked at Shannon and then gave Nathan a warning with my eyes.

He held up his hands and mouthed the word "sorry."

I flipped through the file and found Rachel's picture. I stared at it for a long time and wondered if there was any way I could find her with my ability. I closed my eyes and pictured her face. "Where are you Rachel Smith?"

When I opened my eyes, Nathan was scanning the roof expectantly.

I shook my head. "That's not how it works." But just in case, I glanced around the roof as well.

The two college girls were talking to Warren at the bar. Both were in bikinis and both were spilling out of their tops. The blonde was tracing her finger along the tattooed lines on his shoulder. He waved to get my attention, then pointed at me and spoke to them. Judging by their suddenly smug expressions, he was turning down some sort of proposition.

I frowned. "He's such a chick magnet."

"Yes, he is," Shannon agreed, unable to suppress a weak smile.

Nathan balled up his napkin and threw it at her. "Not you, too!"

She just shrugged her shoulders.

By the time Warren returned to the table with our plates, Shannon had found a nearby empty lounge chair and appeared to be asleep with a white towel completely covering her head. Every now and then she would moan in pain. Nathan was on his cell phone.

I looked over at Warren. "Thanks for lunch."

"Of course," he replied, unrolling his silverware.

I jerked my thumb in the direction of the bar. "Did you enjoy your little fan club over there?"

He blinked with surprise. "My fan club?"

I smirked. "Don't play dumb with me, Warren Parish. You may not have a lot of relationship experience, but you know those talking breasts over there were flirting with you."

He chuckled. "No idea what you're talking about."

I threw a potato chip at him.

He caught the chip in his mouth. "It's your fault," he said as he chewed.

"My fault?"

He held his hands up. "If you weren't here, they'd all run from me."

I scowled. "I somehow doubt that."

He held up two fingers in front of my face. "That's twice in two days you've gotten jealous. I like it."

I pushed his hand away. "Shut up."

Across the table, Nathan ended his call and put the phone down along with the pen he was holding. "That was my buddy in Charlotte."

Warren straightened in his seat.

Nathan leaned on his elbows. "He found the guy from last night and is emailing me his rap sheet." He looked down at the paper in front of him. "The guy's name is Larry Mendez. He's a convicted felon on robbery, assault, and drug charges. He's out on parole."

I was shocked. "That's it?"

Warren caught my eye. "That's just all he's been convicted of. That's certainly not all he's done."

I crunched on a potato chip and nodded my head. "Yeah. There's way more than robbery, assault, and drugs going on with that guy."

"Definitely," Warren agreed. "I'm going to go back out there tonight and look for him again. I want to see if he's at home."

"What are you going to do?" Nathan asked.

"I don't know. See what he's up to for now," Warren said.

Nathan's brow wrinkled with concern. "Don't go and get yourself arrested on stalking charges while we're down here. I really don't want to have to come and bail your ass out of jail."

Warren smirked. "I'll do my best."

"What time should we leave?" I asked.

Warren waved his fork at me. "I want you to stay here," he said. "You can hang out with Nathan and Shannon till I get back. We both know how dangerous this guy is."

I folded my arms across my chest. "Yes. We both *do* know how dangerous this guy is, and because of that, I don't want you going out there alone."

He looked insulted. "Have you met me? Do you not think I can handle him?"

Realizing he was right, I changed tactics. "Well, what if he's not there? You'll need me to find him. I'm coming along."

He shook his head. "No."

I widened my eyes at him and tilted my head to the side. "No?"

"Uh oh," Nathan said. He scooted back a few inches from the table with pure amusement splashed across his face.

Warren leaned forward and put his hand on the back of my chair. "This is too dangerous. It's a bad part of town, and I'm not going to let you—"

"*Let* me?" My voice jumped up an octave. "I don't remember ever giving you the authority to decide what I can and cannot do, Warren Parish."

Like watching a volley being returned across the net, Nathan's head whipped toward Warren.

Warren's eyes narrowed. "And if we find him and you have another meltdown like you did last night, then what are you going to do?"

Nathan looked back at me.

"I'll have my Xanax and I'll stay clear of the guy," I said. "I'm a big girl. I can handle myself. I think I've proven that."

"Nate, tell her what a bad idea this is," Warren said. He picked up a french fry off his plate and dunked it into a pile of ketchup.

Nathan held his hands up and shook his head. "You're on your own, brother. I'm just enjoying the show."

I sat back in my chair. "Warren, if I don't go, you don't go."

Warren stared at me in stunned silence for a moment before shaking his head and picking up his sandwich, signaling the end of the conversation.

Satisfied with my victory, I looked at Nathan. "Are you coming with us?"

"Heck yeah, I'm coming. I don't want to miss seeing how this plays out."

"What about Shannon?" Warren nodded to where she was sprawled across the chair a few feet away.

Nathan laughed. "I don't think Shannon will have any interest in leaving the hotel today."

I picked up another potato chip. "I don't think I've ever been that hungover."

"Me either. I have a feeling she won't be drinking again

anytime soon," Nathan said smiling.

* * *

Late in the afternoon, after we had showered from the pool, I came out of the bathroom dressed in a pair of black tactical cargo pants and a black t-shirt. I had purchased the ensemble for just such an occasion when Warren and I started dating.

He was watching television on the bed when I walked into the room. He shook his head when he saw me. "Well, you certainly *look* the part." He was not amused. He was pissed.

I put my hands on my hips. "Are you going to be mad at me all night?"

He nodded. "Probably."

I kicked the side of the bed with my boot. "Well, get over it."

His eyes were dark and glaring up at me. "Sloan, you can't defend yourself if something happens out there. You can't carry a gun or even shoot one. What happens if we get into something bad and I can't get to you in time?"

"Warren, I think I can handle a simple stakeout. I've been kidnapped, beaten, and shot at, remember?"

He sat up. "Yeah. I remember. That's exactly why I don't want you going. There's no telling what we might encounter out there, and I don't want to put you in harm's way if I don't have to."

I sat down on the edge of the bed and put my hand on his cheek. "I sincerely appreciate you worrying about me, but you're going to need my help with this whether you want it or not. What if you can't find Larry Mendez and he hurts or kills someone when I could have prevented it? I would rather take the risk and help stop this guy, than sit here safe in my hotel room."

He dropped his forehead onto my shoulder. "You're going to cause me to have anxiety."

I kissed the top of his head. "Well, I've got plenty of Xanax for both of us. Come on. Nathan's probably waiting."

There was a knock at our door.

I smiled as I stood, and Warren shook his head.

When I swung the door open, Nathan looked me up and down. "Uh, hi." He awkwardly looked at my outfit and then down at his own black pants and t-shirt.

We both laughed and walked back into the room side by side.

Warren rolled his eyes. "Geez," he said. "Should I change? I feel like I don't fit in with the mob squad." He was wearing jeans and a blue t-shirt.

Nathan tugged on the brim of his ball cap. It still said *Shitstarter* across the front. "All you need is a hat."

"And a bunch of inappropriate patches," I said, smiling. "I feel like we need a dynamic duo name. Maybe Cagney and Lacey."

He shook his head. "Nah. Mulder and Scully."

Warren pushed himself up off the bed. "More like Lucy and Ethel."

"I get to be Ethel." Nathan smiled. "Are you guys ready to go?"

"Almost," Warren said.

He walked to the closet and pulled out the huge black gun case he had brought on the trip. He placed it carefully on the bed and used a key to open the lock. I had never even seen what he carried in it. Nathan stepped over beside him as he opened the lid. Inside, a sniper rifle and two black, semiautomatic handguns were encased in dark gray foam.

Nathan surveyed the rifle while Warren strapped a double shoulder holster over his t-shirt and attached the straps to his belt.

"Is that a Remington MSR?" Nathan asked.

Warren nodded. "Yeah. It's awesome. One of the best

rifles I've ever owned."

While Nathan drooled over the gun case, Warren loaded both Glocks and tucked them into the holster. It seemed excessive.

I crossed my arms and looked at him sideways. "Why do you carry two guns?"

They both looked over at me. Warren's mouth was agape, and his eyes were genuinely puzzled. "Because I don't have three hands," he answered.

Nathan laughed.

Warren shrugged into a vintage blue plaid button up to conceal the holster, and he adjusted his belt. He smoothed the front of his shirt with his hands and looked over at me. "Now, I'm ready."

Warren carried the rifle case to the door.

"You're bringing that thing with us?" I asked.

He looked at me confused. "Of course I am."

At first, Warren carrying guns perplexed me since he had the ability to inflict death with a single glance. It finally made sense the night he shot the serial killer in the woods. He shot Billy three times without killing him because he knew we needed more information. Guns, to Warren, were just a stopping force. Warren himself was the lethal weapon.

"We should find a range while we're here," Nathan said as we walked to the elevator. "I want to shoot that rifle."

Warren pointed at me. "I agree we should find a range, because *she* needs to learn."

Nathan nodded in agreement. "Especially if she's going to dress like that."

I punched him in the shoulder.

* * *

It was almost dark by the time we reached the west side of town. Warren had stopped protesting my coming along, but he made me ride in the back seat of the SUV. We rolled slowly down a street lined with older, one-story, vinyl-siding houses where half the owners did their best to keep up their homes, while the other half did not. Rusted chain-link fences divided most of the properties, and there was graffiti covering the broken sidewalks. An old Hispanic man appeared to be reading a Bible on the porch of one house, while a group of teenagers were drinking forties and passing around a joint on the porch next door.

Warren slowed down as he pointed to a house on the left side of the street. "This is it."

At one time the house had been blue, but most of the paint had peeled away. It had a stone front porch lined with fractures and a swing that was only hanging from one side. Most of the windows were dark, except for the main one in the front that flickered with the light from a television screen.

"Is he home?" I asked.

Warren shook his head and looked up and down the street. "I don't think so. Last night he was driving a maroon truck and he parked on the curb. It's not here."

Nathan looked over at him. "Can't you use your laser vision and see if he's inside?"

Warren scowled. "I don't have laser vision. And that's not even close to how it works." He jerked his thumb toward me. "Besides, Sloan's better at that anyway."

Leaning forward, I cupped my hand around my ear. "What was that? What did you just say?"

He didn't turn to look at me. "Oh, shut up."

I chuckled.

Over the past month, Warren and I had been practicing my ability to summon people. The power was definitely getting stronger, but I still only had a certain amount of control over it. Sometimes it worked. Sometimes it didn't. I sat back in my seat and closed my eyes. Even though it made me a little queasy, I pictured Larry Mendez's terrifying face and his black soul hidden behind his thick glasses. "Where are you, Larry Mendez?" I asked out loud.

When I opened my eyes, Nathan was peering out of his side window. "I keep thinking someone is going to fall out of the sky when she does that."

"Turn left," I told Warren.

He looked at me in the rearview mirror. "Why?"

I shrugged. "It just feels like you should go left."

"You're the boss." He obediently turned left onto Blaine Avenue.

Nathan turned around in his seat and looked at me. "Since when can you find people like that?"

"Warren's been teaching me," I told him.

Warren was better than any bloodhound when it came to tracking down human remains. In total, he had found six of Billy Stewart's missing victims without any aid or equipment at all. Two of them had been dead and missing for well over a decade. His theory was I could apply his same techniques to my connection with the living. My powers were still faulty, but I was getting better.

After a few minutes, I closed my eyes. "Turn right."

We rolled down another street that forked a few blocks ahead.

"Now where?" Warren asked.

"Right again."

The street curved almost in a semicircle around a gas station at the end of the block, and it stopped at a three-way stop sign. "Go right," I said.

Nathan clapped his hands. "Congratulations, we have now almost completed a circle."

"Look!" Warren pointed down the street.

A dark red pickup truck pulled out in front of us a few blocks up ahead.

Nathan straightened in his seat, then looked back at

me with wide eyes. "No shit."

I clapped my hands together. "I did it!"

"Good job, babe." Warren pulled over to the right curb and turned off the headlights.

We watched in silence as Larry Mendez got out of his truck and carried a brown paper bag to his front door. He was talking on a cell phone and didn't notice the brand new, sparkling white SUV parked a block down the street.

I took a deep breath as I felt my chest begin to tighten with panic, but I didn't dare complain and risk igniting a series of I-told-you-sos from my boyfriend.

"I'll bet he's got beer in that bag," Nathan said. "He probably went to that gas station we passed to get booze and come back home. I doubt he's leaving again tonight."

Warren nodded. "You're probably right. Let's give him a minute, and if he doesn't leave again, we'll take off."

After six boring minutes of zero activity at the Mendez home, I pulled out my cell phone and started playing Candy Crush. After successfully completing two levels, I decided to text Adrianne to see how she was feeling. She didn't answer, so I sent a message to my mom.

Mom replied after a few seconds. *Not feeling so great. Gone to bed early. Hope you're having fun in Texas. XOXO.*

After that, I sent a group message to Warren and Nathan. *I'm bored.*

Their cell phones beeped at the same time. They exchanged puzzled looks before checking their messages.

"Very funny, Sloan," Nathan said, tucking his phone back into his jacket.

Warren straightened in the driver's seat and dropped his phone on the console. "Well, what do we have here?" He pointed out the windshield.

I looked up and followed the direction of his finger. A young girl, with long dark hair and light brown skin, was walking up the concrete steps to Larry's front door. She couldn't have been older than fifteen or sixteen. She used a key to open the front door and disappeared inside.

"Could it be his daughter?" I asked.

Nathan snatched up the papers off the dashboard where he had deposited them and flipped through the stapled pages. "It doesn't say he has any kids."

"Huh," I said. "I don't like it."

Warren grunted. "I don't like it either."

We waited for another twenty minutes, but there was no other movement at the house. I was half-asleep with my head propped against the glass.

"Call it a night?" Warren asked, looking around the car.

I leaned in between the two front seats and looked at him. "Can't you just go break down the door and drag him outside?"

Nathan answered first. "No, he can't."

"Well, technically I *could*," Warren said.

Nathan shook his head. "We'll keep an eye on him. If he's the monster you two think he is, we'll get to the bottom of it without getting ourselves killed or worse, arrested."

Warren grinned. "I can't believe you're such a rule follower."

Nathan rolled his eyes. "And I can't believe you're any kind of angel. Let's go."

10.

"Take the gun."

Warren pushed the unloaded handgun against my chest as he glared down at me.

I scrunched up my nose and looked around the dusty wooden box-of-a-room on the pistol range. It was hot, but sweat wasn't rolling down my spine just because of the Texas sunshine. The thought of firing the Glock that Warren kept thrusting in my direction had me perspiring like a turkey on Thanksgiving.

"Sloan," he said again, snapping his fingers in front of my face to get my attention. "If you don't do this, I'm going to leave you at the hotel with Shannon from now on for the rest of the time we are here."

I pressed my lips together and took the gun, holding it with two fingers out in front of me like it was contaminated with some dreadful disease.

He frowned and brought my other hand up to support it. "Hold it correctly." He tapped the side of the barrel with his finger. "See this lever? This is the safety. If you see red, the safety is off." He flipped it and a red mark appeared. He looked at me seriously. "Red is dead. Say it."

"Red is dead," I echoed.

He put the safety back on before putting his hands on my shoulders and turning me around to face the targets downrange. Stepping up close behind me, he extended his arms along mine and looked over my shoulder.

I took a deep breath and sighed. A wave of dizziness washed over me, partly because I was bordering on hysterics but mostly because of the effect he always had on me. I looked over at him. "For future reference, you're not allowed to wear cologne when I'm handling firearms."

"Pay attention." He began repositioning my fingers around the gun. "Keep your finger off the trigger and along the side of the barrel till you're ready to fire. Point it at the target or down, but never point it at another person unless you plan on killing them." He moved my arms down pointing at the ground and then back up toward the target. "Don't forget and start waving this thing around."

I nodded. "OK. Don't point it at you unless I'm ready to shoot you. I got it."

Warren didn't laugh.

"Now, pull it in, keeping the barrel pointed away and remove the empty magazine," he said.

Obediently, I pulled the gun close to my chest.

He moved my thumb over a small button on the side. "This is the button to release the magazine."

I pressed it, and a metal piece slipped out of the bottom. Warren quickly moved and caught it. He shook his head.

I beamed at him. "I did it!"

He handed me the magazine. "Shove it back in there and try it again. This time, *you* catch it."

I pushed the magazine back up into the handle, but it

slipped down again.

He shook his head. "Don't baby it. That's a good way to jam the gun. It won't break. Really slam it in there."

I slammed it hard the second time, nearly knocking the gun out of my other hand.

He smiled. "Better, but don't have butterfingers either." He nodded toward the gun. "Now, drop the magazine again."

I hit the button again and dropped the magazine into my left hand.

"Good." He took the magazine out of my hand and laid on the table. "Now, pull the slide back to clear the chamber."

I pulled on the slide at the top of the Glock, but it wasn't as easy as Warren made it look.

He scowled. "Stop being a baby."

"It's hard!" I whined. "I have nerve damage in my fingers, remember?"

He ignored me. "Yank it back."

I pulled as hard as I could, and it slid back into a locked position. "Hey, I got it!"

"Good job." He put his hands on top of mine again. "Now, push it forward to look down the barrel, and then pull it back to look down the barrel the other way. You've got to make sure it's clear in both directions." He did the motion again. "Push. Pull."

I obeyed, and he nodded with satisfaction. He handed me a loose bullet. "Now, put this in the clip to load the gun."

"So many steps," I grumbled.

I put the gun down and picked up the magazine. I pressed the bullet into it. There was a little resistance, but I did it without invoking more scowls from my beautiful, frustrated teacher. He actually looked pleased. Then he handed me the heavy box of ammo. "Now, load it full."

"I hate you."

"I know."

One by one I pushed the ammo into the magazine, but with every bullet the task became harder and harder. "Geez! How many times do I have to do this?"

"It holds fifteen rounds." His smile was getting wider as I struggled.

I stopped counting somewhere around twelve, and as I neared the end, loading more bullets was almost impossible. The last bullet simply wouldn't fit.

"Help me," I whimpered.

He shook his head. "Nope. If you can't load it, you can't shoot it."

I put my hand on my hip. "I don't want to shoot it!"

He nodded and held out his hand for the gun. "OK. Let's go back to the hotel and I'll book you and Shannon manicures at the spa."

I huffed and turned away from him. "Damn you."

He chuckled as I went back to trying to press the bullet into the magazine. After what seemed like an eternity, I got it to go in.

Warren nodded. "Now take them all out and do it again."

My mouth fell open.

He cracked up and took a step toward me. "I'm kidding." He picked up the gun off the table and handed it to me. "Pop the magazine back in. Hard."

With all the strength I had left, I slammed the magazine back in. And by some miracle, it locked into place on the first try.

"OK. Now pull the slide back to put a round in the chamber."

I yanked the slide back hard and released it.

He slapped me on the back. "Nice! It's ready to fire." He pointed at the target. "Now aim and shoot."

I frowned. "I don't wanna."

"Sloan." His tone was a warning.

I groaned and turned toward the target.

"Hold on." He stepped forward and slid noise-canceling ear protectors over my head. Then he put on his own. After that, his mouth was moving, but I couldn't hear what he was saying.

I leaned toward him and shouted, "What?"

He laughed and pulled the ear protection back from my left ear. "Take off the safety, look down the site to where you want to shoot, and pull the trigger."

He released the ear covering, and it slammed against my ear. "Ow!"

He pointed at the target and took a step backward.

I pulled the gun up straight in front of me, looked down the barrel, and aimed the notch at the top at the center of the black body outline. I pulled the trigger.

Bang!

The recoil knocked me back a few steps.

"Jesus, Mary, and Joseph!" I screamed.

I put the gun on the table and turned to see Warren doubled over, laughing with his hands on his knees. I ripped off my headset. "Why didn't you warn me?" I shouted, stepping over and punching him square in the chest.

He was still laughing. "I thought you knew there would be some kickback."

"There's no kickback in the movies!"

The man two stalls down from us was watching and laughing as well.

I folded my arms over my chest and kicked Warren in the shin.

He straightened and put his arms around me. "You did well though! I'm proud of you." He kissed the side of my head and turned me back toward the target.

There were no holes in it.

My head dropped in defeat. "I didn't even hit it."

He squeezed my shoulder. "But you didn't kill anyone either."

I glared back at him. "Yet."

He smiled. "Do it again. Empty the clip." He pointed down at my tennis shoes. "Plant your feet this time and try to not let it knock you over." He chuckled, and I stuck up my middle finger.

I turned back toward the target and put my ear protection back on. I picked up the gun and fired again, this time not caught so much by surprise. Dust *poofed* up on the embankment behind the target which was still left untouched.

Aiming again, I tried to hold my shaking hands steady. I fired and saw more dust.

Slowly, I blew out a deep breath and squeezed the trigger a third time. This time, the target moved. A small hole was ripped in the top right corner.

I put the gun back on the table, then jumped up and down, squealing as I turned around. I removed my headset and hopped toward Warren. "I did it! I did it!"

Warren laughed and kissed me. "Congratulations."

Nathan and Shannon walked across the wooden floor toward us. They had been inside looking at the selection of guns the place had for sale.

"How's it going?" Nathan asked as they approached.

I grabbed his arm and pointed at the target. "Look! I hit it!"

He chuckled and patted me on the back. "Congrats. That's practically a kill shot."

I smiled. "I hit it though!"

He nodded. "Yes, you did."

Warren nudged me with the back of his hand. "Finish."

I put my headset back on and turned back to the target. With more confidence than before, I didn't stop firing until the magazine was empty. Most of the shots hit the bank, but two more bullets hit in the white space of the paper, and one actually pierced the body outline's shoulder. I turned around and smiled with satisfaction.

Warren clapped his hands before handing me the box of ammunition again. "Now load it back up and practice some more."

I frowned and lowered my voice so only he could hear me as I accepted the box of bullets. "You're never getting sex from me ever again."

He laughed and rolled his eyes. "*Sure.*"

While I struggled with the magazine, Nathan and Shannon got ready to shoot in the stall right beside us. Without instruction, Shannon loaded a small handgun and slipped on a pair of pink ear protectors.

I looked at Warren. He was curiously watching her as well.

Nathan took a step back beside him and leaned toward his ear. "Watch this."

We all covered our ears as Shannon raised her pistol. Like a pro off the hunting channel on TV, she aimed and popped off one bullet after another. The paper target rattled furiously till she stopped and put the gun down.

My mouth dropped open.

Warren clapped his hands—for much longer than he had clapped for me—and laughed. "I did *not* see that coming at all!"

In my head I was screaming, *Oh hell no!* But I kept my mouth shut. Almost every shot Shannon had fired pierced the inner part of the outline's body. Furiously, I began cramming bullets into the magazine.

Shannon turned, smiling with pride.

Nathan kissed her and put his arm around her shoulders. He had never done that in front of me before.

She shrugged. "My daddy started teaching me when I was ten."

"*My daddy started teaching me when I was ten,*" I mimicked under my breath.

Warren was nodding his head. "I have to say, I'm pretty impressed."

I rolled my eyes and turned my back to everyone.

Shannon came over and put her hand on my shoulder. "Don't worry, Sloan. You'll get better with practice."

I thought about punching her in the face.

Forty-five minutes later, I was a little better, but I still couldn't shoot like Shannon Green. I was, however, able to shoot and not feel like I might pee all over myself.

Warren put his arms around my waist after he'd packed up his guns. "I'm proud of you," he said, pressing a kiss to my forehead.

I groaned. "Thanks."

He smiled and tightened his grasp on me. "I mean it. And you look hot holding my Glock."

I rolled my eyes.

"Mind if we go to the rifle range for a bit?" he asked.

I shook my head. "That's fine."

We packed up what was left of our ammo and cleaned up the stall before Warren picked up his rifle case and we headed across the complex. Aside from the Range Master, who was there to observe and enforce safety, we were the only people at the rifle range. It was much longer than the pistol range we had just left. There were three sets of targets, one at a hundred yards, one at two hundred, and one at three hundred.

I leaned against the wooden support post and watched Warren pull the huge rifle out of its case. As he attached the scope, I realized I had only seen anything like his gun in video games and action movies.

The gun rested on a stand on the table. Warren straddled the bench sideways behind it and looked down the scope. He was wearing a fitted gray t-shirt that stretched tight over his biceps when he positioned himself behind the gun.

Shannon was practically drooling next to me.

Warren stood up and looked at Nathan. "Go on, man. It's ready to fire."

Surprised, Nathan smiled. "Thanks."

Warren leaned against the wall beside me and folded his arms across his chest. "You need any help?" Warren asked him as he slipped his ear protection on.

Nathan shook his head and sat down on the bench. "Nah, I'm good."

"Good luck, baby," Shannon said, blowing Nathan a kiss while she covered her ears.

My hands tightened into fists at my sides as I glared at her.

Nathan began firing, and I screamed and clasped my hands over my ears. He stopped shooting and looked back at me while Warren laughed and pulled my ear protectors up from around my neck. My head was ringing, Shannon was giggling, and Nathan was shaking his head.

I hung my head and ducked under Warren's arm, a victim of my own bad karma.

Once Nathan was certain my ears were secured, he fired off a bunch of rounds, but the target was too far away to see how he had done. When he stopped shooting, he looked through the scope. "Six kill shots out of ten. Not too bad." He turned and looked back at us.

Warren had a sly smile on his face as he looked through a pair of binoculars. "Not bad at all. Not excellent, but not bad."

Nathan smirked. "You can do better?"

I wasn't sure what Nathan was thinking. Warren was a trained sniper for the Marines. Surely, he knew that.

Rolling my eyes, I looked at Shannon. "Men and their balls."

She laughed.

Warren pushed himself off the wall when Nathan stood up and moved out of the way. Warren pressed the binoculars into Nathan's hand as they passed. Without a word, he straddled the bench, swapped out the magazine, and looked around with the scope for a moment. Then he pulled on his ear protection and slipped on his black sunglasses before settling over the weapon. A few seconds later, he fired off three evenly spaced shots.

Pow!

Pow!

Pow!

When he stopped, he looked through the scope, and then sat up and cracked his knuckles.

Nathan had the binoculars squashed over his eyes. He laughed. "You didn't even touch it! The target didn't move!"

Warren stood up and walked in front of Nathan. He shifted Nathan and the binoculars just a little bit to the left. "That's because you're looking at one hundred yards and not three hundred."

After a second, Nathan's jaw went slack. "Holy shit." He started laughing again, this time in awe.

I smacked Nathan in the stomach. "Let me see!"

He handed me the binoculars, and I searched the three hundred range. Warren's target had three holes in the face. I pulled the binoculars down and laughed. "That's the sexiest thing I've ever seen in my life!"

He smiled as I passed Shannon the binoculars and then draped my arms around his neck.

Nathan shook his head, resting his hands on his hips.

"I can see now why the Marine Corps wants you back."

When we left, I carried Warren's target proudly to the car. "I think I'm going to frame this and hang it over my bed at home."

Nathan laughed. "You're not going to hang your shoulder shot over your bed?"

I whipped my head around toward him. "Don't make me have my boyfriend shoot you in the face."

"Where are we going next?" Warren asked as he loaded his gun case into the back of the SUV.

I rubbed my hands together with a renewed sense of hope. "Let's go find Rachel Smith."

11.

Rachel Smith wasn't easy to find.

We spent the better part of that week driving all over San Antonio with no sign of her and without gathering any more evidence on Larry Mendez. I was beginning to think the whole trip might be a bust.

On Friday morning, I rolled toward Warren in the bed with a crystal clear look of defeat on my face. "This sucks." I rested my head on his chest and traced my finger along his tattoo. "Maybe we should just call it quits and fly home when Shannon leaves on Sunday."

"You want to go home?" he asked surprised.

"I don't know. I kinda miss Adrianne."

He kissed the top of my head and tightened his arm around me. "We'll do whatever you want."

I pushed up on my elbows next to him. "I want to lie by the pool again for a while today. I'm going to miss the warmth when we go back to the mountains."

"We can do that." He brushed my hair away from my face. "And then maybe we can take one more crack at Rachel

Smith this afternoon."

I nodded. "Yeah. We might as well try. We've covered Nathan's entire list though. I don't know where else we could even look. She could have just been passing through San Antonio, you know? She might not have ever lived here at all."

"That's true," he agreed.

"I mean, we might have just wasted an entire week here for nothing," I said.

Under the covers, he slid his hand up my bare side and smiled. "I wouldn't quite say that any of this week has been a waste. I've had a pretty good time here in Texas."

"I would say you have. You've stayed in bed with me every morning we've been here." I smiled and bit my lower lip. "For that reason alone, I don't want to go back to the real world."

His hand ran down my back. "I'm trying to convince you to be a morning person by making them extra good."

Laughing, I leaned over and kissed his cheek. "You're doing a good job of it. I think getting away from everything was exactly what I needed. The nightmares have stopped, and I don't feel so nervous all the time. You must be a good influence on me."

He rolled over on top of me and pinned my arms down over my head. "You're not sick of me yet?"

"Not even a little bit." I smiled and squirmed underneath the weight of his body.

He nodded. "That's good because I'm not going anywhere," he said, "for the rest of your life." He buried his face in the crook of my neck and nipped at my skin.

I giggled as his hair fell into my face. "Well, if that's true, my daddy is going to insist that you marry me. He's pretty old-fashioned like that."

He pulled back and smiled down at me. "I know. I already talked to him about it."

Wait.

I turned my head and cut my eyes at him. "You what?" The volume of my voice was a little louder than I intended.

He was still grinning. "I might have bounced an idea off him before I came by to see you at work last week."

"Well, bounce it off of me, would ya?" I pushed him back and sat up on my elbows.

He rolled onto his side, propping his head up on his arm. "I just asked him what he thought about letting his only daughter marry a guy who has no job and no family and no history with you at all."

"Are you serious?" I was laughing with an uneasy mix of nerves and excitement.

"Yeah. Why wouldn't I be?" he asked. "You didn't think this was some kind of random fling for me, did you?"

Everything had transpired so quickly, I wasn't sure what I thought. "No, but I didn't think you were talking to my dad about marriage either." I jerked the sheet up over my body. "Are you proposing to me right now?"

He opened his mouth and widened his eyes like he was about to say, *Surprise!* But instead, he laughed. "No."

Strangely enough, I was disappointed. "No?"

He shook his head. "No."

"Why not? Do you want to marry me?" I asked.

He raised an eyebrow. "Are *you* proposing now?"

I smirked. "No."

He cupped my chin in his large hand and pulled on my lower lip with his thumb. His eyes fell to my mouth. "I'm going to marry you, but not just yet."

My brow wrinkled. "What are you waiting for?"

He gave me a half-smile and slid his hand down to my arm. "I guess I'm waiting until I don't wonder where your mind goes sometimes."

I twisted my head in confusion. "What?"

He just stared at me, till a lightbulb flickered on in my mind and I realized what he was talking about. It felt like my stomach fell through the mattress. "Nathan McNamara."

He nodded, and there was a knock at our door.

He sighed. "Speak of the devil."

Warren flung the covers to the side and pushed himself off the bed. As he walked to the door, he slipped on the jeans he'd discarded the night before. Around the corner, I heard the door open.

"Morning," Nathan said. "You guys up?"

"Yeah, but we're not ready yet."

"We're heading up to the pool for breakfast if you want to join us," Nathan said.

"Sounds good. Give us a few," Warren answered.

When he came back into the room, he didn't rejoin me in the bed. "You hungry?" he asked.

It was obvious the subjects of marriage—and Nathan McNamara—were no longer open for discussion. My brain was firing in a thousand different directions. I got up, and we both dressed in awkward silence.

Everything was happening so fast, and for the first time since we'd been together, I felt really overwhelmed. I loved him, but he was right. My mind was still prone to wandering. My ears had been ringing from noise damage all week to prove it.

The silence continued when we got up to the roof. Nathan and Shannon both noticed over breakfast. Nathan pointed his fork at both of us. "What's with you two?"

"It's none of your business," Shannon scolded him from underneath her ridiculous hat.

That was both true and untrue.

I shifted in my seat. "We've just been trying to decide this morning if we should stay for a few more days or not. We haven't accomplished anything at all," I said. "Not with Rachel

Smith or with Larry Mendez."

Nathan's head snapped back in surprise. "You're thinking about going home early?"

I shrugged. "I don't know. Probably, if we don't start getting somewhere pretty fast."

Nathan looked at Warren. "You're just going to walk away from Mendez?"

Warren didn't look up from his omelet. "I might go kill him before we leave and neutralize the problem."

Nathan stared at him with an awkward smile, like he wasn't sure if Warren was joking or if he was serious. To be honest, I wasn't sure if Warren was serious or not either.

My phone rang, and I jumped at the chance to escape from the table and answer it. I looked at the screen. "It's my dad. Excuse me." I stood up and walked to the edge of the roof.

"Hey, Dad," I answered. I leaned my elbows on the chest-high concrete wall that surrounded the area.

"Hey, sweetheart. How's the Lone Star state?" he asked.

I groaned. "A little tense at the moment. Did Warren talk to you about us getting married?"

There was a beat of silence on the other end of the phone. "Why? Did he propose?"

"No, but he said he talked to you."

"He did. He came by my office last week," he said. "Is everything OK?"

I sighed. "It will be. How are you?"

"Well, I'm fine. Your mother, however, isn't feeling too well," he said. "I'm trying to convince her to go to the hospital for some tests, but of course she's being stubborn. If she isn't any better today, I'm going to drag her there if I have to."

"What's wrong with her?" I asked.

"Well, it started with a mild headache. Then a few days

ago she started getting dizzy and throwing up. She thinks it's just an inner ear infection, but I'm not convinced. She started on antibiotics three days ago and still isn't any better. I don't think it's anything serious. I just wanted you to know before someone called you and said your mother was at the hospital."

"Yeah. Thanks for letting me know. Keep me posted on how she's feeling and what you find out. Tell her I said to quit being stubborn and go to the hospital and listen to you," I said.

He laughed. "She hasn't listened to me in twenty-seven years. I'm not sure why she would start now."

I laughed. "Give her my love, OK?"

"I will," he said.

"Love you, Dad."

"I love you too," he said and disconnected.

Warren looked up with concern as I walked back to the table. "Is everything OK?"

I nodded and sat back down. "Mom is pretty sick, and Dad wanted me to know he's trying to get her to go to the hospital for some tests. He's going to keep me updated. What are you guys discussing?"

"Nathan thinks we should go back to the gas station, where the photo was taken, and see if anyone recognizes Rachel," Warren answered.

"I'm kinda surprised we haven't already thought to do that," I said.

Shannon raised her hand. "What's so special about this Rachel person anyway? Why have you spent all week looking for someone you don't even know?"

"It's complicated," Nathan said.

She put her fork on her plate. "I think I can keep up."

Nathan looked at me for an answer.

A bright idea popped into my head. "You remember how I'm adopted, right?"

Shannon nodded.

"Well, Rachel Smith might know something about my birth parents and where I came from."

She adjusted her hat. "Right, because she's a social worker."

Nathan's eyes widened at me. "Yes," he said. "That's exactly correct."

"Well, that doesn't sound too dangerous. Mind if I tag along?" she asked. "I've been in every shop on the River Walk at least twice, and I don't think I can stand another day of being left behind and cooped up in this hotel."

I thought about it. Shannon really hadn't been a pain in the ass all week about staying at the hotel while we went out like I had expected she would. She had actually almost been pleasant to be around. I also knew the chances were very slim we would even find Rachel, so I decided to throw Shannon a bone. "Sure. Come with us."

Warren looked up at me but didn't say anything.

Shannon clapped her hands together and squealed. "Yay! Thank you! I promise I won't get in the way. I'll be as quiet as a church mouse."

I doubted that.

We hung out at the pool until families with a lot of young children showed up just after noon. We decided to go get changed and grab lunch on our way toward what we assumed was Rachel's neighborhood.

When Warren and I got to the room, I grabbed him by the hand. "Can we talk a sec?"

He turned toward me and nodded. "Sure."

"What you were saying this morning." I shifted uneasily on my feet. "Do you worry about me and Nathan?"

He shook his head. "No. I don't think you would cheat on me, if that's what you're asking. But I also know if I weren't in the picture, the two of you would be together."

"But he's with Shannon."

He crossed his arms and frowned down at me.

I sighed. "OK. Yes, we probably would be together, but we aren't because I love you, and I've chosen to be with you."

He put his hands on my shoulders. "I know that, Sloan, and I'm not mad at you. I just want to make sure you're in this 100 percent before we start making permanent plans together. Not 99 percent or 99.9 percent. I don't want the majority of you. I want all of you."

"Do you want me to not be friends with him anymore?" I asked.

"I would never ask you to do that. I just think we need to give it some time to make sure you're never going to look back." His eyes became very serious. "I don't want to be walking in on my wife someday looking at him the way you were looking at him the other night in the pool."

His words were like a knife to the chest. "Nothing happened in the pool."

"Maybe nothing physical." His eyebrows were raised, daring me to argue. I didn't. "I told you, I'm not angry about it. I'm not happy about it either, but I trust you."

I cast my eyes down at his feet. "I'm sorry, Warren."

He shook his head. "There are a lot of layers to this relationship, Sloan. This whole thing with you and me blew up overnight, taking everyone by surprise, including us. You've still got some things to figure out, whether you want to admit it or not."

I opened my mouth to protest, but he kissed me to shut me up. When he let me go, he smiled like the whole conversation hadn't even happened. "Get dressed."

* * *

We drove to the gas station where the surveillance photo was captured and showed both clerks who were there the picture of Rachel Smith. Neither of them recognized her.

When we got back in the SUV, I slammed my door shut. "The clerks at the Texaco near my house would at least recognize my face," I said. "She doesn't live here."

Warren nodded and started the engine. "You're probably right."

I felt a hand on my shoulder from behind. It was Shannon. "I'm really sorry, Sloan."

I nodded. "Thanks."

Warren looked over at me. "Well, you wanna cruise back by Mendez's house before we completely call everything quits?"

I looked up at the sky. "It isn't dark yet." I glanced back at Nathan. "What do you think?"

He leaned against his door and shrugged. "It's your call."

"It wouldn't hurt to take one more look," I said.

Across town, the maroon pickup was parked at the curb outside of Larry Mendez's house. All of the lights inside appeared to be on. We parked a block away and watched.

"Who is this guy? What do you want with him?" Shannon asked.

"He gives me the creeps," I said. "I want to figure out why."

She laughed. "Lots of people creep me out, but I don't sit outside their houses like a stalker."

A blue car that was missing the front fender pulled up behind the truck. Nathan leaned forward between the front seats for a better view. The car doors opened and two men got out and stepped onto the sidewalk. One was a white guy wearing a white tank top and baggy jeans. The other was Hispanic, wearing a red polo and a lot of gold jewelry. They were both covered in tattoos, and they were both about our age.

Warren leaned over the steering wheel and ripped off his sunglasses. He strained his eyes. "That's impossible," he muttered.

I looked over at him. "What's impossible?"

He pointed. "The guy in the white shirt. I think I know him."

"What?" Nathan asked.

"Who is it?" I asked.

Warren cocked his head to the side. "Sloan, do you remember me telling you about the two guys who attacked that girl at the dumpster in Chicago? One died and one got away?"

Warren had told me the story. It had been the second time he had ever used his power. He killed a guy from his group home who was trying to rape a girl in an alleyway near a movie theater. "Yeah. I remember."

"I could be wrong, but I'm pretty damn certain that's the one who escaped. That's Rex," he said.

My mouth fell open. "You're kidding? We're a bazillion miles away from Chicago."

Nathan shook his head. "That would be a huge coincidence."

I groaned and felt my heart start to pound. The word *coincidence* was becoming a verbal red flag. True coincidences never seemed to happen around me. I looked at Warren. "What do you want to do?"

He reclined back in his seat and rested his hand over the steering wheel. He tapped his fingers on the dash. "Let's see what they do."

The two men talked for a moment on the curb, and then the Hispanic guy made a phone call. A moment later, they scanned the street, then walked up the stairs and knocked on the door. They disappeared inside. After a few short minutes, the Hispanic guy came out first holding his car keys.

He scanned the street again before signaling to the front door.

Nathan chuckled. "Not so good as a lookout, is he? Big white SUV right here."

I laughed. Warren didn't.

Rex and Larry Mendez came outside holding onto the arms of two young Hispanic girls. One was the teenage girl we had seen earlier that week and the other was much younger. They both looked sluggish, like they had been drugged, as they were led to the car.

I gasped and covered my mouth with my hand.

"They're trafficking," Nathan said. He moved to reach for his door handle.

Warren reached out and grabbed him by the back of his shirt. "Hold up. Hold up. We should follow them and see where they go."

"I agree with Nathan," I said. "I think we should take them down now before this escalates any further."

"No, Warren's right. We need to see where the hub of this thing is." Nathan sat back and put his seatbelt on.

"What about Shannon?" I asked. "This isn't safe."

Warren put the car in drive and chuckled to himself. "I'll give her my gun and she can protect you."

"Hey!" I shouted and punched him in the shoulder.

Larry Mendez turned and walked back to his house as the car rolled away from the curb. Warren followed at quite a distance behind as it moved through the streets of west San Antonio. We twisted and turned through the city until the car reached the on-ramp for Interstate 10. We were stopped at a red light, but Warren was able to find them again on the interstate. The car was cruising at a safe speed, right at the speed limit.

After about ten minutes of driving, I looked over at Warren. "I don't think they are planning on staying in San Antonio. What if they're going to Houston?"

"Or Mexico?" Shannon asked.

"Do you ladies have somewhere else you need to be?" Warren asked.

I shrugged my shoulders. "I guess not."

"They're not going to Mexico. At least not if that's Rex in the car. I doubt he could even fill out an application for a passport," Warren said.

"Do you really think it could be him?" I asked.

Warren turned his palm up on the top of the steering wheel. "If it isn't, then there are two of him."

"What are you going to do when they stop?" Shannon asked.

Nathan laughed. "Wing it."

I turned in my seat. "Seriously, what are we going to do?"

Warren looked over his shoulder at me. "I really have no idea."

I sat back and rubbed my hands over my face and groaned. "That's great. Just great."

Nathan pointed to the car as it was easing its way toward an off ramp. "They're getting off the interstate."

I sat forward in my seat as Warren slowly moved to the right lane. The blue car was three cars ahead of us. "They're going north, Warren," I said, nudging his arm.

"Yep. Turn left," Nathan added.

"Will you two shut up and let me drive?" Warren snapped.

We headed north on a main highway, winding around till we reached the northeast side. It was an industrial area that had been neglected by the wealth of San Antonio for some time. Buildings were crumbling into disrepair, and there was an unsightly mix of rundown strip malls and gas stations with bars on the windows. The blue car pulled into an alleyway between a two-story building and a warehouse. Warren parked across the street at a liquor store.

"What is this place?" I looked up at the building and noticed the number of broken windows and the flashing red neon OPEN sign near the front door.

"Must be a brothel," Nathan said.

"I believe it might be called a *cantina*. There are lots of them around Texas," Shannon said from the back seat.

At the same time, the three of us turned to look at her, all with the same baffled expression. What in the world could the Baptist traffic reporter from North Carolina know about prostitution in Texas?

Shannon shrugged, noting our skeptical faces. "I've watched a lot of television while you guys have been gone all week. The city has raided a lot of these kinds of places lately. They are bars where girls are bought and sold for prostitution."

"I'll be damned." Warren shook his head and laughed. "Anything else we should know?"

She nodded. "They usually have a lookout posted outside to watch for police."

We all turned to scan the building.

Nathan pointed. "Up there on the roof."

Sure enough, there was a man in a white lawn chair perched on the roof, carefully watching the streets.

I looked back at Shannon in amazement. "I have to say, I'm kinda glad we brought you along."

"How should we do this, Nate?" Warren asked.

"Well, we can't exactly go in there with guns blazing. We'll wind up getting ourselves killed," Nathan said.

"Can we call the cops?" I asked.

Nathan rubbed his chin. "I'm sure the cops already know this place exists. They can't just come in either. They would need someone to investigate and get proof, and then they would have to go through a judge to get a no-knock search warrant. It's a pretty lengthy process."

"Should one of us go in?" I asked.

"Well, I can't go in because if that is Rex, he'll recognize me," Warren said. "And Nate, you can't go in because everything about you screams law enforcement."

"I'll go in," I said, surprising myself as much as I surprised everyone else in the car.

Warren said "absolutely not" and Nathan said "hell no" at the exact same time.

"We can't just sit here and do nothing. Those girls were just kids!" I reasoned.

Warren shook his head. "You can be hard headed and argue all you want, but there's no way I'm letting you out of this car to go in there. I will tie you to the seat if I have to."

Nathan reached up and squeezed my shoulder. "We'll figure something out."

"Maybe no one has to go in," Shannon said. She leaned forward quickly and pointed out the window. "Look!"

Two San Antonio police cars and a police van with blue lights flashing screamed to a stop in front of the front door. Two unmarked SUVs parked along the sides of the building. Cops, some in uniform and others in all black, rushed out of the cars with their guns drawn.

"Holy shit," Nathan said, laughing. "Sloan, did you just summon a police force?"

I scratched my head. "I don't think so."

We watched the police break down the front door and rush in. Like cockroaches scattering, people began to pour out of the building from all kinds of disguised doors and openings. Two of those people were Rex and the man in the red polo shirt. They darted behind the black SUV, took off across the street, and jumped a fence about fifty yards away from us.

"Oh, hell no," Warren said. He wrenched his door open and took off after them.

Nathan followed.

I looked back at Shannon who was cowering in her seat. "What do we do?" I asked.

"You couldn't pay me enough to get out of this car," she said.

Shannon was right. Gun fire sounded inside the building. I hit the lock button on the door and sank down in my seat. A few nail-biting minutes later, Nathan came through a gate in the fence, leading the guy in the red polo shirt by one handcuffed arm. A second after him, Warren appeared, dragging Rex by his blond hair, his arms flailing and his legs trying to keep up. His face was covered in blood—so were Warren's knuckles.

We watched from the car as Warren and Nathan delivered the two to the police officers on the curb. After talking with the officers for a moment, Warren waved for us to come over. Hesitantly, Shannon and I got out of the car. She gripped my arm so hard I winced as we crossed the street. Nathan was still talking to one of the officers. Warren caught my eye and nodded toward the front door.

Scantily dressed girls, some as young as ten or eleven, were being ushered outside and led to a large white police van. Tears prickled my eyes as they shuffled along the curb with their shoulders slumped and their empty stares fixed on the ground. Some of them were bloody and bruised, and others looked drugged or drunk out of their wits.

My heart shattered.

Then, as I watched them, my eyes fell on the woman guiding the girls from the building. She was wearing a gray pants suit and had long dark hair tied back in a no-nonsense ponytail. There was a deep and empty void where I should have sensed her soul.

It was Rachel Smith.

12.

Rachel's eyes locked on mine with the same bewildered expression I was sure was on my face. She tried to refocus on her task of loading up the girls, but her eyes kept glancing in my direction. When she finally closed the door to the van, she said something to a uniformed officer, then walked down the sidewalk toward me.

"Rachel Smith?" I asked as she approached.

She turned her head slightly and narrowed her eyes. "*Abigail* Smith," she said, tapping her name tag which was labeled with *Morning Star Ministries* in bright green letters. She lowered her voice. "I haven't gone by Rachel in years. Who are you?" Then she pointed at Warren. "And who is he?"

"We're like you," I said just above a whisper. I blinked my eyes like they were delivering a secret message.

She laughed. "No, you're not."

I was jolted by surprise. When Warren and I first saw each other, time stood still. Our realization that we weren't alone in the world had been cosmically astounding. Mistakenly, I had expected a similar reaction from Rachel

Smith, and this woman was laughing at me like I'd just told a knock-knock joke.

"Can we talk?" I asked, looking around. "In private?"

She gestured toward the commotion around us. "As you can tell, I'm pretty busy right now." She reached into her purse and produced a business card. "But here's my information. Come by my office in a couple of hours. I'll be there all night."

I smiled. "Thank you."

She stared at me for another moment, and I studied her carefully while I had the chance. She was even more beautiful in person than in her photos. We were about the same age and height, but she was wearing heels. There was an emptiness in her dark brown eyes that I had only ever seen inside of Warren.

She nodded like she was answering a question I didn't ask. "Yes. Definitely come by my office later."

"I will."

Without another word, she turned and walked back toward the police van. Before she got into the passenger's seat, she glanced back over her shoulder to where I was still watching, mesmerized. She waved and gave a slight smile. I waved back, just as the van pulled away.

Warren stepped up behind me. "Well?"

"She wants us to come by her office later."

Confounded and shaking his head, he crossed his arms over his chest. "Well, two birds, one stone."

Nathan and Shannon walked up beside us. "Was that who I think it was?" He was pointing in the direction the van had gone.

With the two of them flanking me, and Shannon clutching to Nathan's arm, we turned back toward the SUV. I nodded as we crossed the street. "It sure was."

"Who are you talking about?" Shannon asked.

Nathan jerked his head back toward the building. "That woman in the gray suit who Sloan was talking to is the same woman we've been looking for all week."

"Seriously?" Shannon asked in amazement. She looked around Nathan at me. "That's a crazy coincidence. Did you talk to her? Was she able to tell you anything?"

I shrugged. "Not yet, but we're going to meet her at her office in a little while."

Warren looked over at us as we reached the car. "The cop told me she's the head of a big human trafficking rescue mission here in Texas. Apparently, she's got a couple of homes here. One in San Antonio and one in Houston."

"That explains why we couldn't find her working for the government," I said as I pulled open my car door.

We all got in.

Nathan was still shaking his head as he fastened his seatbelt. "You know, I don't think I'm ever going to get used to the crazy shit that seems to follow the two of you around."

I grabbed Warren's forearm. "Speaking of crazy, was that the guy from Chicago?"

He laughed as he started the engine and put the SUV in reverse to back out of the lot. "Yes ma'am. What are the odds of that?"

My brain was spinning like a mental Rolodex full of questions as I stared out my window. "Impossible odds."

Behind us, Nathan chuckled. "We should go to Vegas."

I looked at Warren. "Did he say what he was doing here or how long he's been in Texas?"

Nathan poked his head between our seats. "He didn't have a chance to speak. He was kind of busy having his face rearranged." He slapped Warren on the shoulder. "This guy beat the hell out of him."

I blinked. "I'm surprised you didn't kill him."

He stared straight at the road ahead. "Trust me. I

thought about it."

"What will happen to Larry Mendez?" I asked.

"Nathan told the cops we were in Mendez's neighborhood because we got lost, and we saw them leaving the house with the two girls. He said we thought it looked suspicious so we followed them. He gave them Mendez's address."

I laughed and looked back at Nathan. "You told them we were lost? And they bought it?"

Nathan shrugged. "They seemed grateful we saved them a lot of work."

"So they'll go arrest him?"

He nodded, exchanging a glance with Warren in the rearview mirror. "They should have enough to take him into custody, but we may get called in to testify at some point."

I relaxed back in my seat. "Good."

"Where to now?" Warren asked.

"Take me and Shannon back to the hotel and drop us off," Nathan said.

I looked back at him. "You don't want to come talk to Rachel with us?"

He smiled at me. "No. You go and get to the bottom of all this. I've done my part."

"Thank you, Nathan." I reached to the back seat and squeezed his hand.

He squeezed my hand in return. "You're welcome, Sloan."

We took Shannon and Nathan back to the Hyatt before heading back across town to the address of Morning Star Ministries. Night was falling over San Antonio, but the city was so bright it was almost unnecessary to burn our headlights. My vision blurred in and out of focus as we drove through the city. The passing lights left trails behind them as my mind wandered.

We were on the cusp of something big. The answers we had sought our entire lives were dangling right in front of us. There were a thousand different possibilities, but one thing was certain: tomorrow would not be the same.

Warren reached over and took my hand. "You seem tense."

"I don't know why, but I'm a little nervous. And I'm excited." I looked at him. "She's not clueless like us. I told her we were like her, and she laughed and said we're not. She had this certainty in her voice."

"That's interesting," he said.

"I thought so too."

Morning Star Ministries was located next door to a large brick church on the west side of town. Warren parked at the curb, and I sat and looked out the window. It was a nice two story building that was relatively new with two large double glass doors out front. The sign bearing the name had a fresh coat of paint, and orange and yellow mums were blooming at its base.

Warren turned toward me in his seat. "You ready?"

I took a deep breath. "Yep."

Inside the front lobby, there was a receptionist desk to our right, secured behind a large glass window. In front of us was a huge living room, and a restaurant-size kitchen was to our left. The second story walkway looked down on the lobby, and there was a young Hispanic girl watching us. She wore a San Antonio Spurs sweatshirt and blue jeans, and even from where we stood, I could see a large gold and jade cross hanging around her neck. She appeared to be around seventeen years old.

A young blonde in casual dress clothes peeked out from the receptionist area. "Can I help you?"

"We're here to see Abigail. She told us to come by tonight." I held up Abigail's business card.

The woman nodded. "Can I tell her your name?"

"Sloan Jordan," I answered.

She smiled. "You can have a seat," she said, nodding to a padded bench behind us.

We sat down, and Warren held my hand. "This place is nice." He was looking around at the newly tiled floors and professional paint job.

Two girls walked by us speaking Spanish and disappeared into the kitchen.

I lowered my voice. "I think it's a home for them. A home for the girls they rescue."

"Looks that way," he said. "Can you imagine going from that dilapidated cantina to this?"

I shook my head and sighed. "This place is giving them their lives back."

On a table next to us were some brochures. I picked one up and read it aloud. "Morning Star Ministries was founded in 2011 by Abigail Smith." I scanned through the rest of it. "They bring in girls rescued from human trafficking rings around San Antonio," I told him. "This is the main office. The one in Houston is smaller."

The click-clack of heels against the tile, announced Abigail's entrance as she came around the corner, obviously looking for us. We both stood when she saw us. "Hi. I'm glad you came by. Both of you." She smiled warmly as she stretched out her hand. "Sloan, is it?"

When her fingers touched mine, I jumped from the jolt. Every nerve ending from my scalp to my toes sizzled. "Whoa!" I looked down at my finger almost expecting it to be singed.

She chuckled. "Sorry, I should've warned you."

Still rubbing the tip of my finger, I looked up at Warren. "Abigail, this is my boyfriend, Warren Parish."

Cautiously this time, she offered him her hand.

His eyes doubled in size when he shook it, but he didn't freak out like me. "It's nice to meet you," he said.

"The pleasure is all mine." She nodded toward the hallway. "Let's go back to my office where we can talk and have a bit of privacy."

We followed her around the corner and down a long, carpeted hallway. There were plain white doors in groups of two all the way down to the end.

"This is a pretty impressive place you have here," I said as we walked.

She smiled back over her shoulder. "We have sixty beds in this home. We run at capacity all year long. The girls who were brought out of the cantina earlier will be on this floor till they receive proper medical attention. Then, once their physical needs are met, we will start dealing with their emotional ones."

"What happens to them?" I asked. "When they leave here?"

"Most of them are returned to their families, the ones whose families we are able to locate. Others go into a private foster system we have established through the local churches," she said.

"Private? You're not government funded?" I asked as we walked into a humble but nice office.

She shook her head. "We work with the local government, but we are strictly funded through private donations. Once you start accepting government money, you become subject to government red tape. I vowed when I began this ministry that we would operate as an independent agency only." She closed the door and motioned to the two chairs opposite her desk. "Please, have a seat."

Warren and I sat down in the chairs. "Thanks for seeing us. We've looked all over for you," I said.

As she settled behind the cherry wood desk, her eyes

widened. "Why were you looking for me?"

I exchanged a glance with Warren. "We actually thought you were murdered by a serial killer we helped take down a few weeks ago."

She laughed and leaned back against her chair. "A serial killer? Where?"

"In Asheville, North Carolina," I replied.

Her head tilted with confusion. "Why would you think I was murdered in Asheville?"

I shook my head. "We actually thought you were murdered in Greensboro. You were reported missing from your job there, and you seemed to fit with the profile of all the other victims." I looked at Warren again. "We assumed you were dead because—"

"Because when you looked at my photograph, you didn't see my soul?" she interrupted.

I swallowed hard. "Yes."

She leaned forward over her desk and rested her chin on her hands. She carefully studied our faces. "That's because I don't have a soul."

Her answer knocked the breath out of me like a baseball bat to the chest.

"Are you human?" Warren asked.

A thin smile spread across her lips as she tugged at the skin on her hand. "This is human."

The whole scene was a little unnerving. Had I not been so curious and fascinated, I probably would have been terrified. Instead, I was desperate to know more. "Are you an angel?"

She nodded slowly. Then she pointed at us. "And you *are not*."

Warren looked at me as if to say, *I told you so.*

I ran my fingers back through my hair and blew out a deep sigh. "Do you know what we are?" I asked.

She tapped her fingers on her lips. "You are Seramorta."

"Seramorta?" I had never heard the term before. And from the look on Warren's face, he hadn't either. I turned back to Abigail. "What does that mean?"

She sat back in her chair and leaned on her armrest. "You are half-angel, half-mortal."

I had known for quite a while that there was something supernaturally different about me and the hunky man sitting at my side, but I was fully unprepared to have it confirmed out loud by someone in the know. I burst out laughing. Loud, crazy-person laughter.

Abigail's eyes widened. "This amuses you?"

I reigned in my cackles, pressing my palms against the sides of my head. "It's just so…"

"Unbelievable," Warren finished. He rubbed his forehead and squeezed his eyes shut. "So what happened? We had a mortal mother who got knocked up by an angel?"

Her head tilted. "Or a mortal father."

I narrowed my eyes and wagged my finger between Warren and myself. "So, we had angel parents who just abandoned us both to figure all this out for ourselves?"

She shifted in her chair. "They didn't have a choice. It is forbidden for angels to raise their offspring."

I folded my arms across my chest. "Forbidden by who? God?"

She gave a noncommittal shrug. "More so forbidden by nature. The human mind is a fragile thing, especially during its developmental years. The prolonged physical contact of an angel in the early life of a Seramorta would have dire consequences for the child."

I thought of what it felt like when she touched my hand. "Could it kill them?"

She shook her head. "No, but it can cause insanity of

the worst kind."

I pinched the bridge of my nose. "This is a lot to take in."

"I can imagine." She looked over at me. "How old are you?"

"I'm twenty-seven. He's twenty-nine," I answered.

Warren leaned back and rested the ankle of his boot on his knee. "Why do Sloan and I have different abilities?"

"Because of your lineage. Much like the human race, you inherit different traits from your parents." She studied his face. "For example, you, Warren, have the power to end life, don't you?"

His eyes widened.

She pointed at him. "That's because you're the son of an Angel of Death."

I looked at him. "Well, you were right about that."

"So, am I evil?" he asked.

She laughed. "No one, angel or human, is inherently evil. We are all given a choice."

"What about me?" I asked. "Do you know what I am? I seem to be able to talk about people and make them show up."

She nodded. "That's a summoning power, shared by the Angels of Life. You have the power to influence the paths of others around you."

I raised my hand. "Angels of Life?"

"The second choir in Heaven."

I had no idea what that meant.

"She can heal people too," Warren added.

"That's not exactly been proven," I said. "People do seem to get better around me though."

Her face was curious as she nodded. "That's part of your gift."

I pointed at Warren. "He and I can't see each other's

souls. Does that mean we don't have them either?"

She shifted on her chair. "What you call a soul is your eternal spirit that lives in the body on this earth and then lives forever in eternity. Human spirits and angelic ones are entirely different, and you were born with both. Your human spirit and your angelic spirit are so closely knit together that you are blind to each other because your mortality doesn't allow you to see the angelic."

"So, that's why we can't see you?" I asked.

She nodded. "Yes. But your angelic spirit—which is stronger—allows you to see the human souls of others, as can I."

I sighed and closed my eyes. "My brain hurts."

"That's another thing." Warren leaned forward. "Whenever Sloan and I are away from each other—"

She cut him off. "You get a headache?"

"Yes," we answered at the same time.

She smiled. "The connection you have on a spiritual level affects your human physiology. When you remove that connection, your body is starved for that flow of spiritual energy."

"You were right, Warren." I looked over at him. "It's like detoxing off of each other."

Abigail nodded. "That's exactly what it is."

I looked at her seriously. "Is it dangerous?"

She shrugged. "It could be dangerous if your body is already compromised for some reason, I guess. Humans die all the time from complications of detoxing."

"Does it just happen with me and Sloan?" Warren asked.

She shook her head. "No. It happens with all angels who walk among humans. Some angels stay exclusively with other angels, while others, like me, prefer to be alone. I will suffer when you leave town."

"You'll have a migraine?" Warren asked.

She nodded. "Yes."

I sat back in my seat and rubbed my face. "That's fascinating. And I'm really sorry."

The telephone on her desk beeped. "Abigail, Mr. Parker is on line two for you."

"Thank you. Ask him to hold for a moment," Abigail replied. She glanced down at her watch before looking at us again. "I hope I have been of some help. I would like to speak with you more, but I'm sure you understand how busy I am right now."

I nodded. "Of course. Thank you for meeting with us."

She offered me her hand and I shook it, this time less jarred by her powerful energy. "Call me anytime." She examined my face carefully. "I mean it."

I smiled. "Thanks. I probably will." I pointed toward the door. "We will see ourselves out."

Abigail turned and picked up her telephone as we walked out of the office, and Warren quietly closed the door behind us. "Well, that went well," he said.

I looped my arm through his. "We're angels."

He laughed. "You called it," he said. "Are you happy to have some answers now?"

I sighed and rested my head against his shoulder. "So happy I could cry!"

He held the front door open, and we walked out into the warm night air. He squeezed my hand. "I say we go somewhere and celebrate."

I gripped his arm. "I want to go back to the hotel and get Nathan. We've got to tell him the good news!"

He stopped and looked at me. Then he shook his head and laughed.

"What?" I asked as he opened my car door.

He rolled his eyes. "Nothing. Let's go find Nate."

Nathan met us at the bar in the hotel lobby when we got back. Per my request, Shannon wasn't with him. "How'd it go?" he asked as we settled into a booth in the corner.

I shuddered with happiness. "It was awesome." I leaned across the table toward him. "Guess what?"

He produced a bag of Skittles from his pocket and poured a handful. "What?"

"We're angels." I dramatically dropped my jaw.

Nathan laughed and a green Skittle tumbled off his lip. "Sure you are." He tapped his chest. "Hell, so am I."

I threw a sugar packet at his head. "Do you want to hear this or not?"

"Tell me," he said, smiling around a mouthful of candy.

Before I began, a waiter stopped at our table and Warren ordered us all a round of beers. When he was out of earshot, I lowered my voice. "She said we are Seramorta."

Nathan blinked. "Sera-whatta?"

"Seramorta," I said. "Half-angel, half-human."

He started chuckling again. "Are you going to sprout wings?"

I ignored him. "She said Warren is the son of an Angel of Death and I was born from an Angel of Life. I have the power to influence the paths of the people around me."

Nathan nodded and looked at Warren. "That's the truest thing I've ever heard. Wouldn't you agree?"

"Absolutely," Warren said and they slapped a high five across the table.

The waiter delivered our drinks, and Nathan held his high in the air like he was about to propose a toast. Instead, he said, "You're welcome."

My head fell to the side. "Huh?"

He placed his glass back on the table. "Well, if it weren't for me being such a pain in your ass, as you constantly tell me, you never would have known Abigail even existed. So, you're welcome."

I smiled and held my glass toward him. "Thank you, Nathan."

He clinked his beer with mine and winked. "I'm happy for you both."

Warren squeezed my shoulder.

In my purse, my cell phone rang. I pulled it out and saw my father's picture on the screen. It was almost midnight in North Carolina. "That's weird." I answered the call. "Hey, Dad."

"Sloan," he said, his voice cracking.

"Are you OK?" I asked. "It's really late."

"Sloan, it's your mother."

13.

The tone of my father's voice alarmed me even more than his words. "What's wrong with Mom?"

He cleared his throat. "I think it would be a good idea if you came home as soon as you can."

I sat forward on the edge of my seat. "Why? What's going on?"

Concerned, Warren leaned in close.

Dad sighed over the phone. "Maybe we should talk about it when you get back."

"Dad, there's no way I can get a flight home tonight. You have to tell me what's happened!" I demanded.

There was another pause. "It's a tumor, Sloan, in her brain. It's very serious."

I gasped and covered my mouth. "What?"

His voice was shaky. "I've never seen anything this aggressive. The growth rate alone shows it has to be malignant. We are making plans to do surgery to try and remove it as soon as possible, hopefully first thing in the morning. There isn't any other choice."

I closed my eyes and took a deep breath. "OK. I'm going to figure out how to get home," I said. "Can I talk to her?"

"She's not conscious anymore, sweetheart. She fell asleep about an hour ago, and we haven't been able to wake her up," he said.

Tears spilled down my cheeks. "Dad, no!"

"Please come home as quickly as you can, but please be careful," he said. "I promise I'll call you if anything else changes. I love you, Sloan."

"I love you too," I said and disconnected the phone.

"What's going on?" Warren asked.

My mouth was hanging open in shock. "My mom has a brain tumor. It's really, really bad," I said. "She's unconscious, and they are going to try and remove the tumor tomorrow. We have to go." I pushed myself up from the table. "I need you to take me to the airport."

Warren reached for my arm. "You said it yourself. There aren't any more flights out tonight."

"Then we need to start driving!" I cried.

"It's at least a fifteen hour drive, Sloan," Nathan said. "You can sleep and fly home faster than you could drive there."

Warren pulled me under his arm. "We will call the airline and get on the first flight out in the morning," he said. "If we catch the five a.m. flight, we can be home before lunch."

I melted into his chest and sobbed. He rubbed my back and let me cry for several minutes. Then, he finally suggested we go to our room.

When we stopped at Nathan's floor, he hugged me. "I'm so sorry. Call me in the middle of the night if you hear anything."

I nodded and the doors closed behind him.

When we got to our room, I sat down on the bed, and Warren put my purse on my lap. "Take one of your pills so you can relax and get some sleep. You're going to need it. I'm going to call the airlines and figure out what flight we can get on."

"OK," I whispered. My hands were shaking as I rifled through my purse.

While I waited for the anti-anxiety medicine to seep into my bloodstream, I called Adrianne and then packed my suitcase. Warren was on the phone with the airline. I kept picturing my mother in my mind. She was alive, and I could still sense her presence, and that was the only thing that remotely consoled me.

I was still awake when Warren finally stretched out next to me. "We're on the five-ten flight on American Airlines in the morning. That's the first flight out."

"Was it expensive?" I asked.

He smiled. "Not at all."

"You're a rotten liar."

"Come here." He pulled me into his arms and pressed his lips against the side of my head.

Tears leaked from my eyes onto his bare chest. "This is all my fault."

"That's crazy. No, it isn't." He ran his fingers through my hair.

"I told you before we left that I knew something was wrong with her. The tumor has been there all this time. I've felt it for a few months. I just didn't know what it was. I've been keeping her healthy by just being around, and I didn't know it. Why else would she get so bad so quickly right after we left?"

"Shh," he said. "This is a tumor. You didn't cause this."

"You know I'm right," I whispered into the dark.

He was quiet for a moment. "If you were keeping her healthy, then you prolonged her life, Sloan. It's not your fault. We'll get you home and you'll make her better again. You'll see."

I sniffed and nodded my head. The Xanax was kicking in and my eyes were getting heavy. Before long, with my mother still in the forefront of my mind, I was fast asleep.

* * *

The sound of my mother's voice rattled me from a deep sleep. "Sloan," I heard her say.

I opened my eyes. The hotel room was still dark. The clock on the nightstand read two-fourteen. I pictured my mother and felt nothing but a deep void. I sat up and tried harder, but again, I felt nothing. Uncontrollable sobs welled up inside me as I tried, over and over, to find her presence in the dark.

My mother was gone.

* * *

The flight back to Asheville was excruciating. I had called my father in the middle of the night, and he told me they had put mom on a ventilator because she was having trouble breathing on her own. I didn't have the heart to tell him the machines were only keeping her organs functional.

I knew it. Warren knew it. My mother wasn't going to wake up.

Adrianne was in a wheelchair in the waiting room with her father when we got to the hospital. It was the same room where I had slept for several nights when she was in intensive care after the car wreck.

I stopped to hug her. "You should be at home in bed," I said.

She squeezed my hand. "You know I wouldn't be anywhere else."

I wiped my eyes.

"Your dad is down the hall," she said, pointing through the door. "He just came out and talked to us a few minutes ago."

My Aunt Joan, Mom's sister, was talking with Dad in the hallway when we walked through the door. Aunt Joan looked a lot like my mom, except she had more gray hair and was probably thirty pounds heavier. Mom had been extremely health conscious and was an avid jogger. She had always been the healthiest person I knew. It made the whole scenario very ironic.

I released Warren's hand and ran to my dad when he saw me. I cried all over again in his arms. Wet tears soaked my hair as he wept holding me.

He finally pulled away. "She's stable, but she's still on the ventilator. Do you want to go in and see her?"

I sniffed and nodded my head.

Warren squeezed my arm. "I'll wait out here."

Dad and I walked down the hall and behind a curtain in ICU. My mother was tethered to every life-sustaining machine in the room, but I knew it was pointless. I cried as I took her cold hand and kissed it.

My father's hand came to rest on my back. "The results of the tests we did this morning weren't good," he said. "It's grown in such a way that there's not much hope they'll be able to get it all. They are still going to attempt the surgery, but I asked them to wait until you got here because there is a good chance she might not come out of it."

I sucked in a deep breath and leaned down to push some stray gray hairs away from my mother's smooth, peaceful face. "Don't do the surgery, Dad."

He took a step toward me. "But it's the only option we —"

I cut him off and looked back at him. "Mom's gone. These machines are making her heart and her lungs work, but she left early this morning."

The blood drained from my father's handsome face. His blue eyes were bloodshot from worry and lack of sleep.

They filled up with tears again. "How do you know?"

"Because her soul isn't here. This is just a shell." For the first time in my life, I didn't care that I sounded like a lunatic. "She's gone, Dad."

My father crumpled into the chair beside the bed. I went over and knelt down beside him as he wailed. "I'm not ready," he cried. "I can't let her go."

My mother was the first experience I had ever had with death, not counting Billy Stewart. I wondered if something about me had extended the lives of others without me realizing it. Holding her hand on that bed, one thing occurred to me: the word dead was the wrong word. My mother's body may have been lifeless, but my mother, herself, was just gone. I had no idea where she was gone to, but I was certain I didn't have the power to summon her back.

Over the next hour, my dad had to convince my aunt and my mom's doctors to not attempt the brain surgery. He signed a medical release stating he didn't want any more excessive measures to keep her body alive. The doctors turned off the machines. Even though I knew she wasn't there, something about hearing the finality of my mother's last heartbeat devastated me all over again. Warren held me as I sobbed with my dad at her bedside.

Blindly, I walked to the waiting room and sat down next to Adrianne. She reached over and took my hand and rested her head on my arm. "I'm so sorry, friend," she said. "I love you."

I nodded. "I love you too."

My dad walked into the waiting room. Aunt Joan was with him. Warren got up from beside me and offered Dad his seat. "The funeral home is sending someone to pick her up," he said. "We'll need to go down there at some point today or tomorrow and make the arrangements."

"OK," I said, unsure of what else to say.

"Do you want to come to the house? We are going to head that way now since there's nothing left for us to do here," he said.

I squeezed his hand. "Of course, Daddy. We'll be there."

"All right." He pressed a kiss to my knuckles.

Warren hugged my dad. "I'm so sorry, Dr. Jordan."

Dad patted Warren on the shoulder. "Call me Dad, son."

When he was gone, we waited for Adrianne's dad to bring the car around, and Warren helped her into the front seat. "Let me know when the service will be. Come over and have a beer if you need to get away." She held my hand through the car window.

I smiled. "Thank you."

When they were gone, Warren put his arms around me, hiding me from the chill of the mountains. As I shivered against his warm chest, I deeply regretted not wearing a jacket.

His hands rubbed my bare arms. "We need to get you home so you can change. Are you ready to go?" he asked.

"I just need to get my phone. I left it in the waiting room." I pulled away from him and turned back toward the hospital.

A tall black man was standing in the doorway of the waiting room. He matched Warren in size and had a shiny bald head. He was wearing blue hospital scrubs and an I.D. name tag. His eyes sparkled like gold nuggets, but there was nothing behind them. I knew exactly who he was.

An angel of death.

14.

Like a bull being released from a rodeo pen, I charged at the man and slammed my fist into his face as hard as I could. The jolt from touching him nearly knocked me off my feet. He barely flinched, but I recoiled, grabbing my hand and cursing in pain. Warren took hold of my arms and pulled me under his control. Without a word, the man wiped a trickle of blood from his bottom lip.

"It was you!" Undeterred by the possibility of fractured fingers, I fought as hard as I could to free myself from Warren's tight grip. "You took her!"

The man held up his hands in defense and took a half-step back from me. "Yes, I took her." His voice was calm and even.

I lunged at him again, but Warren kept me from reaching him. He shook me and put his lips close to my ear. "Sloan, you need to calm down."

"Shall we talk inside?" The man nodded back toward the building behind him.

Without waiting for us to agree, he turned and walked

through the door. After exchanging a worried glance with each other, Warren and I followed. Once we were inside the waiting room, the man raised his large hand and waved it toward the doors. They slammed shut without being touched, and I heard their heavy locks tumble.

Beside me, Warren froze. Had I not been blind with rage, I probably would have been frozen in awe and fear as well.

"Who are you?" I demanded.

He tapped his name tag and looked at it upside down. "Today I am David Miller."

I narrowed my eyes. "Who are you really?"

He bowed his head and touched his fingertips together. "My name is Samael."

I shoved him in the shoulder. "Why did you kill my mother, Samael?"

Warren bent down to look at me in the face. "The dude just slammed all the doors in the room without touching them and locked us in here. Please stop putting your hands on him."

Samael held up his hand and smiled, clearly amused by my weak show of hostility. "It's OK. I was warned she could be a little volatile if provoked, particularly early in the day."

I was puzzled but still furious. "Who told you that?"

"Your mother." He smiled. "Her exact instructions were to not try and approach you until at least ten in the morning, unless I bring coffee, at the risk of physical assault." He touched his lower lip. "Maybe I should have waited a few hours more."

I cut my eyes at him. "What do you mean my mother told you?"

He motioned to the chairs behind us. "Shall we sit?"

Warren pushed me down into a chair and pulled one over next to me. Samael moved a chair around to face us and carefully sat down. I massaged my sore knuckles.

"I'm Warren, by the way," Warren said, extending his hand.

Samael shook it. "It is my pleasure to meet you both. I am very sorry it is under these circumstances."

I pointed a finger at him. "Cut the pleasantries and start explaining to me why you killed my mother."

He leveled his gaze at me. "I did not kill your mother, Sloan. Mortality destroyed her body. I simply freed her from this world and escorted her into mine."

Warren eyed Samael skeptically. "No offense, but I've killed plenty of people, and there has never been an angel there to take them anywhere."

Samael slowly pointed at him. "You were there."

That was sobering.

Warren sat back in his seat, his jaw a little slack.

Samael had a small smile on his face. "You using your power is just a little more…" He paused like he was searching for the right word. "Explosive."

Explosive was a good way to describe what Warren could do. He was still speechless and even a little pale.

Samael looked at us both. "Typically, when we are present, we are unseen, hidden just beyond the veil of what your mortal eyes can see. I only came here today as you see me"—he motioned down at his body—"because of my conversation with your mother. Are you aware of what you are?"

"Seramorta," I answered.

Samael nodded. "You are very rare. And two of you together, even more so. I had to see for myself if it was true." His finger moved slowly between me and Warren. "This pairing is quite curious."

I looked over at Warren. He cocked an eyebrow but didn't comment.

Frustrated, I rubbed my hands down my face. "Two angels in two days. Now this." I groaned. "I'm not sure how much more I can stand."

Samael perked in his seat, his golden eyes wide with intrigue. "You met another angel?"

Warren nodded. "A woman named Abigail in Texas."

Samael shook his head. "There is no *Abigail* in our world."

I crossed my arms over my chest and smirked. "You know everyone in your world?"

"Yes. We have been together from the beginning of time," he said.

Warren nudged me with his elbow. "Abigail probably isn't her real name. Remember, we originally thought her name was Rachel."

I shrugged. "Yeah, I'll bet you're right. I didn't even think to ask."

Samael smiled. "We rarely go by our real names when we walk among you. Their obscurity makes us more conspicuous than we would prefer, and you can rarely pronounce them properly. Samael is my real name."

Warren shifted in his seat. "Abigail said I was the son of a death angel. Could you be…?" He was almost cringing.

Samael laughed. "I am not the only angel in charge over the dead, and I have no children. If I did, I would not be able to cross the spirit line."

"Why not?" I asked.

"Having a child on Earth binds the spirit here. While the child lives, the parent cannot leave," he said.

My eyes widened. "So our parents are still here?"

He nodded. "Absolutely. As long as you live, they will remain here on this side of the spirit line."

I sat forward in my chair. "Do you know who they are or where we might find them?"

He looked at us both carefully before finally shaking his head. "I'm sorry. I cannot say that I know."

Warren sat back and crossed his arms. "So, what do you want from us, Samael?"

"Nothing," Samael answered. "I just wanted to see if it could be true."

There was a note of wonder in his voice that made me a bit nervous, though I wasn't sure why.

He pointed at both of us again. "This is not a likely occurrence."

I groaned and looked at Warren. "In other words, it's not likely a *coincidence*."

Samael had a knowing smile. "The mortal often dismiss too much as coincidence."

I rolled my eyes. "Tell me something I don't know."

"My time here must come to an end." Samael slowly rose and extended his hand to me. "I am truly sorry for your loss, Ms. Sloan. But please know your mother no longer suffers. And she is not far away."

"So, it's real?" I asked. "Heaven is real?"

"More real than this very room."

The notion was only mildly comforting. I wanted my mother in *my* world, no matter how glorious the other side was. "Can you give her a message?" I asked.

He nodded.

"Tell her I love her and I'm sorry I didn't get back in time to make this right," I said.

Like a grandfather comforting a child, he put his hand under my chin. "It was time for her suffering to end, Sloan. Someday you will understand."

Something about his words brought me a strange sense of comfort. I believed him and I doubted him in equal portions.

Warren and I stood, and Samael waved his hand and

reopened the doors. A nurse stuck her head into the room as if trying to figure out what had happened in the waiting area, but she quickly disappeared again.

Samael paused before walking outside and looked at us with a serious expression. "I must implore you to exercise extreme caution. There are some to whom you will be a great threat, and they will do everything in their power to overtake you or destroy you."

Chills ran down my spine. "Why?"

"Because you are more special than you realize."

My shoulders slumped. "I don't want to be special."

With a smile, he bowed his head. "Until we meet again." Without another word, he disappeared through the door outside.

I pointed toward the exit. "Warren, did that really just happen, or am I so stressed out and exhausted that I'm hallucinating?"

He wrapped his hand around mine. "That really just happened."

We walked outside, but Samael was nowhere to be seen. "Do you think he was being honest? Do you think he really talked to my mom?"

Warren slipped on his sunglasses and pulled the car keys out of his pocket. "I don't see why he would have any reason to lie about it," he said. "And I'm pretty sure lying is a sin and angels can't sin, right?"

I leaned my head against his arm. "Please take me home and lock me away before anything else weird happens. I've had enough supernatural crap in the last twenty-four hours to last a lifetime."

"Are we going to your dad's?" he asked.

"Yeah. There's going to be a whole lot of stuff that needs to be taken care of, I'm sure. And I don't want him to be alone."

We drove in silence to my parents' house. My brain ran through the events that had transpired like a horror movie reel that I was unable to stop. We helped take down a human trafficking ring. We found Rachel Smith and she was an angel named Abigail. She informed us we were angel half-breeds. My mother died and crossed into the spirit world. And we met an Angel of Death who told us some other angels might try and kill us. My head was beginning to throb. I longed for the morning before when we were enjoying omelets by the pool and my biggest concern was a marriage proposal.

We rolled to a stop on the cobblestone driveway next to Aunt Joan's sedan, and it occurred to me it would be the first time in as long as I could remember that I would walk into the house and not smell anything delicious coming from the kitchen. I had never learned how to make Mom's mashed potatoes. My heart sank and tears would have flowed had my eyes not been all cried out. It's the little things that hurt the most when the most important things are suddenly gone.

I looked at the house, pausing with my hand on the car door handle. "I never should have gone to Texas." I sighed and pushed the door open with my shoulder.

Anticipating at least a one night stay, Warren carried our suitcases into the house. Aunt Joan was at the bar in the kitchen when we came in, and she looked at us and pressed her finger over her lips. We quietly walked in and she nodded to the den where my dad was stretched out across the leather sofa.

I gave her a side hug and lowered my voice to a whisper. "How long has he been asleep?"

"About ten minutes." She looked up at Warren and stuck out her hand. "I'm Joan Thornton. Audrey's older sister."

"Warren Parish," he answered.

I touched her arm. "Sorry, Aunt Joan. This is my boyfriend."

She nodded. "I assumed so. Audrey mentioned him a

time or two. You're a detective for the county."

I hung my head and felt Warren gently squeeze the back of my neck. "No ma'am," he answered quietly. "You're thinking of Detective McNamara."

She smacked her forehead. "Oh, I'm sorry. You're the other one. Military is it?"

"Yes, formerly," he replied and kissed my forehead.

Her cheeks were flushed with embarrassment, and she flashed me an apologetic, wincing smile. "Please forgive me."

He shook his head. "Don't worry about it."

Desperate to change the subject, I tapped my watch. "Do you know what the plan is for the day?"

She sighed. "I don't think we are going to try and do anything today. Your father was up all night long and has been very worried all week. I called the funeral home, and they suggested we come first thing in the morning to make the arrangements. We'll need to talk about what you and your dad want for the service. A pastor, flowers, and such. I'm just guessing, but I think we will try and have the funeral on Tuesday."

I had never been to a funeral before.

She held up her cell phone. "I've just been making calls to everyone who needs to know."

I picked up the list she had scribbled on the back of a receipt. "Can I help you?"

She patted my hand. "Go lie down, sweetie. I know you've not gotten much sleep either. I can take care of this. You're going to need your rest. It's going to be a trying few days ahead."

I hugged her again. "Thank you for being here."

She sniffed and rubbed my forearm. "I just can't believe how fast this happened. A week ago we were at the farmer's market picking out pumpkins and now she's gone."

I wanted to apologize, but that would sound crazy. "I

can't believe it either," I said. "I can't imagine what Dad is going through."

She shook her head. "Or what he will go through in the days ahead. Those two have been inseparable since the day they first met."

My eyes turned toward my father who was on his back with his arm draped over his eyes. Mom had not only been his wife of twenty-seven years, but she was also the head nurse in his office, his cook, his bookkeeper, housecleaner, and grocery shopper. I wondered if Dad even knew where to begin with paying bills at home or keeping up with the accounting at work. My heart broke for him all over again.

"I'll have to start taking better care of him myself," I said.

She smiled. "We'll all pitch in."

I kissed the top of her gray head. "I'm going to try and rest for a while. We'll be up in my old room if you need me."

"OK, sweetie. I'll come get you if necessary," she said.

Warren and I walked upstairs to my former bedroom that mom had converted to a guest room when I moved out after college. I sank down on the edge of the magnolia print comforter, and Warren gently sat down next to me. I dropped my head and a rogue tear slipped down my cheek. "I just can't believe she's gone."

He turned toward me and gathered me into his arms. "Come here," he said.

I silently cried against his chest, listening to the even thump of his heartbeat and savoring the warm buzz of energy that flowed between us. I wanted to lose myself in him and hide from the pain that threatened to consume me. In his arms, he gently rocked me as his fingers trailed up and down my spine. Warren was my safe haven from all the horrors outside of that very moment. I pulled back to look up at him.

His eyes were soft and pleading for a way to remove

my burden, and we both knew he would if it were possible. Instead, he cradled my face in his hands and leaned his forehead against mine. "I'm sorry," he whispered, his thumbs stroking my cheeks.

Please, was the only coherent thought in my head as I stretched up until my lips met his. My fingers tangled in his hair as his mouth parted and moved against mine.

Perhaps Warren was as desperate as I was to escape from reality together because there was no pause for foreplay as his hand slid up the inside of my thigh underneath my skirt. As he bent over me and pressed me back against the pillows, his fingers slid my panties down my legs. A moment later, my skirt was pushed up around my waist and he was inside me. I was pretty certain he hadn't even kicked off his boots.

My vision went in and out of focus until I finally closed my eyes and melted into the intoxicating surge of our connection. The world went black around me, and the chaos that had fueled everything leading up to that moment was squelched by his touch. I dug my nails into his back, gathering the fabric of the shirt he was still wearing.

"I love you, Warren."

His black hair spilled down across my face as he rocked against me. "I love you too."

15.

The ensuing days were a nauseating blur, like a week-long hangover from the world's worst party. There was a visitation and a service at the funeral home where I met more people than I had ever seen in my life. Between countless patients of my father and at least half of the staff at the hospital, people and flowers spilled into every crevice of the building. My dad would have casseroles in his freezer until the apocalypse.

During the service, the pastor rattled on about comfort and grief and encouraged us all to not waste the days we are granted. Considering the amount of people who had shown up to offer their condolences, it was comforting to know not one second of my mom's life had been squandered. The impression she had made on the world was immeasurable, and even greater was the void she left behind.

After the minister shared a final prayer, we rode in the back of a black town car to the graveside. There, they placed my mother's mahogany casket in the ground. It was all surreal, like I was stuck in a nightmare that even the bitter cold couldn't shake me from.

When the formalities were over, a large group of people gathered at my parents' house where the staff from the hospital brought over enough food to feed the entirety of downtown Asheville. Nathan, Adrianne, and even Shannon all came over. Warren and I sat on the porch swing with them on the back deck that overlooked the sparkling city. Warren held my hand and gently swung us back and forth.

"Are you going to stay here with your dad for a while?" Adrianne asked.

I looked inside to where my father sat at the table with a few of his friends. His mouth was smiling, but his eyes were sad and tired. I nodded. "I'm probably going to stay till he kicks me out," I said. "This was so sudden. He had no time to prepare for it at all."

"I'm really sorry, Sloan," Shannon said gently.

Nathan came over and knelt down in front of me. He placed his hands over mine. "You want some good news?"

I sighed. "I would love some good news."

"I made a call to Houston today. They rescued nineteen girls total out of that trafficking ring, and they arrested Larry Mendez," he said.

I forced a half-smile. "That is good news."

He squeezed my hands. "We're going to take off. Will you call me if you need anything at all?"

Nodding, I rose to my feet. I put my arms around his neck and hugged him for a tad bit longer than was probably appropriate. "Thanks for being here, Nathan."

He rested his cheek against mine and spoke softly in my ear. "I wish I could fix it."

I smiled. "I know."

Shannon stepped over and hugged me also. "I'll be praying for you and your family," she said as we embraced.

When they were gone, I sat back down by Warren and

put my head on his shoulder.

Adrianne rolled her wheelchair closer and pointed at me. "You just hugged Shannon Green."

"And neither of them burst into flames. Aren't you shocked?" Warren teased.

I tried to laugh, but it came out as a throaty cough.

Adrianne leaned on her elbow. "You want some more good news?"

I straightened and looked at her. "Absolutely."

Biting her lower lip, she put her hands on the armrests of her wheelchair. She locked the wheels and pushed herself up.

"Whoa, whoa, whoa!" Warren shouted as he jumped up to grab her arm.

She swatted his hand away. "Don't touch me."

He kept his hands close just in case, and I sat forward on the swing and watched her as she straightened all the way up. I covered my mouth with my hands and teared up all over again. I stood and put my arms around her. "Congratulations!"

She laughed and pushed me away. "I can't stand up forever." Warren and I helped her settle back into her chair.

"But you can stand!" I cheered.

"I took five steps at physical therapy yesterday without holding on to anything." She smiled with pride. "I'll be wearing my stilettos and dancing again before you know it."

Genuinely happy for the first time in days, I leaned over and hugged her. "I can't wait! I'll let you dress me up like a paper doll and put as much makeup on me as you want. We'll dance until we're dizzy."

She squeezed me. "I love you so much."

I smiled. "I love you too."

* * *

The next morning when I came downstairs, I smelled coffee and sausage cooking in the kitchen. For a split second, I completely forgot Mom was gone. I stepped around the corner and saw Warren at the stove. I walked over and put my arms around his waist and rested my head against his back.

He rubbed my forearms and looked around at me. "Good morning," he said. "The coffee is ready."

I squeezed his waist, then crossed the kitchen to retrieve a coffee mug. "Have you seen Dad yet this morning?" I asked.

He shook his head. "He's not up yet."

Glancing up at the clock, I put the mug down next to the coffee maker. It was after nine. "That's strange. I'm going to go and check on him."

"OK."

I walked back out of the kitchen and down the hall past the stairs to the door of the master bedroom. Gently rapping my knuckles against it, I pushed it open just a crack. Dad was sitting on the edge of the bed in his flannel pajama pants and a white t-shirt, staring at the carpet. I pushed the door open farther. "Dad?"

He looked up. His eyes were red, and there were dark circles beneath them. I walked over and sat down beside him, looping my arm through his. For a while, neither of us spoke because there was absolutely nothing to say.

Finally, Dad sucked in a deep breath. "It's just so hard to even get up in the morning now." He was shaking as tears streamed down his cheeks.

I turned and put my arms around him, our roles for once reversed.

After a moment, his weeping subsided and he pulled away. Wiping his eyes on the back of his hand, he shook his head. "I'm sorry. I'm trying to keep it together," he said. "I just never even thought about a life without her in it."

On the nightstand was a box of tissues. I grabbed one for Dad and one for myself. "Me either."

He sighed and stood up, dabbing his eyes with the tissue to dry them. "Come on. Let's get some coffee. I'm going to need it. I've got to figure out how to pay the mortgage today."

* * *

The fourth day of what I had dubbed *Dad Intervention Week* was laundry day. When I got back to his house after putting in a few hours at the office, we spent ten minutes discussing the importance of sorting the colors from the whites and figuring out which buttons did what on the washing machine. While Dad gathered the laundry from the house to practice, Warren carried boxes of Mom's stuff to the garage.

When we passed in the hallway, I grabbed Warren by the arm. "How do you think he's doing?"

He nodded his head. "He told me a dirty senior citizen joke over breakfast this morning, so I would say he's doing better."

I squeezed his forearm. "Thank you for staying with him so I don't get fired."

He shook his head. "Stop thanking me." His eyes widened. "Guess what today is."

"Laundry day?"

He smiled. "Halloween."

"Oh geez. We'd better get candy today," I said.

He nodded. "Remind me and we'll pick some up on our way back from dinner."

"Sloan, honey! Can you come up here please?" Dad shouted down the stairs.

"Coming!" I called back and headed up the steps. When I got to the top, I looked into his office, but it was empty. "Where are you?"

"Your room," he answered.

I walked down the hall and found my father sitting on my bed holding a file folder. "What's up?" I asked.

He held up the photograph of Abigail Smith. "I found this on top of your clothes. Do you know this woman?"

Puzzled by his intrigue, I walked over and peered over his shoulder. "Yeah. Her name is Abigail. I met her in Texas. Why?"

He looked out the window and rubbed his hand over his mouth. Finally, he snapped the folder shut and looked back at me. "Nothing, honey. She just looks really familiar." He put the folder back in my suitcase.

"She was a missing person in Greensboro for a while, but we located her in San Antonio," I explained. "You might have seen her on the news."

"That must be it." He stood up. "Excuse me for a second."

He walked out of the room and left the laundry on the bed. "Dad, you forgot—"

The sound of his office door closing cut me off.

I looked down at the clothes and at the file folder, then scratched my head. "That was weird."

A half hour later, Dad was still in his office, and because I'd skipped lunch to leave early, I was starving. I went back upstairs and knocked on his door. "Dad, we're going to go out and get some food, do you want anything?" I shouted through the wooden door.

"No, thank you!"

"Are you all right in there?" I called back.

"Just fine!"

I shook my head and galloped down the stairs. Warren was holding my jacket at the bottom. "He's not coming?" he asked.

"Nope," I answered, shrugging into the black coat. "He's acting really strange."

"How so?" He opened the front door and stepped aside to let me exit first.

The brisk October air slapped me in the face. "Brrr." I zipped my jacket closed and shoved my fists into my pockets. "I don't know what's up with him. He saw that picture of Abigail up in our room earlier, and he's been locked in his office ever since. He looked like he had seen a ghost or something."

"Do you think he knows her?" he asked.

I looked up at him and tried to hide my face behind the collar of my jacket. "How would he?"

"I don't know." He clicked the button to unlock the Challenger.

I held out my hand. "Can I drive? I haven't driven a car in weeks."

He hesitated for a second. "Will you be careful?"

With a hand on my hip, I reached for the keys. He held them up away from me, his eyes demanding I answer the question.

"Yes, I'll be careful!"

He laughed and handed them to me.

When we climbed inside, I sank down in the leather driver's seat and moved it up so I could reach the pedals with my feet. My eyes closed involuntarily as I started the engine and felt the beast roar to life underneath me. An unstoppable moan slipped out.

When I looked over at Warren, he was frowning. "Please don't make me jealous of my own car."

I laughed and put the transmission in reverse. "Oh, I love driving this thing."

He pointed at me. "No hot-rodding it while I'm gone."

Gone.

The word reverberated in my skull like a clanging cymbal inside a racquetball court.

I slammed my foot down on the brakes, and my hands released the steering wheel in shock. "Oh my gosh! With everything going on, I completely forgot you're leaving. When is it again?"

"Seven days."

I muttered the worst of all curse words and pressed my temple against the ice cold window. "What am I going to do?"

He reached over and put his hand on my thigh, and I realized an entire year without the calming zing of his touch was going to feel like an eternity.

"I'm sorry. I shouldn't have brought it up," he said.

"No, I'm glad you reminded me. But seriously, what am I going to do while you're gone?" Panic was pushing my voice a full octave higher.

"You could take up knitting," he suggested.

My eyebrows scrunched together. "The Angel of Death is suggesting I adopt knitting as a hobby?"

Warren's shoulders shook with silent laughter.

I stared out the windshield. "Maybe I'll just stay with Dad for a while. Maybe till you come back," I said. "I don't think either of us are going to be able to tolerate being alone."

He stretched his arm over the back of my seat. "I would feel better if you weren't in the house by yourself."

"Can't you just tell the military to buzz off?"

He laughed. "Sure, I can. Then I'll wind up in the brig and we still won't be able to see each other."

I looked both ways before backing the car out of the driveway and turning down the hill. "And you still have no idea why they're calling you back?"

"No, but I'll start digging more in the media this week to see if I can figure out any leads," he said.

"Did you ever check the FBI's Most Wanted list like Nathan suggested?" I asked.

"I actually forgot all about it." He pulled out his phone. "I'll do it right now."

I drove as Warren searched the Internet on his cell

phone.

The houses in the neighborhood were all decked out with pumpkins, tombstones, and ghosts made out of bedsheets. I had always loved Halloween—the dressing up, the plethora of chocolate, and the thrill of haunted houses and scary movies. Almost every year since high school, Adrianne and I had celebrated with an Exorcist movie marathon before dressing up and hitting the hottest costume parties in town. The year before, we'd been a pair of severely underdressed angels. The irony was not lost on me. Along with so many other things in my world, Halloween would never be the same.

After a few minutes of driving, I pulled the Challenger into a parking space at the Sunny Point Cafe just down the road.

Warren was flipping through web pages on the screen with his index finger. "Huh," he finally said as I turned off the engine.

"What is it?" I asked.

He handed me his phone. "Check this out."

In my hand was a mugshot of a Middle Eastern man, with more thick black hair in his beard and eyebrows than on his balding head. There was emptiness behind his eyes. "Is he alive?" I asked.

Warren shrugged. "I don't know. Normally, I would say no, but we were wrong about Abigail, so I'm not sure."

An interesting thought occurred to me. All my life I'd seen photos and videos of people I assumed were dead. I suddenly wondered how many times I'd been wrong.

Warren was still reading. "He's wanted for terrorist attacks in Palestine and threats against the U.S. as recent as two days ago. It says he's responsible for the deaths of over 1,500 Israeli civilians."

I cocked my head to the side as I tried unsuccessfully to pronounce the series of S's, A's, B's, and K's. "How do you say his name?"

He shrugged his shoulders. "Beats me." He looked at me, the sides of his mouth dipping into a deep frown. "What do you want to bet this freak-show is my dad?"

I laughed, but it wasn't exactly funny. I examined Warren's face and shook my head. "You don't look Palestinian to me."

He laughed. "I'm not sure genetics works the same with supernatural creatures. And I could have taken after my mother."

A sickening feeling settled in my stomach. "Oh no." I groaned. "What if you're right and genetics with angels doesn't work the same? What if the DNA test we had done was faulty? Even Dad said they aren't absolutely accurate as it is. What if we really are related?"

His face twisted with disgust, and he wrenched his car door open. "Why, Sloan? Why would you go there again?" he shouted as he angled out of the car.

I got out and skipped around the back fender to meet him. "Eww…what if you've been sleeping with your sister all this time?" I squealed.

He grabbed me by my collar and jerked me under his arm. "You're not my sister."

I laughed and clicked the lock button on the Challenger's remote. "You'd better hope so or that's just sick."

The cafe was buzzing with early bird diners when we walked inside. We followed the hostess to an empty table by the window and sat down across from each other. I opened my menu and looked it over. When I settled on my usual, a sweet potato waffle and a side of chipotle cheese grits, I placed it down in front of me.

I folded my hands under my chin and leaned on my elbows. "So, *brother*, I'm thinking they might send you to Palestine or Israel instead of back to Iraq or Afghanistan."

He bit his lower lip and playfully smacked me across the head with his menu. "No more talk of war or incest. I'm hungry and you're killing my appetite!"

The sun was setting when we got back to the house after stopping at the store to stock up on candy for the inevitable flood of trick-or-treaters. My father was sitting in the kitchen with my file folder on Abigail Smith spread out before him when we walked inside. Perplexed, I dropped our Halloween haul on the table and leaned against his chair. "OK, Dad. Why are you so fascinated by this?"

Warren plopped down on the couch in the den and turned on the television.

Dad tapped his finger on the bottom corner of the surveillance photo. "Is this date correct?"

I nodded. "It was taken just a few weeks ago."

He looked up at me. "And you met this woman?"

"Yeah. We met her the night you called me in Texas and said to come home. Why?" I asked.

He dropped his head into his hands. "It would be impossible," he mumbled.

I squeezed his shoulders. "I'm learning there isn't much in this world that is truly impossible."

"You being pleasant in the morning is impossible," Warren called from the den.

Dad and I both laughed, but I was rolling my eyes. "Dad, what do you know about Abigail Smith?"

He turned around in his seat to look back at me. "You're going to think I've lost my mind."

I gave him a reassuring smile. "Try me."

His mouth fell open, but it took him a moment to form words on his lips. Finally, he spoke. "If this is who I think it is…this woman might be your biological mother."

16.

Looking at my dad, I was keenly aware of how others must feel when I reveal I can see and manipulate souls. I stumbled back a few steps till I slammed into the kitchen bar. Warren was on his feet and suddenly standing next to us. I gripped the counter for support as my mind struggled to process what my dad had just said.

Dad pushed himself up out of his chair and paced the kitchen, wringing his hands over and over. "When I knew her, her name was Sarah. She was a nurse at the hospital where we worked. I remember her well because she was such a likable person. Everyone loved her. She got pregnant while she was there and stayed through most of her pregnancy, but one day she just didn't show up for work. The hospital received a letter by mail that she was relocating to be closer to her family."

He turned to look at me from across the kitchen. "About three days later is when Audrey found you outside the hospital. Even back then, your mother and I wondered if you might be Sarah's child because of the timing of her disappearance and your arrival. But no one could ever locate her. We tried for a while."

I looked to Warren for help, and he shook his head. "It can't be," he said. "Abigail can't be much older than you are right now, and we're talking about twenty-seven years that have passed. Nobody ages that well."

Dad stopped pacing and leaned against the countertop. He tapped his finger on the granite. "I'm as certain as I am standing here that the woman in the photograph is the same woman I worked with at the hospital in the early eighties." He walked back to the table and picked up the folder. Underneath it was another photograph of a large group. "Here. This was taken at our department Christmas party."

I had seen the photograph before. My parents, just in their twenties at the time, were at the front of the group, standing together. Dad reached over and tapped his finger in the middle of the picture. Abigail Smith was smiling in the center.

My breath caught in my chest, and my eyes slowly rose to meet Warren's. "That's her. That's her, Warren!" My voice was slightly frantic. "I remember seeing this photo when I was a kid. I told Mom the lady was dead, and she completely freaked out on me."

Dad nodded. "Audrey told me about that when it happened. And we both talked about it again the night you came over a few weeks ago and told us you were different." He held up the photo. "She was pregnant when this was taken."

Perhaps fearing I might pass out, Warren grabbed my arm. His eyes were as wide as mine. "Whoa," we said at the same time.

After a moment, Dad looked up at us with imploring eyes. "Who—or what—is Sarah? I mean Abigail...or whoever she is."

Scrunching up my nose, I looked at my dad sideways. "She's a social worker."

He cut his eyes at me over the rim of his glasses and frowned. "Sloan, tell me the truth."

Warren stepped in between us. "She's an angel. When we met her, she told us that Sloan and I are like angel hybrids. Part angel, part human. In the angel world, we are called the Seramorta."

Dad sucked in a deep breath and held it in his mouth causing his cheeks to puff out. Finally, he released it slowly, like hot air leaving a balloon. "Angel hybrids, huh?"

I held my hands up cautiously. "Don't freak out."

He shook his head. "I'm not freaking out." His shocked eyes glanced around the kitchen. "I do, however, need a drink."

"Me too," I agreed.

"Let's all have a drink." Warren moved to the cabinet where Dad had stashed a bottle of Tennessee Honey Jack Daniels. I'd only ever seen him drink it when he was sick with severe chest congestion. Warren poured three tumblers and passed them out to us. Dad's was gone before my glass even touched my lips.

The warm whiskey burned its way down my throat, making me cough. Warren chuckled as he poured my dad a second share.

"Shut up."

Still laughing, he shook his head. "I didn't say anything."

I began to pace around the room, tapping the rim of the glass against my bottom lip. I stopped and looked at Warren. "If this is possible, how do you explain the age thing?"

He shrugged. "You said it yourself. Maybe angel genetics is different."

"Don't you think Abigail would have mentioned she might be my mother? I mean, if she suspected I might be her daughter, she would have brought it up, *right?*"

Warren drank a big gulp of whiskey. "Maybe she was as surprised by it as you are right now. We did kind of broadside her by showing up out of nowhere like we did."

"That's true, but still." I tossed my free hand up in the air with a frustrated huff.

"Call her. You've got her number," he reminded me.

My eyes widened, and I handed him my glass before I ran out of the kitchen. I took the stairs two at a time and jogged till I reached our bedroom. Abigail's business card was tucked into the front pocket of my suitcase. I dialed the number as I walked back downstairs.

A woman answered as I reached the kitchen. "Morning Star Ministries, how may I direct your call?"

My heart was pounding in my chest. "Hi. Can I speak with Abigail, please?"

"I'm sorry. Abigail is out of town on business. May I direct you to her voicemail?" she asked.

I resumed my nervous shuffling around the kitchen. "Do you know when she might be back in the office, or do you know of another way I might contact her? I really need to talk to her."

"May I ask who is calling?" the woman asked.

"Sloan Jordan."

"Oh! Hello, Ms. Jordan." Her tone had completely changed. "Ms. Smith directed me to give you her cell phone number if you happened to call here looking for her while she was away."

"Great! What is it?"

I scribbled the number down on the corner of an old newspaper and thanked the woman profusely before ending the call. Staring at the number on the paper, I froze as the gravity of the situation hit me. I hadn't paused to think about it before, but I was about to potentially find out the identity of my birth mother. This day had been on the back burner of my mind for as long as I could remember.

Warren must have noticed the shift in my demeanor. "Are you OK?" he asked.

Slowly, I sank down onto the barstool. "This is just… *huge*."

He crossed his arms over his chest. "You don't have to do it."

Yes, I do.

I dialed Abigail's cell phone number before I could change my mind. As the line rang, I gnawed on a hangnail.

She answered on the fourth ring. "Hello?" Her voice was smooth and melodic, nothing like my own.

"Abigail, it's Sloan."

"Hello, Sloan. I've been hoping to hear from you again," she said.

My finger started bleeding. "Are you my mother?" The words were out of my mouth before I could stop them.

There was silence on her end of the line. "Perhaps this is a conversation you and I should have in person."

Her response wasn't a confirmation or a denial.

"I know you've already left Texas," she continued, "but do you think you could come back for the weekend? I'll be back in town in the morning. I would be happy to pay for your plane ticket."

Caught off guard by her proposition, my brain scrambled for a response. "I'll have to talk to Warren, but maybe. I don't know. You didn't answer my question."

"I will clear my schedule for you if you can come," she said.

My frustration was growing. "Abigail! I'm not hanging up this phone before you tell me the truth. Are you my mother?"

Silence.

"I am."

My phone slipped from my grip, bouncing off the counter before clattering onto the kitchen tile. I was paralyzed by shock.

Warren spread his hands out in front of him. "Babe, you're kind of leaving us hanging here."

Finally, I looked up at them with eyes so wide I thought they might pop out of my skull. I picked up my glass and finished off my whiskey with one painful gulp. "It's her."

Their jaws fell slack in unison.

"Holy shit." My father's words came out slowly. I had never heard him curse before.

Suddenly, I felt dizzy. "I might fall off my chair."

Warren crossed the room in two steps and put both of his strong hands on my shoulders to steady me. I slumped over the counter and thumped my head on the countertop. I rolled my forehead back and forth against the cool stone. "I'm losing it. I'm officially losing my mind." I watched the granite swirl in and out of focus just an inch below my eyes.

His hand came to rest on my back, and I trained my attention on the warm buzz of comforting energy it transmitted. I slowly lifted my head as my nerve endings settled back into place.

"This is impossible," my father stammered again. He made a few laps around the kitchen island before he turned on his heel and walked back to the table. He picked up Abigail's photo again and thrust it toward me. "She has to be at least my age now!"

Warren groaned. "Dr. Jordan, something tells me she's been looking at your age in the rearview mirror for quite some time."

Everything made sense. Abigail was an Angel of Life. She had a very attractive personality. Everyone loved her. I was found at the hospital, and Abigail disappeared because angels are forbidden to raise their offspring. If I was a summoner, then Abigail was too. All this time, all the coincidences…

"She was summoning me."

Warren stumbled back a step into the side of the counter. "Oh my god. Do you think so?"

I held out my hands. "How else do you explain all of the crazy stuff that's happened lately?"

He didn't have an answer.

I took a step toward him. "But why wouldn't she tell me? I think if I were sitting across the room from my daughter, I would say something!"

He was quiet for a while. "I don't know." He shook his head. "I don't know about any of it. We need more information before we start making big assumptions."

I rubbed my hands over my face. "This is too much. I can't process this."

Dad leaned over the counter toward me and raked his fingers through his hair so hard the tendons in his hands strained with tension. "You don't think *you* can process this? How do you think I feel? You've had a chance to get used to all this supernatural stuff, and I'm still trying to get my head around the news that you can see people's souls!" He almost sounded maniacal.

He must have realized he was starting to go a little Jack-from-The-Shining on us, and he walked over and pulled me into a tight hug. "I'm sorry. I'm rattled right now. We'll figure this thing out together. What can I do for you?"

"Will you be all right here for a couple of days if I go back to Texas? She wants me to come talk to her about it in person. Or, you can come with me?" I suggested.

He shook his head. "No, sweetheart. I think I need to sit this one out. This is a lot for an old man to handle. You and Warren go. I'll be fine."

My heart was torn between desperately wanting to talk to Abigail and not wanting to leave my father alone. I also felt guilty that this revelation had come so soon after my mother's death, like she might be looking down on me and fearing I had already found her replacement.

Maybe my father heard my anxious thoughts. "This is something you need to do, Sloan. Honestly, I want to hear what this Abigail woman has to say."

I smiled and nodded my head. "OK."

Warren refilled my father's empty glass for a third time and looked over at me. "When do you want to go?"

I turned my palms up. "She said she'll be home tomorrow. Could we leave right after I get off work?"

He shrugged his shoulders. "I'll get online and look at flights tonight."

My eyes widened. "You'll come with me, won't you?"

He smiled. "You don't really think I would let you go alone, do you?"

I shook my head. "I hope not."

My dad's arm was still around my shoulders. He seemed to be leaning, ever so lightly, on me for support as he sipped his drink. He held his glass toward Warren. "Sloan, I really like this young man. You need to get your act together and marry him."

Laughing, and a little bit embarrassed, I patted his chest. "I like him too, Dad. Have you eaten today? You wouldn't let me bring you dinner."

He shook his head. "Nope." The word popped off his lips.

I patted his hand and then pried the tumbler from his grip. "No more whiskey till you've got some food in your system. Daughter's orders."

I prepared a turkey and provolone sandwich and put a bag of chips on the plate. Dad was sitting next to Warren at the counter. "Here," I said, placing it in front of him. "Eat this before you get sick."

"Buzz kill," he grumbled with a smile.

After a moment of looking around for my phone, I realized I had never picked it up off the floor. When I retrieved it, the screen was cracked. "Damn it."

Warren looked over. "Uh oh. Does it still work?"

"Yeah. I'll have to replace it soon though. It's busted pretty bad." I turned it around to show him the spider-webbed glass on the front.

He shrugged his shoulders. "You can have my phone switched to your number. I won't be needing it for a while."

I frowned. "You'll need it while you're still in the States," I said. "I'll just get a new one when we get home from Texas. I have insurance on it, so it's not a big deal."

My dad picked up his sandwich and put it back down again. "I forgot you're leaving us," he said, looking at Warren. "I don't like that at all."

I kissed Dad's cheek. "I don't like it either."

I pulled up a new group text message on my phone and put in Nathan's phone number and Adrianne's. *Here's a spooky Halloween story for you: Abigail Smith is my biological MOTHER.*

Adrianne called first. "You're kidding me?" she asked without saying hello when I answered the phone.

"Nope. Dad figured it out. Get this, she used to work with my parents at the hospital in Florida," I told her. "And she hasn't aged a day. Apparently angels don't age."

She laughed. "*You* age. I'm going to have to start covering up gray in your hair soon if you don't cool it with all of the intergalactic drama you seem to get yourself into."

"That's the freaking truth." I sighed. "How was physical therapy today?"

My phone beeped with an incoming call. It was Nathan, so I ignored it.

"You just found out your biological mother is an angel

and you want to hear about me doing leg lifts and squats?" she asked.

"Of course I do. You're still more important."

"Physical therapy was fine. But back to you. What are you going to do?" she asked.

"I think Warren and I are going to try to fly to Texas tomorrow and meet with her. She asked me to come so we can talk in person," I said.

"The bitch dropped you off outside a hospital as a newborn. She could at least fly to you."

I laughed. "I hadn't really thought about it that way. She did offer to buy me a plane ticket."

My phone beeped again, and again it was Nathan.

I sighed. "Nathan's blowing up my phone. I'll call you back later."

She laughed. "Bye, freak."

I swapped calls on my phone. "I was on the other line. You know I'll call you back," I told him without a greeting.

"You can't send a message like that and then not answer your phone!" He was shouting. "How did you figure it out?"

"I didn't. My dad did," I said. "Her name was Sarah when he knew her. They worked together at the hospital back in the eighties. Isn't that the craziest thing you've ever heard?"

"It's right up there with everything else I've ever heard from you, Sloan. How is it possible she's the same person? She would have been maybe two years old when you were born," he said.

I sat down on Warren's lap at the counter. "Nathan, weren't you the one who originally asked how any of this is possible? Why are you still asking that question?"

"Good point," he said. "Are you going back down there?"

"We are going to try and go tomorrow. You wanna

come with us?" I asked.

"As intriguing as it sounds, some of us have to go to work to pay the bills," he said.

"It's just for the weekend," I told him. "We'll be back in plenty of time for you to go to work on Monday."

"Three's a crowd, babe," he responded.

Warren leaned his mouth close to the microphone. "I heard that. You're not allowed to call her *babe*, Nate."

"Hi, Warren," Nathan said. "Sloan, let me know how it goes." He raised his voice. "Maybe you can come over when you get back and tell me about it over dinner and a bottle of wine!"

"I'll bring the dessert!" Warren replied.

I rolled my eyes. "I'll talk to you later, Nathan." I laughed and disconnected the call.

The doorbell rang. I pushed myself up and crossed the room, grabbing the giant bag of candy on my way to the front door. When I pulled the door open, a small girl and her even smaller brother were dressed as an angel and a devil respectively. "Trick or treat!" they sang together, holding up their plastic pumpkin buckets.

A chill ran down my spine.

Truly, Halloween would never be the same again.

17.

For the first time—and probably the last time—I was out of bed and getting dressed before Warren that next morning. At four a.m. he walked into the bathroom in his boxer shorts, sleepily rubbing his eyes. I had already showered, dressed, and put on my makeup.

He squinted at me. "Did I wake up in the wrong house?"

I brushed my long hair back into a ponytail and wound an elastic band around it. "I couldn't sleep at all last night."

He shook his head and pointed his toothbrush at a me. "I think all the stress lately is taking its toll on you. Are you cracking up on me?"

I put my arms around his waist as he brushed his teeth. "We are so close to answers, Warren! Aren't you excited?"

He paused, watching me carefully in the mirror. "I'm more terrified of you right now than I am on normal mornings when you're hateful and sadistic."

I hopped up on the edge of the counter and swung my

boots off the side as he finished brushing. "I think I should get a reward for beating you out of bed."

He shook his head. "It doesn't count if you never went to sleep. Besides, I don't get rewards when I sleep in with you."

I winked at him. "Yes, you do."

He laughed. "Touché."

I kicked my heels against the cabinet beneath me. "Are you going to pick me up at the office since I'm closer to the airport?"

"Yes. Are you sure it won't be a problem for you to leave at noon?" he asked.

"I'm sure. Most everyone leaves early on Fridays anyway."

He nodded. "Good. We need enough time so I can check my guns at the baggage counter."

I narrowed my eyes. "Why do you need guns this time? This is a social visit, not a man hunt."

He packed up his travel case. "Babe, you should just go ahead and get used to the fact I'm going to be carrying heat no matter where we go. It's what I do."

I sighed. "It just seems like a big, unnecessary hassle."

"Was it worth it when I took Billy Stewart down in the woods?" he asked.

I crossed my arms over my chest. "That was different."

He reached in the shower and turned the water on steaming hot. "Hope for the best, but have your guns locked and loaded for the worst." He leaned over and gave me a minty kiss.

I drummed my nails on the counter and smiled as he dropped his shorts and stepped under the water.

He wiped the fog off the glass shower door and looked at me. "Should I charge admission for this?"

I bit down on my lower lip. "You'd make a killing if you did." After a moment of enjoying the show, I pushed myself up. "I'm going to go make breakfast."

He shook his head. "We didn't remember to pick up cereal at the store yesterday."

"I'll cook something then," I said.

"Oh God. Does your dad have a fire extinguisher handy?"

I laughed. "Shut up!"

The house was still and quiet downstairs. Dad was still sleeping. I started a pot of coffee, then yanked open the refrigerator and immediately regretted we hadn't made a list before going shopping the day before. I wondered what Dad was going to eat while we were gone. I pulled out the carton of eggs and carried it to the stove.

The cabinet above the cooktop was where mom kept her small, brown Rubbermaid file box full of her recipes. I was sure the box was older than I was. Inside were hundreds of index cards, most were yellowed with age. I found the breakfast tab and searched for scrambled eggs. I pulled out the entire stack of cards and couldn't find it anywhere. Frustrated, I slammed the cards back into the section.

Then I noticed another tab labeled "For Sloan." I carried the cards over to the kitchen island and sat down on a barstool. Dad's bottle of Tennessee Honey was still on the counter and significantly more empty than it had been the day before. I pushed it out of the way and pulled the index cards from the section.

My mother's handwriting, the familiar curve of her S's and the peculiar cursive style of her E's, brought tears to my eyes. I stroked the paper with my thumb like I was touching her very hand. The first card was the detailed recipe for sausage gravy with step-by-step instructions she knew I would need. The second was for made-from-scratch biscuits. The third was for her roast beef. And the next one was for her secret-recipe mashed potatoes. There was an asterisk by the ingredient—

cream cheese. I dropped my face into my hand and cried.

After a moment, I felt a hand on my shoulder. I looked up at my father's sympathetic smile. He leaned down and gave me a side hug. "She wrote them down because she knew you were never coming to learn in person. She figured someday you might want to cook for someone else."

I wiped mascara on the back of my knuckles and covered my dad's hand with my own. I sniffed and glanced up at him again. "There aren't any recipes for eggs."

He nudged me with his arm and smiled. "Come on. Your old man can handle that one without a recipe card."

He pulled a glass bowl out of the cabinet and picked up the eggs.

I snatched the carton right back from him. "I can crack them."

"OK. Go ahead and crack eight into the bowl. Warren strikes me as a man who can eat more than two," he said with a chuckle.

I smiled over at him. "I think Warren could eat the whole dozen."

"Well, then crack the whole dozen," he said as he walked to the refrigerator.

As I worked on the eggs, he carried butter and sour cream back to the stove. I shot him a quizzical glance. "Sour cream?"

He nodded. "Your mother swears a tablespoon of sour cream makes them fluffier."

When I finished cracking the last egg, he put a huge dollop of sour cream into the bowl. He handed me the salt and pepper. "Sprinkle them with just a little." After I added the seasoning, he handed me a large metal whisk. "Now, whip them around till it's all mixed together and frothy."

He pulled out a large frying pan and put it on the stove. He cut off a hunk of butter and dropped it in the pan.

"How much butter are you putting in there?" I asked.

He grinned and winked at me. "The more, the better."

I wagged a finger at him. "I don't think doctors are supposed to say that."

He laughed as he turned the stove up to just higher than medium heat. He tapped the temperature dial. "Don't turn it too high or you'll burn them. Wait until the butter starts to melt, then swirl it around to coat the bottom. Once it sizzles just a tad, pour the eggs in and keep stirring till they're done."

Dad poured us two cups of coffee while I followed his directions. I dumped the contents of the bowl on top of the melted butter and grabbed a wooden spoon. When the eggs were finally solid, he turned off the stove eye.

"See? That wasn't so hard." He kissed my forehead. "Now put some bread in the toaster and we'll have a real, bonafide breakfast."

I turned around and Warren was leaning in the doorway to the kitchen smiling. He winked at me before coming over and pouring himself a cup of coffee. "I was prepared to call the fire department," he said over his shoulder.

"Shut your face," I said.

Dad put a jar of peach preserves on the table along with the butter. "What time does your flight land in Texas?"

"Around six," Warren answered.

I dished out three small plates full of scrambled eggs, giving Warren the largest portion. "Dad, are you sure you're going to be all right here for the weekend?"

Dad sat down at the table with his newspaper. "Sloan, I really appreciate your concern, but I am a fifty-five-year-old renowned physician. I think I can handle a weekend alone in my own home."

I flashed him a coy grin. "Two days ago I had to show you where the toilet paper is kept."

He nodded and pushed his reading glasses higher up on the bridge of his nose. "And now that I know where it is, I'm sure I'll be fine."

I kissed the top of his head and sat down next to him.

He tasted the eggs and nodded with approval. "They're perfect."

Warren swallowed a forkful. "Best eggs I've ever had," he agreed.

I laughed and launched a napkin across the table at him.

Dad's expression melted into seriousness. "Sloan, are you holding up all right? You have been hit with a lot of huge, life-changing stressors in a very, very short period of time."

I sighed and sipped my coffee. "I try not to over-think it, Dad. That's the only way I'm still functioning. If I stop long enough to consider the whirlwind that has become my life, I'm afraid I would be sucked up in it and spat out somewhere in the stratosphere."

He pointed his fork at me. "Well, be sure to find some time to relax. That much stress—good or bad—will wreak havoc on your body if you aren't careful. You might just wind up making yourself very sick."

"I'll be fine, Dad," I insisted. "When I get back home, life will go back to the same old same old. I'll go back to work and resume cranking out press releases and preparing the county newsletter. And I'll be having dinner with you on Mondays. Maybe we can even tag team the cooking duty."

He smiled. "I would like that."

* * *

Instead of staying at the Hyatt on the River Walk again, we checked into a hotel closer to Abigail's neighborhood. I called her from the room once we got settled, and she answered on the first ring. "Hello?"

"Hey, it's Sloan. I just wanted to let you know we're

back in town. We're staying at the Holiday Inn Express near your ministry."

"Wonderful." She sounded anything but wonderful herself. "How was your trip?" she asked.

I sat down on the bed. "It was uneventful, which is always good when you're on an airplane. Are you all right? You don't sound well."

"I'm fine. Just a bit of a headache from traveling," she said. "And I'm swamped trying to get a number of our girls transferred to our home in Houston. Tomorrow, however, I have blocked out the entire day for us. Would you like to come over to my house around lunch?"

An involuntary smile crept across my face. "I would love that."

"Wonderful. I'll text you my address," she said.

"Great."

"I'll see you tomorrow then?" she asked.

"Yes. See you tomorrow," I replied and disconnected the call.

Warren came out of the bathroom and stretched out on the bed next to me. "Tomorrow, huh?"

I nodded. "Yeah. She's busy today, but she's open all day tomorrow. She wants me to come to her house. Are you going to come with me?"

He shrugged his shoulders. "I think it would be good for you to spend some time with her on your own. I'm sure you have a ton of questions."

"Well, yeah, but what are you going to do?" I asked.

"I was thinking of trying to get on the visitation list at the jail tomorrow. I'd like to go have a chat with Rex and make sure Mendez is locked up. Of course, if you really want me to stay with you, I will."

I patted his arm. "No, I'll be fine. You can just drop me off at her house and do what you need to do," I said. "Why do you want to go and talk to Rex?"

He laughed. "I don't know. Morbid curiosity, maybe."

He rolled over enough to work his cell phone out of his blue jeans pocket. He searched on the Internet before dialing a phone number and pressing the phone to his ear. When his call was answered, he sat up a little. "Yeah, I'd like to find out how I can get on the visitation list to see an inmate you have. His name is Rex Parker." He waited for a few moments and then cocked his head to the side as he listened to the person on the other end of the line. "Really?" he asked with surprise. "OK. Thank you. How about a Larry Mendez? Is he still in custody?" There was another pause, and I watched his face darken. "No records?"

My stomach twisted in a knot at the thought of Mendez out on the street.

"Thanks anyway for checking." He disconnected the call and dropped the phone onto the mattress.

I pulled my knees up to my chest and peered down at him. "What is it?"

"Neither of them are in jail," he said. "Rex bonded out and they haven't had Mendez at all."

"Are you serious?" I asked. "Nathan said they arrested Mendez."

He shrugged. "He must have gotten released somehow."

"I hate the justice system."

He nodded. "I should have killed Mendez when I had the chance." He looked up, lost in thought. "I wonder what the hell happened."

I wondered the same thing.

"Well, do you want to go out and look for them tonight? I can find them for you."

He reached for my hand, then held it against his chest. "No. Your dad was right about taking it easy. We both need a break. For one evening, I want to be normal and do some normal-people shit like go to the movies and out to dinner."

I laughed. "Have we ever done anything normal?"

He shook his head. "No."

I pulled out my cell phone and searched for things to do in San Antonio. "OK, here we go," I said. "Thirty Most Awesome Things to do in San Antonio."

"That sounds promising," Warren said.

"Number one on the list is the Six Flags theme park. Too bad we didn't get here earlier," I said. "Ooo, there's the San Antonio Botanical Gardens."

He chuckled. "Next."

My eyes skimmed the list. "What about a ghost tour? I've never done that before."

His brow wrinkled in confusion. "We're both part-angel and you want to go hear ghost stories?"

I smiled as I clicked on the tour website. "I think it sounds like fun."

"We'll do whatever you want to do, babe," he said.

I leaned down over him. "I really want to go to the botanical gardens."

He rolled his eyes. "We'll do anything but that."

I lay down on my stomach beside him and propped myself up on my arm. I twirled a strand of his long dark hair around my finger. "Do you think ghosts are real?"

He thought for a second. "Two weeks ago I didn't believe in angels. So, stranger things have already happened."

"I wonder if human spirits can cross back into our world. Maybe they can walk around on Earth like angels do," I said.

He offered a sympathetic smile. "Are you thinking about your mom?"

Releasing his hair, my hand flopped onto the mattress. "I'm always thinking about my mom." The words seemed to trip some emotional wire in my brain, and before I could stop them, tears spilled out as I pressed my eyes closed.

He quickly rolled toward me and touched my arm. "I'm sorry. I didn't mean to make you cry."

Unable to hold back, I buried my face in the pillow and cried. Warren curled into me, but even his touch couldn't ease the pain that was twisting my heart into knots.

"Let it out, babe." His voice was gentle as he rubbed my back.

When my muffled wailing subsided, I turned my face on the wet pillow to look at him. We were nose to nose. "I'm sorry," I whispered.

He tucked my hair behind my ear. "Don't apologize. God knows, if anyone needs a good cry, it's you."

My lip quivered as I nodded.

"You've been through so much. Adrianne's accident, Billy Stewart, all the shit with me and Nate, then your mom..." His hand rested against my face. "It's more than anyone should have to survive."

I covered hand with my own.

He leaned over and kissed my forehead. "I'm here anytime you need fall apart."

I squeezed his fingers. "Why are you so good to me?"

"Because you're everything to me. I don't have a choice in the matter."

I closed my eyes again. "Talk about something else before I start crying again." Somehow I managed a depressing chuckle.

He sat up on his elbow, and I rolled onto my side to look at him.

After a moment, he spoke. "You should start making a list of questions to ask Abigail tomorrow."

I sniffed and dried my eyes on the back of my hand. "That's not a bad idea. Maybe we could do it over dinner."

He looked at his watch. "What time is the tour?"

"Ten. Are we even going to have time to eat?"

He grimaced. "Not if we don't leave right now."

I turned my palm over. "Are you ready to go?"

He thought for a second, then smiled and shook his head. "Absolutely not."

"No?"

He leaned over me. "I haven't had you all to myself in two weeks. We can be a little late." His eyes were twinkling with mischief as he untucked my t-shirt.

* * *

We caught up just in time with the ghost tour group behind the Alamo. There was one family with two small children, two other couples about our age, and a group of teenage girls who immediately began whispering and giggling when we approached. I looked up at the object of their attention and admired him as well.

Warren noticed me staring. "What?"

"You haven't shaved in a while," I said.

He rubbed his chin. "I'm enjoying the option of not shaving while I can," he said. "Do you hate it?"

"Are you kidding?" I shook my head. "It looks so hot on you, I'm thinking about not shaving myself."

His face melted into a frown. "Let's not get carried away."

I laughed and playfully backhanded his arm. He pulled me against him and pressed a kiss against my temple.

A tall man in his early forties approached our group. He had a thin black beard and thick black eyebrows. He was dressed in character, wearing a top-hat, black pants, a shiny red vest, and a Western necktie.

Warren looked down at me and frowned. "What the hell have you dragged us into?"

The man at the front of the group jumped up on top

of a concrete planter that was built into the sidewalk. He cleared his throat, and a hush fell over our group. "Good evening, ladies and gentleman. My name is Patrick Henry Jameson, and I invite you to walk with me tonight through a history of violent death and mass murder."

I leaned into Warren and lowered my voice. "Just another night in the office then."

I felt his body shake with laughter.

Patrick Henry continued his spiel. "Tonight, I implore you to stay close as we make our journey back in time, for we will, I guarantee you, brush elbows with the dead and come face to face with troubled spirits!"

"We paid forty bucks for this?" Warren asked.

I nudged him in the ribs with my elbow. "Shush."

Patrick Henry was making grand gestures toward the Alamo behind us. "As many as a thousand souls were lost right here on the ground where you stand." His voice dropped to a dramatically low octave as he swept through our small crowd. "Many of the decimated remains are still buried under your feet."

My eyes shot up at Warren. "True?"

"True," he said. "I could have told you that for free."

"And that doesn't creep you out, even just a little bit?"

He shrugged. "I told you. You get used to it."

A chill ran down my spine and I shivered. "I don't think I could. And time really doesn't affect it? Like, can you feel prehistoric remains underground?"

"I don't know that I would go that far. Bodies disintegrate over time and, after a lot of time, it diminishes what I feel." He grinned down at me. "Whole bodies are much easier to find."

I shook my head. "You're such a freak."

He rolled his eyes with a grin. "Hi, Kettle. This is Pot. You're black."

I giggled and tugged on his arm. "Oh, shut up."

The rest of the tour was even less interesting than the Alamo. Warren was able to debunk most of the guy's claims, but he only told me. Patrick Henry said a woman was buried in the wall of a hotel. That wasn't true. He also said the body of an actress was buried under the floor of a theater. That wasn't true either.

Finally, I looked up at Warren. "Searching for Rex Parker would have been more fascinating than this."

"Wanna head back to the car? Maybe stop somewhere for a drink?" he asked.

"Please," I begged.

We abandoned our group and headed back toward the Alamo. When we crossed into the square, an odd movement in the crowd caught my attention. Rex Parker had seen us and was running in the opposite direction down the street.

I released Warren's hand and took a step back, preparing for him to break into a sprint, but he didn't. I was puzzled. "You're not going after him?"

He shook his head and watched Rex dart down an alleyway. "I'll hunt him down tomorrow. Tonight I'm spending with you."

18.

Abigail lived in a nice neighborhood near the ministry where she worked. She had a beautiful two-story brick house with a two-car garage and elaborate stone work around the front entryway. The lot was professionally landscaped and water from the sprinkler system arched across the lawn. The house seemed big for just one person, but then it occurred to me that I didn't know if she lived alone or not. She could have an entire family inside that I knew nothing about.

"You look nervous." Warren reached over and gently squeezed the back of my neck as we sat in the car at the curb in front of her house.

I realized I was wringing my hands in my lap. I stretched out my tingly fingers which felt stiff with tension. I blew out a heavy sigh. "I guess I am. What if she doesn't like me?"

He laughed. "When has anyone in your life not liked you?"

"Shannon doesn't like me," I reminded him.

"I think she likes you more than you believe she does,"

he said. "Sloan, Abigail is going to love you. You're finally going to get all the answers you have looked for your entire life. This is a good thing."

I nodded. "I know. OK, I'm ready."

We got out of the car and walked up the path to the front door. I rang the bell and a moment later, Abigail opened it.

"You made it!" she cheered as she stepped out to give me a hug.

When the initial shock from her embrace subsided, her arms just felt awkward around me, like I was hugging a radioactive stranger in the supermarket. She pulled back and grasped my hands. Her eyes searched mine like she was looking for my soul…maybe she was. "It's true. I can't believe this moment is finally here." She looked close to tears as she studied my face for a moment so long it creeped me out a bit.

I pulled my hands away.

She took a deep breath and let out a sing-song sigh as she stepped to the side. "Well, come on in."

I looked at Warren.

He brushed a loose strand of hair from my cheek. "You good?"

I nodded. "Yeah. You can go."

Abigail's eyes widened. "You're not staying?"

He shook his head. "No ma'am. I think you two should have some girl time." He leaned over and kissed my lips. "Call me when you're about ready to go and I'll come back over here to pick you up."

"I love you," I said.

He squeezed my hand. "I love you too." He lowered his voice and whispered in my ear. "Relax."

When he turned to leave, I followed Abigail inside. The inside of the house was beautiful and very tastefully decorated in hues of blue and brown. She had the same

Pottery Barn formal dining table that I did, which made me laugh. I wondered if she didn't use hers either. There was a large, brown leather, sectional sofa in her huge living room that faced a sixty inch television screen on the wall. The kitchen, with tall white cabinets and marble countertops, overlooked the living area.

I ran my hand over the soft leather of the sofa. "Your house is amazing."

"Thank you. I'm leasing it. I don't tend to stay in one place long enough to justify buying anything. I'm a bit of a vagabond." She walked into the kitchen. "Have you eaten lunch?"

I shook my head. "No, ma'am."

She waved her hand toward me and smiled. "You don't have to be formal. We're family."

Awkward.

I watched her move around the kitchen. She had long dark hair, the same as mine. Her skin tone was similar as well. We had the same thin frame, but I definitely hadn't inherited her boobs. They were ginormous. She carried two green plates to the dinette table in the kitchen.

"I made enough for your boyfriend. I hope he didn't feel like he would be imposing here. The invitation was certainly for both of you."

I walked to the table and placed my purse on the floor. "He had some things he wanted to do today, and he thought it would be best for us to spend some time alone."

She nodded. "Well, that was very thoughtful of him. We do have a lot to catch up on." She motioned to the table. "Shall we?"

I pulled out a chair and sat down. "Thank you. I know you're really busy, so I appreciate you taking the time to see me."

She laughed and waved her hand in my direction. "Are

you joking? I've been dreaming of this day for twenty-seven years."

I had too, but the fruition of the dream lacked the fireworks I'd always expected.

"I hope deli turkey is all right," she said. "I also have wine if you would like some."

I nodded to the full water glass to the right of my sandwich and kettle-cooked chips. "Water is fine."

She sat down across from me and stared for a moment. Her eyes were brown, but outside of that, I didn't see much semblance in our faces.

She smiled. "You're very beautiful, Sloan."

"Thank you," I said again.

"Have you enjoyed your time here in Texas?" she asked.

"We just got in yesterday. Last night we went on a ghost tour through the city, but it was pretty lame. My boyfriend has the ability to find dead bodies, so he kinda squelched the mystery of it all," I said.

She laughed. "I'm sure he did."

"Are ghosts real?" I asked, thinking of my mother.

She shook her head. "No. Human spirits do not come back across the spirit line." She must have noticed when my face fell. "Why do you ask?"

"My mother died last week," I said. "The day after I met you."

She put her hands down on the table. "Oh, I am terribly sorry to hear that. Was she ill?"

I stared at my plate. "Not when I left to come here. But she got really sick while I was gone. The doctors found a brain tumor, and it was growing out of control. She was dead before I got back home."

She reached over and took my hand. "I'm terribly sorry."

"I feel like it was my fault. That maybe if I hadn't left, she wouldn't have gotten so bad, so quickly," I admitted.

"It's true you probably kept the cancer at bay. You would have inherited life and health promoting gifts from me. However, that doesn't mean it's your fault. Cancer destroyed her body. Not you." She smiled and squeezed my hand.

I sighed and crunched on a potato chip, still unconvinced of my responsibility in the matter. I blinked back tears. "I'm sorry. Can we talk about something else?"

She picked up her sandwich. "Of course we can. I'm sure you have a ton of questions for me. Where would you like to begin?"

I thought about it for a moment. There were so many questions floating around in my mind, and I was having trouble picking a starting point. Warren was right. I should have made a list. Finally, I just blurted out the question that had been bugging me the most. "Did you know you were my mother when I was here the last time?"

She swallowed the bite in her mouth and slowly nodded her head. "Yes."

My jaw went slack. "Why didn't you tell me?"

She shook her head. "It wasn't the right time. You wouldn't have believed it."

With that, I really couldn't argue.

I inhaled a quick breath. "Did you summon me here?"

Her face was unreadable. "I planted the seed long ago for you to find me, but I didn't directly summon you here."

"I don't understand."

She was thoughtful for a moment. "I have much more control over my summoning power than you do. I can use it in different ways. So yes, I summoned you many years ago, but in a way that was very gradual and natural."

I looked up at the ceiling. *Nothing about any of this is natural.*

She continued talking. "I created you for a purpose, Sloan. And as much as I hated having to leave you as a child, I knew someday the pieces would fall into place for you to find me again. And in the meantime, I knew you would be well loved by whoever took you in. You would have inherited that from me as well. It's part of who we are."

"So, people liking me is part of this gift or whatever?" I asked. "I've always wondered about that."

She nodded. "People are attracted to the life power inside you. It can be a blessing and a curse at times."

I sighed. "That's the truth." I thought of Nathan. His attraction to me was cosmic coercion after all.

"Would you like to know more about your gifts?" she asked.

My eyes widened. "Absolutely."

She straightened in her chair. "First, you must understand your powers are not as strong as mine because you are also human."

"Like with genetics, I only inherited part of your gifts?" I asked.

She shook her head. "Oh no. You inherited all of my gifts. Your humanity, though, limits what you can do with them."

"OK. So what can you do?" I asked.

She leaned toward me. "I am an Angel of Life. All angels of the second choir—"

I raised my hand. "Choir?" In my head, I envisioned the singing variety.

"It's a division of angels. There are seven different choirs, all with different jobs, if you will," she clarified.

I nodded.

"All angels of the second choir have the power to influence the human spirit. The human spirit—or what you call a soul—is like the powerhouse of the human body.

Without the spirit, the body doesn't function."

The vision of my mother's body lying on the hospital bed came to mind. "The body is just a shell."

"Correct," she said. "In addition to being able to summon and heal, I can also prolong the lives of humans past their normal life expectancy."

"Is that why your body hasn't aged?" I asked.

She shook her head. "Aging happens as cell death begins to outpace cell reproduction. My body was created with a similar genetic makeup to yours, but my cells are programmed to continually reproduce. Therefore, I do not age."

I examined her face. "How old are you?"

A small smile played across her lips. "I'm twenty-nine and holding." She pointed to my empty glass. "Would you like some more water?"

I hadn't even realized that I had finished all of it. "Please."

She picked up the glass and walked to the refrigerator.

I leaned on my elbow. "So, the summoning thing... How does it work, exactly?"

She thought for a moment. "Close your eyes."

I hesitated.

She laughed and put my water back down in front of me. "Trust me," she said as she sat back down.

Obediently, I closed my eyes.

"Picture that handsome boyfriend of yours," she said.

I smiled. "That's easy."

"Now, imagine there is a string connecting you to him."

My eyebrow peaked with skepticism. "OK."

"Pull the string."

I couldn't help it—I laughed. My eyes popped open. "You want me to pull Warren's string?"

Frowning, she rolled her eyes and pointed at me. "This is exactly why you have a hard time controlling your gift."

I crossed my arms over my chest. "And you can just do this at will?"

She nodded. "Absolutely. If I wanted your boyfriend to return right now, all I would have to do is call out to him, and he would be here as quickly as his feet could carry him. I could summon him here from across the world if I so desired."

I shook my head. "My gift doesn't work that well. It's getting stronger, but most of the time it still feels a lot like coincidence."

She smiled. "It's certainly not coincidence."

"Warren thinks I'm getting better at using my power because I'm exercising it more. Is that true?"

She nodded. "Yes, and just your exposure to him strengthens your ability to access your gifts. It's also a matter of discipline, and I can teach you."

That was an interesting prospect, but I doubted we would get to it over lunch. "Can you just summon humans?" I asked. "Or can you summon angels too?"

She shook her head. "Only human spirits."

I picked at a stray sliver of turkey. "Have you created anyone else? Do I have any brothers or sisters?"

She settled back in her seat. "No. We do not have the ability to create more than one offspring."

That settled the debate over whether or not Warren and I were related.

I sipped my water. "What about my father? Who is he?"

She thought for a moment and closed her eyes like she was trying to remember. I found it offensive that she had to think about it, but I didn't say so. Her eyes fluttered beneath her eyelids. Finally, she looked at me. "He was a remarkable man. One of the most intelligent and resourceful humans I've ever encountered. I chose him because I wanted you to have the best genetic makeup possible from your human line."

Anticipation was compounding inside me by the second. "And who was he?"

She pressed her lips together and searched my face carefully. After a moment, she shook her head. "I don't believe you're ready to know."

I folded my arms across my chest and sat back hard in my seat. "Excuse me?"

She folded her hands in front of her. "Someday I'll tell you, perhaps. But not today."

My jaw went slack. "You're kidding, right?"

Her expression didn't change. "Sloan, there are many things about my world you can't comprehend. This is one of them."

I tossed my hands up in the air. "Does he know about me?"

She shook her head. "No. I doubt it would even be possible for him to remember the act of your conception."

Surely, I misheard her. "What?"

"I have full control over my summoning powers, Sloan. When I summon someone for a purpose, they often don't remember it."

"You raped him?"

She laughed and squeezed my arms from across the table. "Stop being so dramatic. It wasn't rape."

"How do you possibly arrive at that conclusion?" I started counting on my fingers. "You coerced him against his will, and he has no memory of it. Here in America, that's a felony!"

"I apologize if you're offended. You must understand, it's just different in our world. Copulation is a means to an end, not an act of love." She forced a smile. "Let's change the subject. Tell me about your boyfriend."

It was hard to change the subject. I was confused and pissed off. Her rationalization of her actions baffled me. She could have just as casually been telling me why she chose turkey for our lunch.

I stared at her for a moment before deciding to let the issue of my birth father rest till later. "What do you want to know about Warren?"

She shrugged. "How did you meet? How long have you been together?"

"He saw me on the news rescuing a little girl out of a drug house. He couldn't see my soul, so he came to Asheville to find me and figure out why. It was only a couple of months ago," I said.

She leaned forward on her elbow. "I wish you knew just how unique your relationship is with him." She took a sip of water. "Are the two of you pretty serious, then?"

"Yeah. Certainly as serious as two people can become in such a short amount of time. He moved in with me a few weeks ago when his job ended out on the coast," I told her.

"What does he do?" she asked.

"He was a mercenary, and he's a sniper for the Marines," I said. "He's being deployed next week."

She laughed and covered her mouth with a napkin. "Being an Angel of Death and being a sniper is a little heavy-handed, isn't it?"

My face broke a smile. "I think the same thing all the time."

"Where are they sending him?" she asked.

I shrugged my shoulders and pushed my half-eaten sandwich away from me. "They haven't told him yet."

"Well, I hope it all works out for the best." With a long fingernail, she was drawing circles around the rim of her glass. "You should know, Sloan, there could be serious repercussions if you are committed to another Seramorta."

I frowned. "Another angel kind of said the same thing to us recently."

She stopped drawing circles. "Another angel?" Her eyes were wide and questioning.

"When my mother died, I met an angel named Samael. He warned me and Warren that we should be very careful," I said.

"Samael?" She sat forward on her chair. "Really? He doesn't come to this side of the spirit line very often at all."

"That reminds me, he didn't know who you were. What is your real name?" I asked.

She stared at me for a moment. Then, she relaxed. "My name is Kasyade."

"Kahh-see-ahh-day," I repeated. "That's very pretty."

"It means, The Siren," she said.

My brow lifted. "Like the sirens in Greek mythology?"

She smiled. "Exactly." She leaned forward and lowered her voice. "Would you like to know the name I gave you?"

My eyes widened. "I have a different name?"

She nodded. "Of course."

I straightened in my seat. "Yeah, I guess."

"Praea," she answered.

The name fell flat. "Pray-yah," I echoed slowly.

She leaned close as if to tell me a great secret. "In my language, it means something like a gift."

"A gift? Really?"

"That's what you are, Sloan."

I turned my palms up in question. "What's the big deal about me and Warren? Why is everyone so fascinated by us being together?"

She hesitated for a moment. "Because there are billions of people on this planet and very few Seramorta. It's mathematically improbable that two of you would find each other in the time of a human lifespan. It's only ever happened a couple of times in history. And neither of those pairings combined the powers of life and death."

I almost giggled. "We'll be a power couple like Brad and Angelina."

Her eyes were serious, and when she gripped my arm, my skin began to crawl. "This no laughing matter, Praea."

I recoiled from her grasp, suddenly feeling hot and dizzy. "I'm sorry. Can I use your restroom?"

She nodded, still watching me carefully. "Certainly. I need to check in at the office anyway. The bathroom is down the hall, the third door on the left. Take all the time you need."

Forcing a smile, I stood up. "Thank you."

I picked up my purse and carried it down the hallway on the other side of the living room to the bathroom. The bathroom was painted a deep red, and it had elaborate golden fixtures. It felt like the walls were closing in as I braced myself against the sink. I pulled my cell phone out of my pocket and brought up a text message to Warren. *I think I'm ready to go. I know I'm cutting this terribly short, but it's too much for me, and I have a bad feeling I can't shake. Starting to feel sick.*

A moment later, my phone beeped with a response. *Be there in ten. Are you OK?*

Yes. Don't make a big deal out of it when you get here, I replied.

When I walked out of the bathroom, my feet froze outside the door. Something unseen was pulling at my attention, but I couldn't place what it was. A feeling of foreboding was growing inside my chest like a cancer running rampant. Then I heard it. Not exactly an audible voice, but a clear message from somewhere. *Go to the office.* It was as plain as I could hear Abigail on the phone back in the kitchen.

Across from the bathroom was a home office. The room was dark, save for a small amount of light coming through the cracks in the blinds over the window. There was a large cherry desk, a desktop PC, and piles of neatly stacked paperwork. There were no pictures on the wall. It was as impersonal as a broom closet. I tiptoed across the carpet toward the desk, and right on top was a lone sheet of paper. Quietly, I turned it around so I could read it.

It was an invoice from The Law Offices of T.R. Shultz for the criminal representation of...Larry Mendez.

Oh hell.

My mind scrambled. Why would Abigail have an invoice for Larry Mendez's attorney? He had been linked with a human trafficking operation, and she had the largest human trafficking rescue mission in Texas. Nausea began to churn through my stomach. I backed out of the office as quietly as possible. Once I was safely back in the hallway with my snooping undetected, I leaned against the wall and struggled to slow my rapid breathing.

My phone rang, causing me to jump. It was Warren. "Hey," I answered.

"Tell her the hotel found my guns and they need you to come and handle it because the room is booked in your name," he said. "My ETA is six minutes."

My shoulders relaxed. "You're brilliant. Hurry."

The line went dead in my hand.

Sucking in a brave, deep breath, I walked back to the kitchen. Abigail was talking to someone about airfare when I returned. She held up her index finger indicating she was almost finished. When she ended the call, she let out a frustrated huff.

"Is everything all right?" I asked.

She rolled her eyes. "It's so hard to find good help, Sloan." She gestured toward me. "Perhaps now that we've found each other, someday you'll be interested in coming to work with me. I need someone I can trust to get things done right."

Uneasily, I laughed. "I've never been very good at keeping up with paperwork."

"I'll bet you would be better than the minions I have working for me now," she said.

I held up my phone before tucking it into my purse. "I just got some bad news. I'm going to have to run back to the hotel. My boyfriend insisted on bringing half of his arsenal with us on the trip, and the hotel cleaning staff apparently found it. They need me to come handle it because the room is in my name," I explained. "Could we maybe continue this over dinner tonight?"

She deflated. "Oh, I hate to hear that. Yes, dinner would be wonderful. There's a great Italian place not too far from here that would be perfect. Perhaps Warren could join us, and I can get to know him better."

I forced a smile. "That would be great." I already knew I wasn't going to make it to dinner. In that moment, I hoped to never see Abigail—Kasyade—ever again.

My heart fluttered with relief when the doorbell rang. I slung my purse over my shoulder. "That must be Warren," I said as we walked to the front door together.

She pulled the door open, and he was standing there with his hands stuffed in his pockets. I could have cried at the sight of him.

He rolled his eyes. "I'm really sorry I screwed up girls' day."

Abigail waved off the apology. "Things happen." She smiled brightly. "Sloan and I were talking about all of us getting together for dinner this evening."

He nodded. "Sounds good to me." His eyes locked on mine. "You ready?"

"Yes." I turned toward Abigail, and she pulled me in for a tight hug. I felt like I might barf over her shoulder.

"I'll call you about dinner plans. It was really

wonderful spending some time with you today, even if it was cut short," she said.

When she released me, I stepped out of her personal space and into Warren's. "Me too. I'll call you later," I lied.

She watched us from the door as we walked to the car. I turned back and waved when Warren opened the passenger side door for me. She waved back and stared at us from the doorway.

When he got in the car and started the engine, I whipped my eyes toward him. "Drive."

He pulled away from the curb as I buckled my seatbelt. "What happened?"

I turned to face him in the seat. "I have a really, really bad feeling about all this. First of all, her name isn't Rachel or Sarah or Abigail. It is Kasyade, and guess what!"

He turned out of her neighborhood onto the main street. "What?"

"My birthday is a day earlier than I thought it was, and my real name is Praea."

He raised an eyebrow and shook his head. "Your real name is Sloan."

I had no desire to get philosophic about my name. "From the moment I walked into the house, I had a weird feeling. The conversation was all right until I asked about my biological father. She refused to tell me who he is."

He cut his eyes over at me. "Are you serious?"

I leaned toward him. "Oh yeah. She said I'm not *ready* to know, whatever that's supposed to mean. She said she 'chose' him for the purpose of getting pregnant, and he probably wouldn't even remember it. She talked about it like she was just visiting a sperm bank."

"Is that why you wanted to leave?" he asked.

I shook my head. "I wish. That's just the beginning of when things started to go downhill!"

He blew out a deep sigh.

"She asked some questions about me and you, and then she grabbed me and said how serious it is that we're together. And it was the way she said it, like the world was going to end or something. I don't know. That's when I started to feel sick."

"Well, what do you want to do?" he asked.

I held my hands up and shook them furiously near his head. "Wait, I'm not done!"

"There's more?" he asked in disbelief.

"At that point in the conversation, I was ready to go. I snuck off to the bathroom and sent you the message to come and get me. Then, when I left the bathroom, I heard this voice in my head telling me to go into her office, so I did."

"You heard a voice?" he asked. "Whose voice?"

I shrugged. "I have no idea, but I know I did. Guess what I found in her office."

He looked at me with a raised eyebrow.

"An invoice from a criminal attorney for Larry Mendez," I said.

The car swerved, kicking up gravel from the shoulder of the highway. He brought the car to a screeching halt on the side of the road. "What?" he shouted.

"I saw it with my own eyes, Warren. She's the reason Mendez was released. She paid for his defense," I said. "That makes no sense!"

He stared out the window, lost in thought. I could almost hear the gears in his mind turning. "It only makes sense if he's working for her," he said.

"What?" I asked.

He turned toward me. "Think about it. If Nate and I hadn't been there that day, Rex and the other guy would have gotten away. They were prepared to get out of that building and disappear. They had to have known the cops were coming to be able to slip out of there the way they did."

I squeezed my forehead. "But why hire criminals to sell girls to sex rings just to rescue them?" I asked. "If it's about money and getting donations, I don't think she has to create a human trafficking problem. There's already plenty of it."

His eyes widened. "What if she's not rescuing them at all? What if she's just shutting down her competition and selling them herself?"

My nausea returned. "You think she's just monopolizing the industry?"

He nodded. "You're talking about a lot of girls with no families and no one who would miss them. Most of them don't even speak English, I would guess."

I covered my mouth as I began to connect the dots. "And she's not funded by the government, so she wouldn't be subject to their watchful eye. No one is checking up on her. She can send those girls right back out and claim they were released from the program or put into her private foster system because no one would follow up."

He gripped the steering wheel so tight his knuckles went white. "She releases some success stories, pulls in donations, and then sends these girls only God knows where." He looked over at me. "My guess is she bailed Rex Parker and his buddy out of jail too."

I gasped. "She's a monster."

The blood drained from Warren's face. "Do you remember what that old priest told us?"

Father John floated to my memory. I quoted his haunting words verbatim. "*If you are on a quest seeking angels, take great care. Even Satan himself masquerades as an angel of the light.*"

19.

My fingers dialed Nathan's phone so furiously the screen cracked even more, and a piece came off in my hand. The touchscreen was useless after that. I held out my hand toward Warren. "I need your phone to call Nathan. Mine is officially broken." I dropped the phone into the cubby between the front seats.

He adjusted in his seat and pulled his phone from his pocket. I found Nathan's number in his contact list and hit dial.

Nathan answered on the third ring. "Aww, it's my favorite Prince of Darkness. What's up?"

I rolled my eyes. "It's Sloan."

"Oh, hey," he said.

"I need your help."

"Sure. What's going on?"

"We're pretty sure Abigail is a fraud."

"She's not an angel?" He sounded confused.

"Oh, no. She is an angel. Actually, I'm starting to think she's a demon, if those are real too. You need to convince the

FBI to investigate her. Larry Mendez is not in jail, and I found an invoice in her home office from his attorney."

"What?"

"You heard me." I gripped the phone tighter. "Nathan, we think she's using her ministry to sell those girls herself."

"Shit, seriously?" he asked.

"Seriously," I said.

His tongue was clicking on the other end of the line. "I'm going to need some kind of evidence to pursue this. Did you get a copy of that invoice?

"No, of course not."

"Sloan, I can't go to the FBI with a hunch from *my friends the angels.*"

I looked at Warren. "He needs evidence."

"I'll bring Rex to him," he said.

I spoke back into the phone. "Rex Parker was bonded out of jail, probably by Abigail. Warren is going to bring him to you."

He was quiet for a moment. "If Rex is out on bond, he can't leave the state. I'll come to you," he said. "Let me see if I can get on a flight today. I'll call you when I've got something."

"Thanks, Nathan."

"I'll be in touch," he said and disconnected the line.

I looked at Warren. "What do we do now?"

He pointed to the road ahead. "I need you to find Rex Parker."

We caught up with Rex an hour later at a liquor store not far from the home of Larry Mendez. He took off running again when he saw Warren angling out of the rental car, but this time Warren didn't allow him to get away. Several people stopped and stared as Warren dragged him, again by the hair of his head, back to our car. Rex wasn't a tiny guy, but you would have thought he was judging by the ease with which

Warren slung him around. Thankfully, we weren't in the type of neighborhood that would call the cops for a thug.

Warren opened the back door and tossed Rex in like a sack of potatoes. "Babe, I'm going to need you to drive," he said.

I got out and ran around to the driver's side and got back in. Warren climbed in the back with Rex and pulled his Glock out of his side holster.

Rex Parker looked like he had been run over by life a few times. His face was badly scarred from acne, and his nose looked like it had been broken more than once. A couple of cuts, one across his cheekbone and the other across his forehead, were still healing from the beating Warren had given him the week before.

"What the hell you want with me?" Rex shouted. He was hopelessly trying to open the child-locked back door. "This ain't cool."

I looked over my shoulder at Warren. "Where are we going?"

"Let's go back to the hotel," he said.

I nodded and pulled out of the parking lot, back onto the highway.

"Who are you working for?" Warren demanded.

"Man, I'm not tellin' you shit. Why don't you tell me who *you're* workin' for? Why you keep poppin' up and beatin' the hell outta me?" Rex asked.

"Because you're still a no good piece of shit," Warren said. "Who are you working for?"

"I don't work for nobody." Rex spat at him.

Warren lowered his voice to a menacing octave. "Do you remember what happened to Travis? Do you really think it's wise to lie to me?"

"What the hell are you, man?" Rex asked, no longer able to hide his panic.

"Who are you working for?" Warren roared, making even me jump.

I swerved the car a little.

Like a frightened puppy being backed into a corner, Rex scrambled as far away from Warren as he could in the close confines of the back seat. "Shit man, calm down," Rex said, his voice trembling. "I work for that broad Abigail Smith."

"What do you do for her?" Warren asked.

"I'm a delivery guy," he said. "I'm her freakin' errand boy."

"Delivering little girls?" Warren asked.

Rex held his hands in front of his face. "And some older ones, man. Calm down!"

"And she bonded you out of jail?" Warren asked.

He nodded. "Yeah, I'm supposed to be drivin' the van back to Chicago tonight. She's gonna have me killed if I ain't there."

"Trust me. You shouldn't be worried about *her* killing you," Warren hissed. "Who are you taking to Chicago?"

"A few of the girls she's got ready to go," he answered. "All I do is pick 'em up and drop 'em off."

"So, she picks these girls up here in San Antonio and sends them to Chicago?" Warren asked.

"She gets 'em here and in Houston. Then she sends 'em to Chicago, LA, and New York," he said. "That's all I know, I swear. Warren, man, please let me go. We used to be like brothers!"

I could hear Rex's gold jewelry rattling behind me as he quivered with fear.

Warren laughed. "Brothers? I don't think so. And you're not going anywhere except for on a little trip with us to talk to one of our friends."

"You're never gonna bust her. The cops around here

think she shits rainbows," Rex said. "You're wastin' your time."

"We'll see about that," Warren said. "Sloan, when did you say our friend will be here?"

I turned my head to speak over my shoulder. "His flight gets in at 7:30. I told him I'd pick him up at the airport." I turned onto the interstate.

My cell phone rang. It was Abigail, but I couldn't answer it with the broken screen even if I had wanted to. And I didn't want to.

"Parker, you've got the next three hours to decide how this is going to go down," Warren said. "You either help us bring down your boss, or I won't be as merciful to you as I was to Travis in that alleyway. Do we understand each other?"

I glanced in the rearview mirror.

"She's gonna kill me," Rex said. I thought he might burst into tears.

Warren shook his head and glared at him. "Not if I kill you first."

* * *

At 7:43 p.m., I rolled to a stop at the curb where Nathan was waiting outside the airport. I honked the horn, and he waved to me.

He opened the back door and tossed the backpack he was carrying onto the seat. He paused for a moment with his hand on the doorframe. "Is that blood?"

"Probably."

Groaning, he slammed the door. "Do I want to know?" he asked as he got in the passenger's seat.

"Nope."

He looked over, his gray eyes genuinely baffled. "You must be terrified to wake up every day. Just hanging out with you stresses me the hell out."

I laughed. "It's getting that way. How was your flight?"

He pulled the seatbelt across his chest. "Expensive."

I cringed. "How much?"

"$1,498. The only seats left were first class."

"I'll pay you back." I did the math in my head. "By February."

He laughed.

"It's a good thing you find that funny because I was being serious."

He winked at me. "I know where you live."

I glanced up at the patch on his hat. It had a picture of a missile and the letter *F*. I shook my head and pointed at it. "I don't get it."

"F-Bomb."

I laughed and pulled away from the curb.

He sat back in his seat. "So, where is this guy?"

"Tied to a chair in our hotel room."

He turned his shoulders toward me. "You know that's illegal, right?"

I shrugged. "You know Warren doesn't care, right?"

"Well, if Warren goes to prison, I guess he doesn't have to worry about getting deployed."

My bottom lip poked out, but Nathan didn't notice.

"Don't use my name around this guy we're questioning. I don't want any of this shit blowing back on me and ruining my career," he said.

I shook my head. "We won't let it get back to you. Speaking of careers, what did you ever decide about the FBI?"

He shifted in his seat. "I turned them down."

"Really?"

He nodded. "Yeah, I told them I want to stay in Asheville because you're way more interesting than anything that could ever happen anywhere else." He laughed and stretched his arm across the back of my seat.

Sadly, he was probably right.

"I'll bet Shannon was excited you didn't take it."

He looked ahead down the road. "I broke it off with Shannon when we got back. You were right. I was using her and it wasn't fair."

My head snapped back in surprise. "Wow. That's huge. How did she take it?"

He laughed. "How do you think?"

I smiled over at him. "Well, I'm excited you're sticking around, even if I don't understand at all why you turned down the FBI."

"I'm glad I'm staying too. Although, you and I both know how much less complicated things would be if I just left town."

My heart dropped a few inches. "Then why did you decide to stay? It would make life a lot less complicated for you too."

The corners of his mouth twitched. "You wouldn't believe me if I told you."

My eyes widened, and I looked over at him. "Don't tell me Warren asked you to stay."

He laughed. "OK, I won't tell you."

"What? Are you serious? Does he think I need a babysitter?"

"He's really worried about leaving you with all that's going on." He looked out his window. "Hell, even I'm worried about him leaving."

I swallowed the lump in my throat. Warren always seemed to be a little more clued in on the happenings around us than I was. Perhaps it was because he'd always been an outsider, observing the world from a distance. Sure, Samael's warning had rattled me a bit, but if Warren was concerned enough to leave me in the care of Nathan McNamara, that was frightening on a whole different level.

"Personally, I don't know how you've not been locked up in the looney bin yet," Nathan was saying when I realized he was still talking. "Tell me the truth. Are you doing OK? Especially about your mom and all."

My hands twisted around the steering wheel. "I just can't even think about it. In a way, I'm actually thankful for all the drama in my life right now because I'm afraid if I slow down long enough to really process mom being gone..." Tears threatened to spill.

He squeezed my shoulder. "I wish I could help."

I forced a smile. "Thanks." I needed to change the subject. There was no time for me to have a meltdown. "Warren must be really worried if he's entrusting me to you."

He nodded in agreement. "I definitely think this defines absolute desperation."

I pointed a finger at him. "I still hold you personally responsible for all this. My life was almost normal before you landed me on television. I distinctly remember telling you I wanted to stay out of it."

He looked out the window and took a deep breath. Surprisingly, his voice came out serious and somber. "I actually feel really bad about it, Sloan. Capturing Billy Stewart was huge and all, and we probably saved a lot more lives, but you're right. I got this huge boulder rolling, and now it seems like it's rolling right over you." He turned his eyes back toward me. "I'm very sorry."

Suddenly, I felt bad for teasing him. "You had no way of knowing. Neither of us did. I just have to keep focusing on the good things like Kayleigh Neeland and all the women we probably saved. We'll save a lot more when we stop Abigail."

"Can you even stop an angel?" he asked.

"We've got to try," I said. "This sex trafficking thing is a whole lot bigger than just the state of Texas. Warren's guy says she's moving the girls to at least Los Angeles, Chicago, and New York."

"No shit?" he asked.

I shook my head.

He started laughing. "Now, hopefully I can figure out a legal way to bring her down."

I shrugged. "Legal, schmegal."

He rolled his eyes. "You're starting to sound like Warren."

I laughed. "I guess I am."

"Does he really have this Rex guy tied to a chair?"

I shot him a knowing glare.

He sighed and shook his head. "Someday I'm going to be able to teach a training class on manipulating evidence and looking the other way."

When we got to the hotel room, I used my key and opened the door. Inside, Warren was stretched out on the bed watching football. Rex was facing the wall in the corner, his hands tied to the chair with strips of Warren's white t-shirt. The sight was pretty comical. Nathan shook his head and dropped his bag on the floor.

Warren clicked off the television and stood up to shake Nathan's hand. "Thanks for coming, man."

"I can't let you guys have all the fun without me." Nathan nodded to the corner. "So, you found him."

Warren nodded. "Let's just say I made a citizen's arrest."

Nathan sighed. "You make my job and my life very complicated," he said. "Is he ready to talk?"

"Oh, he'll talk, sing, tell you a joke...whatever you want him to do. Isn't that right, Rex?" Warren called over his shoulder.

The back of Rex's head nodded.

Nathan sat down at the table, and Warren spun Rex's chair around to face us. His eyes were wide with terror, and he had a tube sock shoved in his mouth. Nathan looked him over. "Well, at least he's not bloody this time."

Warren reached over and pulled the sock out of Rex's mouth, then he and I sat down on the edge of the bed.

"Who the hell are you?" Rex barked at Nathan.

Nathan scowled. "You'd better watch how you speak to me because I may be the only reason you walk out of this room instead of being carried out in a body bag. Do you understand?"

Rex withered a bit.

Nathan pulled a small notebook out of his pocket along with a small pen. "How long have you been working for Abigail Smith?"

"About three years," Rex answered.

"How did you meet her?" Nathan asked.

Rex shifted uncomfortably against his restraints, and looked up at Warren. "She worked for the state when we was kids, remember?"

Nathan and I both whipped our heads toward Warren. "What?" I asked.

Warren was looking at Rex like he'd sprouted a second nose on his pitted face. "What the hell are you talking about?"

Rex rolled his eyes. "Ms. Smith? They's no way you could forget her, dude." He huffed. "She was a case worker for the group home."

Bewildered, Warren looked at us and shrugged. "I have no idea."

My eyes narrowed. "She was in Chicago?"

He held his arms up in question. "Not that I'm aware of. I would remember."

Rex looked pleased that he knew something we didn't. "I can't believe you don't remember her, dude."

Nathan leaned his elbow on the table. "And you didn't notice anything strange about the way she looked after what, ten years?"

A sleazy grin spread across Rex's dry lips. He was

missing a side tooth. "Man, I didn't notice nothin' except that bitch is fine as hell."

My skin was crawling.

Obviously frustrated, Nathan held up his hand. "Forget about it for now. How did you end up working for her?"

"She came back a few years ago, was volunteerin' at a rehab center downtown. She looked me and a few of the other guys up. Asked us if we wanted to do some work for her."

I was skeptical. "She pulled some random punks off the streets and put them to work trafficking girls across the country? She's not that stupid."

He shook his head. "Nah, bitch—"

Rex didn't get another word out before the back of Warren's fist slammed against the side of his head so hard it rocked the chair sideways. He yelped in pain. I expected Nathan to at least shoot Warren a reprimanding glare, but his fist was balled at the ready to go next.

I grabbed Nathan by the shoulder and Warren by the arm. "He's no use to us dead."

Warren pointed a sharp finger at Rex, and he flinched.

"Sorry, sorry!" Rex looked at me, his eyes a little off-center from the blow. "No, *ma'am*." He shook his head from side to side like he was trying to clear his muddled thoughts. "The work was legit at first. Me'n a few other guys was rehabbin' an old building in South Chicago. She said she was turnin' it into some kind of halfway house or somethin'."

"How did you wind up in Texas?" Nathan asked.

"When the place in Chicago was finished, she said she had some girls in San Antonio who needed to get outta town, and she was gonna move them into the building we just squared away. She sent me and another guy down here to drive 'em back up to Illinois. He'd worked with her for a while," Rex explained.

Nathan was taking notes. "Who was the other guy?"

"Mendez," Rex said. "It wasn't till we brought the haul back from Texas that I realized what was really going on. Mendez is a pretty sick, twisted bastard. For a while, I thought he was playin' the broad and sellin' those girls behind her back. Then, he got busted for breakin' into his ex-wife's house in Texas and went to jail, and everything continued on just the same without him. I started making the runs with Tito."

"Who's in charge in Chicago?" Nathan asked.

"Tito's mom. This bitch named Marisol."

"What about New York and Los Angeles?" Warren asked.

"I don't know, man. It's not like we do company picnics and shit, ya know?" he said.

Nathan pointed his pen at Rex. "If you're running girls to Chicago for her, why were you taking girls from Larry Mendez to the cantina?"

"Since Larry's been on parole and can't leave the state, he's been workin' at pickin' up runaways and sellin' them to buyers around town. We gather intel on the buyers, and after a while, Abigail will claim that one of her girls ratted out another pimp somewhere. Then the cops bring it down, and Abigail is right there to bring the girls in."

I did the math in my head. "So, she makes money selling them, she gets them back for free, and then she pimps them out." I dropped my head into my hands. The whole thing was starting to make my head pound.

Warren looked at me. "And she doesn't have to do the leg work finding the girls and breaking them into the business."

"What is she planning on doing next?" Nathan asked.

Rex shifted in his seat and tipped his chin up defiantly at Nathan. "Are you gonna send me back to jail or what? What the hell am I gettin' outta this?"

"You get to exist for a little longer," Warren interjected. "Answer the question."

Rex was clearly terrified of Warren. He looked back at Nathan. "Me and Tito are supposed to be taking a haul back later tonight. She's been movin' almost all the girls out of Texas lately."

"Why?" I asked.

"Do I look like someone who sits at her conference table?" he asked. "I don't know what she's doin'."

"When are you supposed to leave tonight?" Nathan asked.

"We leave from the ministry at eleven," he said.

"Driving what?"

"A big white van with Morning Star on the side."

Nathan looked at us and then back at Rex. "Sit tight." He grabbed the sock out of Warren's hand, wadded it up, and shoved it back into Rex's mouth.

Rex groaned and struggled again.

Nathan looked at Warren, then nodded toward the door. The three of us got up and walked outside. Once the door was closed, Nathan leaned against it. "We need to cut him loose," he said.

"What?" I asked, my voice cracking.

He nodded. "We need to let him make that haul. Once he crosses the state line, he will be in violation of his bond agreement, and it will become a federal offense. We can call in an anonymous tip. Maybe that will get the ball rolling with the FBI and give them enough probable cause to dig into this and bust Abigail and the rest of them," he explained. "I don't have anything else we can use. Everything he has said in that room would be inadmissible in court because you freaking kidnapped him."

Warren folded his arms over his chest. It was obvious he didn't like the thought of letting Rex go either. Finally, he sighed. "God, I hate it when you're right."

"How do we know he's not going to blab all this to Abigail as soon as you let him go?" I asked.

"I'll make sure he doesn't," Warren said.

We went back inside, and Warren sat down in front of Rex. "Are you listening to me?"

Rex nodded with frightful eyes.

Warren leaned in, inches from his face. "I'm going to let you go, but I'm going to be right on your ass. You're going to make that transport to Chicago, and I'm going to have my eyes on you the whole time. I have the ability to track you down, so you will not get away from me. Do you understand?"

Rex nodded again.

"I'm going to take down your boss, and if you get in my way or try to warn anyone involved in this, you will no longer have amnesty with me. What you saw me do to Travis fifteen years ago will be merciful compared to what I will do to you," Warren warned.

Rex's head furiously bobbed up and down.

Nathan leaned toward me and lowered his voice. "Who's Travis? What did Warren do to him?"

I just shook my head and closed my eyes.

He sighed and folded his arms over his chest.

Warren ripped the sock out of Rex's mouth, causing him to gasp for air.

"I'll keep my mouth shut. Swear to God," Rex said.

Warren took out his knife and cut the straps holding him to the chair. "God doesn't hear you anymore." He pointed the knife at Rex's neck. "Where are you supposed to meet them?"

"The van's already at the ministry." Frantic, he looked over at the alarm clock on the nightstand. "I'm supposed to be there in half an hour."

Warren stood and stepped out of his way. "Then I

suggest you get a move on."

Rex bolted from the room like the devil himself was after him. My eyes settled on the door as it closed in his wake. "Think we can trust him?" I asked.

"Not a chance," Nathan said.

Warren shook his head. "I should have just handled this myself."

"Ehh." Nathan shrugged his shoulders. "Even though they're scum, they're still entitled to a judge and jury."

Warren's gaze could have set the room on fire. "Someday, Nate, you're going to understand that I see guilt as clearly as you see skin color." He folded the blade of his knife back into its handle. "Some villains don't need a justice system. They need an executioner."

20.

Nathan and I stood there staring in stunned silence until Warren walked over to the window and peeked through the blinds. Out of the corner of my eye, I saw Nathan gulp.

"Is there a way to confirm if Abigail was actually in Chicago ten years ago?" Warren asked.

Nathan snapped out of his daze. "I can make some calls this week."

"Warren," I said.

He turned to look at me.

"I don't think he was lying."

He shook his head. "He wasn't. The question is, I was in that group home in '98. I didn't leave Chicago until 2002."

Nathan's head tilted. "That doesn't sound like a question."

Warren tapped his finger on his temple. "The migraines. There's no way we stayed within thirty miles of each other for that long, especially without me ever seeing her."

"Thirty miles?" Nathan asked.

Warren nodded toward me. "The migraines seem to

start around the thirty mile mark. That's been roughly the distance we've been apart each time it's happened."

"What if they don't work the same with her?" Nathan asked.

I considered it. "No, she told us she'd have a migraine when we left town. We would have too had we not been together." I looked at Warren. "You never had migraines before me?"

He laughed with sarcasm. "No. I definitely wouldn't forget that."

"Interesting," Nathan said. "I'll see what I can dig up when we get home."

Warren nodded. "OK. How are we going to handle the current mess with the cops?"

Nathan blew out a sigh. "I'm not sure."

I sank down on the edge of the mattress. "An anonymous tip isn't going to work. You know Rex is right. The police and the community love her. They're going to need a solid reason to call her into question." My breath caught in my chest as I realized what we had to do. "I'm going to have to report this."

Warren didn't seem to hear me.

Nathan laughed. "And what are you going to say? That the woman who is the same age as you is actually your mother and a demon?"

I frowned. "No, but I can tell them I met her that day at the bust and she invited me over to her house to talk about a job or something. I'll say I found the paperwork on Mendez by accident. That's all partially true."

Warren and Nathan exchanged glances.

Nathan pulled off his ball cap and scratched his head. "I don't know. That's a pretty unlikely story."

I smirked. "Not as unlikely as the truth. Do you have a better idea?"

He shook his head.

Warren looked at me. "I don't like it."

"We don't have another choice." I held out my hand toward Nathan. "Give me the phone number."

He pulled his phone from his pocket. "I'll call first and find out where the local office is here. This isn't the kind of thing you can usually do on the telephone." He walked out to the hallway.

Blood oozed into my mouth, and I realized I had nervously chewed a hole on the inside of my lower lip. I shuddered.

Warren walked over and sat down beside me. "You all right?"

My legs were bouncing. "We need a vacation to recover from this one."

He squeezed my knee. "I couldn't agree more, babe."

After a few minutes, Nathan reentered the room. "I gave them the short version and told them to be on the lookout for the van, but she's going to need to go in and make a formal statement in person." He held up a slip of paper. "We're supposed to ask for Agent Silvers."

My cheeks puffed out as I exhaled slowly.

Nathan looked at Warren. "I think I should take her. It would probably look weird to have a mercenary tagging along."

Warren's eyes narrowed. "I'm not a mercenary."

Nathan held up his hands in defense. "I'm sorry. It would look weird to have the Angel of Death tagging along."

We both laughed and it eased the unbearable tension in the room.

Warren looked over at me. "He's probably right, and he knows more about the legal process of all this than I do. Will you be OK if I sit this one out?"

I sighed. "I just want to get it over with."

Nathan motioned toward the door. "Well, I'm ready to go when you are."

I covered Warren's hand with mine. "If I wind up in federal prison, I expect you to use all your badass recon skills to get me out."

"I'll burn the jail down if I have to." He tucked my hair back behind my ears.

I kissed him quickly and stood up. "All right, Detective. I'm all yours."

Nathan raised his eyebrows and grinned. "Really?"

Warren pointed at him. "Watch it."

Nathan glanced at the clock. "We should be back here in time to catch them before they leave the ministry at eleven. Do you want to try and follow them to see how this thing plays out?"

Warren shook his head. "As much as I would like to, I'm afraid we would be too conspicuous. All it would take is for one person to recognize us, and the whole thing could fall apart."

Nathan nodded. "You're probably right. We'll just come back here once we are finished then."

Warren stood up. "Please bring me back some food. I forgot to eat today."

I kissed Warren once more before we walked outside to the car.

As we pulled out of the parking lot, Nathan looked over at me. "Are you nervous?"

I held up my hands. They were trembling. "I'm keeping the makers of Xanax in business this year all by myself."

He laughed. "I'll bet. Don't be nervous though. You'll be fine."

"You'd better not leave me," I warned him.

He shook his head. "I wouldn't dream of it."

We rode most of the ten miles in silence. When we finally arrived, there were more lights on in the four story building than I expected for almost nine o'clock on a Saturday night. I stared out my window until I felt Nathan squeeze the back of my neck.

"Take a deep breath, Sloan."

I turned to face him and sucked in a huge gulp of air and blew it out slowly.

The confidence on his face was only mildly reassuring. "Remember, we're here for the weekend so you could talk to Abigail about a job."

I nodded and picked at my fingernail. "A job doing what?"

"I don't know. Publicity. That's what you do," he said.

It had been so long since I'd gone to work that I'd almost forgotten my job description. "Oh yeah."

"Just tell enough of the truth to make this all sound believable without bringing up all the angels and demons stuff."

I swallowed the lump in my throat.

He smiled to ease the tension. "I'm going to tell them I'm your boyfriend if they ask."

I rolled my eyes. "Of course you are." I pointed a finger at him. "You'd better not let me wind up in jail."

He reached over and wrapped his hand around mine. "You're not going to wind up in jail. I promise."

I wasn't so sure I believed him.

When we walked in the front door, an armed security guard in the lobby stopped us. "Can I help you?" he asked.

I looked down at the notes Nathan had scribbled during his phone conversation earlier. "We're here to see Agent Silvers," I said.

He nodded and walked behind the desk. "Your name?"

"Sloan Jordan," I answered, but the name Praea came

to mind.

He motioned toward an empty row of plastic gray chairs along the wall. "Have a seat."

When we sat down, Nathan put his arm around me and curled his body toward mine.

"What are you doing?" I whispered.

He smiled. "Playing the part."

"You said, 'if they ask,'" I reminded him.

He winked at me. "Gotta make it believable."

I shook my head. "I'm going to tell on you."

He chuckled but didn't remove his arm. Instead, he leaned in closer. "I have some news, but I didn't want to call you last week in the middle of everything with your mom."

"What is it?" I asked.

His eyes were fixed on the carpet. "They are finally releasing my sister's body to our family."

"Wow. Are you OK?"

After a second, he nodded. "Yeah. It's good to have some closure."

"Is there going to be a service?"

"Yeah. Mom is talking about doing it around Thanksgiving while the family is all in town." He was still staring at the floor. "It will be small."

I nudged him with my shoulder. "Well, if you want me to come, I will."

He looked at me and smiled. "Thank you."

There was a loud buzz and the door behind the desk opened. A black woman in khaki pants and a blue polo shirt walked through it. She had a neatly edged bob and the most perfect, full red lips I had ever seen on another human. A blue and white lanyard hung around her neck with her FBI credentials.

She extended her hand as she approached. "I'm Agent Sharvel Silvers. Are you Sloan?"

I stood up and shook her hand. "Yes, ma'am."

She offered her hand to Nathan.

"Detective Nathan McNamara, her boyfriend," he said.

In any other situation, I would have rolled my eyes. Or maybe punched him.

Agent Silvers offered a polite smile. "Nice to meet you both. Let's go back to my office."

We followed her through the door, down a bleak hallway lit up with painfully bright fluorescent lights. The walls were white and covered in plaques and department photographs. My stomach felt queasy, and I hugged my arms to my chest.

Agent Silvers' office was bland and impersonal. A half-dead plant was shedding its brown and shriveled leaves on the corner of her desk near the chairs where she motioned for us to sit. She sat down in her padded office chair, and the wheels squeaked as she rolled across the floor. "Detective McNamara, I read the report you called in earlier," she began. "We've alerted the state highway patrol to be looking for the van you described on the phone. If, in fact, it does cross into Oklahoma, they will stop it and see if the suspects are driving."

I sighed with relief. "Good."

She looked carefully at both of us. "I am very curious to know why you believe Morning Star Ministries is involved with human trafficking across state lines."

I looked at Nathan, and he reached over and wrapped his hand around mine. I cleared my throat. "I met Abigail Smith during a sting operation that we sort of fell into the middle of a few weeks ago."

"Fell into?" she asked.

Nathan leaned forward. "We helped capture a couple of guys who were escaping from a raid during a prostitution bust."

Agent Silvers was making notes. "Why were you at a prostitution bust? This says you're an officer in North Carolina."

He nodded. "That's correct. We were here on vacation, and we got turned around in the wrong neighborhood. It was there I noticed some odd behavior happening on the street. Being the investigator that I am, I insisted on following two men who appeared to be transporting two underage girls." He squeezed my hand, signaling my turn to talk.

I looked at him. "We followed them to an old building and that's when the raid happened. Nathan and another friend of ours chased down two men who escaped through a side door."

"There's a report with the San Antonio police department with all the details," he added.

My hand was sweating inside his. "Anyway, I met Abigail there. We talked for a while, and I expressed an interest in a job with her ministry. She invited me to her house for a lunch meeting earlier today."

She blinked up at me. "A business lunch at her private home?"

I smiled nervously. "Yes."

She looked skeptical, but she gestured toward me with her pen. "And then what happened?"

"I found an invoice from a lawyer representing Larry Mendez in her office. He's one of the men involved in the same raid where I met her. I believe she paid for his defense."

"You just happened to find it?" she asked.

I shrank back in my seat. "I was snooping." Her eyebrow twitched, but she didn't comment so I continued. "After that, I heard her on the phone making arrangements to have some girls sent to Chicago. She said Rex Parker was going to be taking them."

She was still writing down the details. "Who is Rex

Parker?"

"One of the two guys my friend and I apprehended at the raid," Nathan said.

Agent Silvers put her pen down and massaged her temples. "Abigail Smith is a very highly respected member of this community who has been very proactive in taking girls out of sex slavery. And now you're telling me you just happened to hear her detailing the specifics of an interstate sex trafficking exchange?"

I shrugged. "She thought I was in the bathroom."

Her smile was mocking. "What exactly did she say about Chicago?"

"I heard something about someone named Marisol and that a new group of girls would be arriving with Rex Parker soon. She said they were leaving for Chicago at eleven tonight. Then, she wanted to know how much money had been brought in the night before."

Agent Silvers made a few more notes, then looked at Nathan. "Can you corroborate this story? Were you there?"

Nathan shook his head and leaned forward. "I wasn't there, but if you search her home office, you will find the invoice for Larry Mendez. And I suspect if you dig further, you'll find that Rex Parker and Tito Juarez were both bonded out with a cash bond."

She tapped the end of her pen against the desk. "You think she bonded them out of jail?"

Nathan turned his palm up. "It makes sense. She could kill two birds with one stone, if you ask me. Get the girls sent to Chicago and get the two of them out of the area to skip trial and not take the risk of them implicating her."

Agent Silvers folded her hands in her lap and raised her brow with blatant skepticism. "You think she would put up possibly hundreds of thousands of dollars in bond money and encourage them to go FTA?

He nodded. "If this is all true, you and I both know a few hundred grand is a drop in the bucket compared to what she's made off all these girls."

She sighed and returned her attention to the papers. Finally, she leaned on her elbows over the desk and stared at me. "If this is all true and we do find reason to indict her, are you willing to testify against her in court?"

Hesitantly, I nodded. "Yes."

"And you realize making a false statement is a felony criminal offense, correct?" she asked.

Nathan's hand tightened around mine.

I swallowed and nodded again. "Yes. I'll do whatever necessary to help stop her. I believe she's a very dangerous woman who definitely isn't the saint she has convinced everyone that she is."

After signing the paperwork, Nathan and I were allowed to leave. I dug my nails into his arm when we got outside and pulled him close to me. "I'm not tough enough to make it in prison," I said, just above a whisper.

He laughed and patted my arm. "You did the right thing."

I dug my nails in deeper, causing him to wince. "She doesn't believe me. You saw her face."

He shook his head. "It doesn't matter. You'll see. They'll take down the transport, get a search warrant for Abigail's house, and find that invoice. This will all be over very soon, and we can go back home to your normal messed up life with boy problems, superpowers, and a boring day job."

I leaned into him. "Thanks for coming all the way down here. I do promise I'll pay you back."

He draped his arm around my neck and smiled down at me. "I'm starting a tab with you, Sloan. Someday I'm going to ask for a really huge favor."

Oh boy.

"I don't think I like being in your debt."

His grin made my stomach flip-flop. "I like it just fine."

* * *

The next morning, the shrill ring of the hotel phone jarred me from my sleep. The room was still dark, but light was peeking around the corners of the blackout curtains. I heard the shower running in the bathroom, and Warren wasn't in bed beside me. I rolled over and lifted the phone off the receiver. "Hello?"

"Morning, sunshine."

"Geez, Nathan. Do you know what time it is?"

"The FBI called."

I sat up straight in the bed. "Oh! What did they say?"

"The Oklahoma Highway Patrol stopped the Morning Star Ministries van early this morning near the city of Ardmore. Rex Parker and Tito Juarez were arrested on violating the terms of their bond, and seven girls were taken into custody."

I let out a deep sigh. "Thank God. What about Abigail?"

"Silvers said they're moving forward with the case. She's going to try and get the search warrant for Abigail's house and business pushed through this morning."

"And Larry Mendez?" I asked.

"She didn't say, but at this point, I doubt they have any substantial reason to arrest him again, but maybe they'll dig something up during the investigation." He yawned on the other end of the line. "I'm going back to sleep for an hour. I'll see you downstairs for breakfast."

I hung up the phone and swung my legs off the bed. Twisting around to the right, I felt my spine crack all the way down to my tailbone. I got up and went to the bathroom, gently knocking before pushing the door open. Steam and light spilled out into the room.

Warren peeked around the shower curtain. "You're up early. Is the hotel on fire?"

I picked up my toothbrush and slathered it with paste. "Nathan woke me up. The FBI called."

"Really?"

"Uh huh." I brushed for a minute and spat toothpaste in the sink. "They caught Rex and Tito in Oklahoma this morning," I said and went back to brushing.

"That's good news. Did they say when they are going after Abigail?" he asked.

I shrugged my shoulders.

"What about Mendez?"

I shrugged again.

His wet head tilted to the side. "Did you sleep in my shirt last night?"

Gripping the brush with my teeth, I glanced down at the black 5.11 Tactical t-shirt and dribbled toothpaste down the front of it. I turned my wide eyes back toward him.

He shook his head. "I was going to wear that today."

"Sowwy," I said around the toothbrush.

I rinsed out my mouth and packed up my toiletry bag. Before leaving the bathroom, I pulled the shower curtain back just enough to stick my face in. "Kiss me," I said. "I'm going to lie down till you get out."

Water trickled from his face onto mine as he kissed me. Then he reached out and hooked his wet arm around my waist, pulling me into the shower.

I laughed and pounded my fists against his bare chest. "What are you doing?"

He pulled his t-shirt off me and tossed it out onto the bathroom floor. "Keeping you from going back to sleep. We have a plane to catch."

After a bland continental breakfast in the hotel lobby,

the three of us loaded our bags into the trunk of the rental car, and Warren headed in the direction of the airport. I looked in the back seat where Nathan was popping Skittles into his mouth.

"Isn't it a little early for that?" I asked.

He shook his head. "It's never too early for Skittles."

I laughed and rolled my eyes. "Do you think they'll be able to bust Abigail today?"

He nodded. "If they get the search warrant signed by a judge. They'll have to find a judge at home though because it's Sunday."

Warren shook his head. "That's exactly why I don't do law enforcement. Too many rules and way too much paperwork."

I relaxed back in my seat as Warren pulled the car onto the freeway. The buildings of downtown looked small in the distance, and a light haze from the morning dew loomed over the city. I looked at the clock on the dashboard. It was eight thirty, and our flight was at eleven. The thought of curling up in my quiet bed at home was intoxicating. I could almost feel the soft bamboo sheets and smell the lavender fabric softener in my pillowcase.

Nathan's voice snapped me out of my daze a few minutes later. "Dude, you missed your exit."

"Crap," Warren muttered. "I'll have to find another exit where I can turn around. I was off in la-la land."

I pulled my knees into my chest. "Me too," I said, still thinking of home. "I can't wait to get back to my bed, in my house. I think I might just sleep all week long."

"Don't you have to go back to work at some point?' Nathan asked.

My heart sank. "Oh, I hadn't even thought about that. I've almost forgotten I even have a job."

"When do you have to go back?" Warren asked.

"I guess tomorrow. I need to save my last couple of personal days to take you to Charlotte." I groaned. "I can just see the inbox on my office door overflowing into the hallway." I turned toward him. "Hey, speaking of jobs...did you tell Nathan to stay in Asheville and not take the job with the FBI?"

Warren glanced back in the rearview mirror at Nathan. "Do you just not have the ability to keep your mouth shut?"

I crossed my arms over my chest. "So, you did?"

He looked at me over his shoulder. "Not exactly. I just told him I would feel better if he stayed close by while I was gone."

"What's he going to do? Patrol my front porch like Scotland Yard?" I asked.

His eyes turned serious. "We haven't had a very good track record lately, and if we're making enemies somewhere in the spirit world, it would be a lot safer for someone who knows our secret to keep an eye on you."

I knew he was right, and it terrified me.

"It's fine, Sloan," Nathan said. "I like working for the county. And I have no desire whatsoever to go through another brutal training academy. I promise I'm not missing out on anything."

I looked back at him and scrunched my eyebrows together. "Asheville's not that exciting. You're going to get bored."

"Not true," he said. "I have you."

"Well, don't pin all your adventurous hopes on me. I'm taking the year off of supernatural B.S. while Warren's gone. I need a break." I flopped my head back against the headrest.

Warren got off the interstate and turned left, but he didn't get back on the on-ramp in the opposite direction.

Nathan chuckled in the back seat. "Warren, man, do you need me to drive? You're failing miserably at navigation this morning."

"Shut up," Warren said. "I think we can get there by going this way."

"You'd better be sure, or we aren't going to have time to get through security at the airport," Nathan said.

"Let me drive, Nate."

As we wound around the city seemingly further and further away from civilization, I was becoming very doubtful of my boyfriend's sense of direction. I looked at him out of the corner of my eye. "Maybe we should turn on the GPS."

"I know where I am," he assured me. "We're going the right way."

"Okie dokie." I turned my wide eyes back at Nathan, and he covered his mouth to squelch a laugh.

Warren turned the car left down a small street lined with run-down buildings, and I waved my hand in front of his face. "Where are you going?" I asked.

Before he had time to answer, a bright flash, like an explosion of light with no sound, happened all around us. About fifteen feet ahead, a man was kneeling in the remnants of the spot where the light had dissipated. Warren slammed on his brakes so as not to run him over. I screamed as the car lurched forward, throwing the three of us toward the windshield. When the seatbelt slammed into my chest and my eyes came back into focus, Samael was standing at our front fender.

21.

"What the hell was that?" Nathan shouted. He was rubbing his head where it had smashed into the back of Warren's seat.

I scrambled for the handle on the car door and pushed it open. "Samael!"

He met me in two long strides and grabbed me by the shoulders. "Sloan, you are in great danger." He gently shook me and pleaded with his captivating golden eyes. "You must leave. You must get out of here right now."

Warren and Nathan were out of the car. "What's going on?" Nathan asked, confused as he walked toward me. "And where the hell are we?"

Seemingly in a daze, Warren walked past the front of the car, then broke into a jog down the road away from us.

"Warren!" I yelled. "Where are you going?"

He didn't even flinch in my direction.

Samael shook me again. "It's no use. You must let him go and leave this place!"

I pushed Samael away from me. "I'm not going

anywhere without him!" I took off in a sprint toward my boyfriend.

Warren rounded another corner, and when I caught up with him, he was stopped dead in his tracks.

Abigail—Kasyade—was standing in the middle of the street with her arms folded across her chest. Her long dark hair was blowing back behind her, yet there was no breeze. Her face was set like stone, and her skin seemed to glow with some unnatural, radiated brilliance.

"Warren!" I shouted again, yanking on his arm with all the strength I could muster.

Samael caught up with me. "This was a trap to lure you here. The Siren has summoned him. He's under her control now."

"The hell he is," I argued. "Warren!"

He didn't respond.

A blue sedan was approaching in the distance behind Abigail. She didn't turn to look. Instead, she raised her hand and the car flipped backwards about twenty feet into the air before crashing down onto its roof.

I grasped Warren's arm and screamed his name again.

Nathan reached us as Samael tried to pull me away. "It is no use," Samael insisted as he closed his arms around me. "We must go!"

"*En magna, Samael,*" Abigail hissed.

My head snapped up at the sound of the bizarre language. It sounded like an odd mix of broken Latin and Klingon.

"*Retribues pro, Kasyade!*" Samael shouted over my head. "*Adduces enim super te formidabilis vindictae! Tuum erit dies!*"

I wrenched my body free and grabbed Warren by his head. I forced his face down to look at me and peered into his black eyes. His pupils were completely dilated and blank with incoherence. But there was something else. For the first time ever, I saw his mortal soul.

"Warren!" I shouted, shaking his skull. His glazed eyes stared right through me.

An unseen force knocked me sideways, and I landed hard on the concrete. Nathan rushed toward me, and my hip burned with a deep pain as he helped me to my feet.

"You believe you can defy my will, Praea?" Abigail roared, her voice echoing against the buildings with a hollow, inhuman pitch. "Did you not think I would know it was you? You betrayed me! Your very own mother!"

"You're not my mother!" I screamed.

Her hand waved through the air, and a ghostly slap across my face knocked me back against Nathan's chest. He pushed me back behind him with one hand and yanked his handgun from its holster with the other. He aimed and fired twice at Abigail, striking her in the chest. She faltered back a few steps, but straightened...and laughed. The two entry wounds were bloody and should have been fatal, but Abigail was far from neutralized. She raised her hand again and knocked the gun out of Nathan's hand.

She looked back at Warren, and he began slowly walking toward her again. I scrambled to my feet. The pain in my hip seared through me, but I hobbled to him as quickly as I could.

Abigail turned toward me, but before she could act, Samael launched a fiery ball of light at her. The blow knocked her off her feet just as I reached Warren.

I grasped him by the face once more and forced him to meet my eyes. Without a thought in my brain other than the desperation of calling him back to me, I pressed both of my palms to his heart and screamed, "Warren!"

The familiar zing of electricity that regularly flowed between us was suddenly like the shock from a defibrillator. We both fell backward onto the street, and the skin was torn from my elbows by the asphalt.

Suddenly, Warren was on top of me. "Sloan!" Whatever control Abigail had on him was broken.

Samael grabbed Warren by the back of the shirt and hoisted him into the air like my 220 pound boyfriend was nothing more than a flimsy rag doll. He placed Warren on his feet and grasped his shoulders, leaning so close they were nearly eye to eye. "You must sever the connection between her spirit and her body," he said. "I cannot kill her, but in spirit form, I can remove her from this place if you help me!"

I rolled onto my knees and tried to push myself up, but the pain was too great. Then Nathan's arm hooked around my waist and he pulled me up.

"Are you all right?" He was panting as he helped me stand.

Before I could answer, Nathan was ripped off his feet and pulled through the air. Abigail's palm was outstretched toward him, drawing him like a magnet. When his neck collided with her hand, she dangled him inches off the ground.

"Nathan!"

In horror, I watched as she lowered Nathan's face toward her own. Her fingers went white with tension as she closed them around his throat. Her mouth opened to a shockingly abnormal width that dislocated her jawbone. A screeching hiss and a high pitched sucking sound were released from deep inside her. Nathan's shoulders convulsed violently for a moment before going limp. She discarded him, slamming his body onto the nearby sidewalk.

I screamed again and pushed myself up off the road. Stumbling over my own feet, I took off in a clumsy, painful sprint toward him. Her hand flew up again, sending up an invisible wall in front of me. I slammed face-first into it and fell backward with a warm gush of blood flowing from my nose into my gaping mouth. I coughed and spewed a shower of blood into the air.

In my peripheral, I saw her move again, and then Warren and Samael were knocked backward out of my view.

Before I could turn and look for them, my body began to slide across the asphalt, the rocks ripping the back of my shirt open and tearing into my flesh. I slid to a stop at Abigail's feet, and her black shoe came down hard on my throat. "My daughter, Praea." The words dripped like poison from her mouth. Her eyes were a glowing golden color as she ground the back of my skull against the rough pavement. "The events have already been set in motion, and there is no stopping it now. You'll see. This is only just the beginning."

She leaned down, pressing her foot harder against my throat. Burning pain began to throb behind my eyeballs as my body starved for oxygen. "And whether you like it or not, this is your destiny. It is what you were born for, Praea."

I clawed at her shin, struggled in to breathe. "My name is Sloan," I choked out.

She removed her foot, and then her hand sliced through the air above me. The intangible force hit me so hard that I rolled four times down the yellow center line of the street. I came to rest with my face in the gravel dust facing her. She slowly walked toward me, her feet seemingly not connected with the ground.

"You will greatly suffer, my daughter. I will destroy you and those whom you love. I will destroy your future and take what is rightfully mine!" Her hands shot forward, and my body lost its connection to gravity.

"Warren, do it now!" Samael screamed behind me.

As I levitated into the air, I caught a glimpse of Warren dropping down to one knee. Blood was running into my eyes, but I saw his hands shoot forward in my direction. A bright surge of electricity blasted through the air, rippling the space between us. The force spun me out of Kasyade's ethereal grip, and I slammed into the concrete again.

The distinctive clap of lightning exploded and was accompanied by the shrillest shriek I had ever heard. My head rattled with the splintering sound, and I covered my ringing ears. Kasyade's body crumpled to the street, then a cloud of energy rose and pulsed over her lifeless corpse. Suddenly, Samael vanished and a violent, hurricane-force wind rushed over me and collided with what I assumed was her spirit. With an audible *crack,* they disappeared like they had been sucked from this world into a black hole.

The street fell silent.

As I tried to push myself up off the ground, I felt Warren's large hands close around my middle. He pulled me to my feet and into his strong arms. My legs felt limp underneath me.

"Are you all right?" He was panting.

I winced as I tried to hold my weight. "I'm broken."

Out of the corner of my eye, I saw Nathan's contorted figure bent at an unnatural angle between the side of a building and the broken sidewalk which had cracked under the sheer force with which she had thrown him. "No!" I tried helplessly to work myself free from Warren's grasp, but he held me still until he turned and saw Nathan for himself.

A choking gasp caught in his throat. "Oh God, Nate." He wrapped his arm around my waist, and I winced as he carried me across the road.

When we reached Nathan's lifeless body, I sank to the ground beside him as Warren rolled him onto his back. His eyes were open and bloodshot and staring into nothingness.

Nathan McNamara was gone.

Though I knew I wasn't going to find one, I checked for a pulse in his neck.

"Sloan," Warren said.

Instinctively, I tilted Nathan's chin up and opened his

mouth to begin CPR. I covered his mouth with my own and breathed into him.

When I straightened, Warren reached over and closed Nathan's eyes. He put his hand on my back. "It's no use."

I threw my fist at him. "You can help me or you can leave!" I shouted. "I'm not just going to give up on him!"

Patronizing me, Warren got on his knees beside Nathan's torso and pressed his large hands against Nathan's sternum. When I breathed into his cold mouth again, the audible grind from his broken rib cage as it expanded was almost enough to turn my stomach. Warren compressed Nathan's chest a few more times, and tears mixed with blood streamed down my face and dripped onto Nathan's lips. I breathed again. And again.

Nathan's lower lip quivered ever so slightly, and I pulled back. "Check his pulse," I said.

"Sloan, it's no—"

"Check his pulse!"

Warren pressed his fingers against the side of Nathan's pale neck. "Nothing."

I bent and forced more air into his lungs. His chest rose and collapsed. My heart twisted as I hopelessly breathed into him again. When Nathan's chest fell a second time to its lifeless resting place, painful sobs erupted that I couldn't control. Warren reached to console me, but I pushed him away. I clambered to my knees and clasped my hands one on top of the other and placed them over Nathan's heart. With all my strength, I pushed.

A deep and hollow *boom* echoed all around us. I toppled forward as all the windows in the abandoned buildings around us exploded. Warren shielded me with his body from the falling glass where I lay with my head on Nathan's chest. And I heard it.

Thump. Thump. Thump…

Warren and I slowly rose up. Warren must have sensed it as well because he moved around me and pressed his fingers to Nathan's jugular again. His eyes widened.

"Call an ambulance," I said, pushing him out of my way.

Warren moved a good distance away from us and pulled out his phone.

I cupped Nathan's face in my hands. "Nathan! Nathan, can you hear me?"

His eyes fluttered open ever so slightly. "Sloan." It was barely a whisper.

I cried and bent and kissed him on the mouth, not even pausing to think of the consequences that might follow. "Oh my God, Nathan!"

I sat up and looked at him again. Blood stained his mouth. I wasn't sure if it was his or my own.

"Sloan," he said again.

"Shh," I said. "Just breathe."

A bright flash of light lit up the street, and I looked back to see Samael standing over me. "Put your hands on him," he said with a voice so calm it was haunting. "Cast your life into him. You have the power now."

"I don't know how," I said.

"You don't have to know how. Your power is not limited by your ability," he said. "Put your hands on him."

Carefully, I placed my trembling hands on Nathan's chest and closed my eyes. Like something out of a bad, low-budget sci-fi movie, I concentrated on sending whatever energy I had into Nathan's broken body. Either to my surprise or to my horror, I wasn't really sure which, my hands warmed slowly against his chest. Heat surged through all of my fingers —even the ones I hadn't been able to feel in weeks. Underneath my palms, his bones were moving and grinding like rocks stuck in the chain of a bicycle.

Nathan cried out in pain.

"Don't stop," Samael said.

His joints popped and snapped. I felt his spine crack, but much more violently than the way mine did in the morning. Nathan was screaming and writhing in pain, but once again Samael instructed me to continue. Finally, the angel's hand came to rest on my shoulder, and I relaxed.

Nathan's breathing was even, and when I pulled back and looked in his face, his eyes were calm and no longer streaked with broken blood vessels. His lip quivered as he reached up and pulled my head down to his shoulder. We both cried.

For the second time, I had almost lost this man that I loved. I pressed my head to his chest just to hear his heartbeat. When his sobs subsided, I sat back up to examine his face. He was in pain, but he was going to live. I picked up his hand and pressed my lips to his palm, leaving a bloody kiss behind.

Warren and Samael were talking quietly behind us. "How are we going to explain this to the first responders?" Warren asked.

I looked back, curious as to Samael's response.

"Easy," Samael said with a wink.

He turned and looked down the street we had come from, and a moment later, our rental car turned the corner and was rolling toward us. My mouth dropped open, as there was no one in the driver's seat. "What the hell?" I mumbled.

When it neared us, Samael raised his hand, and our rental car floated off the ground. He waved his arm and sent the car careening into the front of the blue sedan Kasyade had flipped earlier.

Warren's mouth dropped open in amazement. "God, I want to learn how to do that." He nodded toward a man sitting on the curb whom I hadn't even noticed in all the confusion. "What about him?"

Apparently, the driver of the blue sedan had crawled to the curb and had witnessed the whole crazy ordeal. He was visibly shaking, and blood streaked the side of his tanned face.

Samael outstretched his hand in the man's direction. The man slowly and gently slumped to the concrete. "When he wakes, he will have no memory of what happened," Samael said. "The accident report will show that the brakes on your rental car were defective."

Warren was shaking his head, staring at the mangled cars. "That's one hell of an impact for a backstreet accident."

Samael put his hand on Warren's shoulder. "Do not worry."

I pointed to Abigail's lifeless corpse sprawled out across the center of the road. "And her?"

"Her, I will make disappear." His steady voice sent chills through my body.

Samael walked over and knelt down next to the body that had once carried me and given me life. He gently placed his hand on the back of the skull, and his eyes seemed to roll back into his head. The body at his fingertips began to disintegrate. In a matter of seconds, what remained of Kasyade's earthly form was reduced to a pile of dust. Samael leaned over it and blew with a force no human could muster, sending the particles sailing into the atmosphere.

Warren shook his head as Samael walked back toward us. "You're good," he said in awe.

Nathan squeezed my hand, and I looked down at him. "You saved my life," he whispered.

Samael knelt down next to us. "She did more than that. She brought you back."

Nathan closed his eyes and shook his head. "I always knew you would get me killed."

I looked up at Samael. "How did I bring him back?"

His face was somber, but his eyes were glowing gold.

His hand rested on my shoulder. "For a time, you will have powers greater than you've ever known."

"What about Abigail…uh, Kasyade?" I asked.

He sighed. "The Siren is not gone. She is tied to the earth for as long as you live. She will procure another body, but it will take some time for her to recover. She will come after you again, as will others."

An uneasy feeling was growing in the pit of my gut. "Samael, what did she mean that it was too late to stop it? What events have already been set into motion?"

Samael squinted his eyes against the sunlight as he seemed to search the horizon. "For that, I have no answer. I have many powers. Unfortunately, omniscience is not one of them."

Warren caught my eye. "What are you thinking?"

I didn't like what I was thinking. "I have a feeling we've only scratched the surface on what Kasyade was up to. It had to be about more than the money she was making."

Samael nodded. "The fallen are motivated by suffering, not monetary gain."

I gulped down his words with a hard swallow and shuddered. "How did you find us?" I asked. "How did you know she would lead us here?"

He took my hand. "The entire spirit world can see you now, Sloan. That is why you must be very careful. You've learned here today that not all spirits are friendly. And they are extremely powerful. Unfortunately, I am afraid this will not be the last attempt on your life."

Warren knelt down next to me and rested his hands on my shoulders. "What do we do to stop them?"

"You will have protection unseen," he said. "But I do suggest to not go looking for trouble. Trouble will find you easily enough on its own."

Sirens blared in the distance. Samael looked around. "I

must go. Peace be with you," he said to us. "We will see each other again."

"Samael, wait!" I called.

He turned his golden eyes toward me. "Yes?"

"Kasyade is a demon, right?" I asked.

He nodded. "She is a fallen angel. That is correct."

"Then what does that make me? She said she created me on purpose." My frantic heartbeat was audible in my ears.

His smile was benevolent and kind. "We are all given the choice between the side of good and evil, Sloan. No one but you can decide."

I reached out and grabbed him by the hand. "Thank you."

He shook his head. "No. Thank *you*."

And with another flash of light, Samael was gone.

22.

Nathan was taken by ambulance to St. Luke's Baptist Hospital. I rode with him, and I suspected I needed medical treatment of my own. On the ride there, I winced in pain as I felt the bone in my hip crack and snap back into place.

Nathan's eyes were fearful. "Are you OK? What's happening?" He clasped his hand around mine.

I forced a nod as the ribs on my right side began to grind against each other. I squeezed his hand and cried till they popped back together. My nose, which the EMT had said was obviously broken, began burning and pouring blood once again. I dropped my face into my lap as it shifted back into alignment. I cried out as my eyes flooded with tears.

The paramedic who was caring for Nathan put his hand on my back. "Ma'am, are you all right?"

I sat up, and blood poured down my face, splattering all over the floor of the ambulance. The paramedic's eyes widened with horror, and he quickly grabbed a towel and held it to my face. Bright dots speckled my vision as the pain slowly faded.

I couldn't even imagine what was happening to me other than somehow my body was rejuvenating itself. It hadn't done that when I was beaten by Billy Stewart. Perhaps somehow Abigail had unintentionally unlocked some of my power. By the time we reached the hospital, I was able to climb out of the ambulance without any help.

Warren had ridden with a San Antonio police officer to the hospital, and he was waiting in the transport bay at the emergency room entrance when we arrived. I stopped and squeezed Nathan's fingers. "I'll be back there in just a minute."

He nodded. "I'll be OK."

As they wheeled Nathan inside, Warren walked over and tilted my chin up to examine my face. "You're a mess. We've got to get you cleaned up."

I could feel the blood crusting on my skin. "I look worse than I feel now."

"Thank God." He took my hand and led me inside.

A nurse stopped us. "Honey, let's get you to triage." The plump woman in scrubs took my arm.

I shook my head. "I'm OK. I just look like a mess. Can you point us to the bathrooms?"

Her eyes were wide. It was obvious she didn't believe me. "You're covered in blood."

"I know. We were in an accident, but most of this blood is my friend's," I said. "Can I get some towels, maybe?"

She nodded. "Absolutely." She walked around the nursing station and returned with a towel and two washcloths. "Come with me. A sink isn't going to be enough. You need a shower."

Her kindness almost moved me to tears as she led us down another hallway to a room with a private bath. She winked at me. "This will be our little secret. I'll try and find you something to wear."

I sighed and smiled. "Thank you."

Warren tugged me toward the bathroom. "Come on."

Once we were inside, I caught sight of myself in the mirror as Warren turned the water in the shower on. I looked like an extra from a Night of the Living Dead movie. My face was splattered and smeared with blood. It covered my mouth and was all down my neck and the front of my shirt. Dark circles from my broken nose were already forming under my eyes. My t-shirt and my jeans were shredded like I had been through a wood-chipper. Tears streaked through the blood on my cheeks.

"I think you should let a doctor look at you." Warren pulled some matted hair away from my face. "Just to be on the safe side."

I shook my head. "No. I felt my bones come back together in the ambulance. It was excruciating." Holding up my hands, I flexed and straightened my fingers. "Even the nerve damage seems to be gone."

He stared at me for a moment. "What's happening to you?"

I turned to face him. "I don't know, Warren. But there's something else."

"What?" he asked, his eyes growing with alarm.

"I can see your soul."

His head jerked back in surprise. "Really?"

I nodded. "Really."

He scratched his head. "Something must have happened back there with Abigail. Maybe she transferred some of her powers to you."

"A lot of things happened back there with Abigail, but I don't think that's it." I leaned back against the sink. "The other day at her house, she told me that you and I were born with all of our angelic powers from our parents. We just aren't able to use them as well because we are human."

His head tilted. ""Does that mean—"

"That I'm becoming less human?" I interrupted him. I held my hands up. "I have no idea what's happening."

He shook his head and laughed, though he clearly didn't think it was funny. "It's like the more we find out, the less we understand."

I sighed. "I know."

He reached over and untucked my shirt. "Let's get you cleaned up."

Gently, Warren eased the torn fabric over my head. My bones might not have been broken anymore, but that didn't mean they didn't hurt like hell.

I stepped into the shower and winced as the hot water ran over the open cuts in my skin. There was a light knock at the door, and the hinges creaked as Warren pulled it open.

"These might be a little big on her, but here are some extra scrubs I had in my locker. And here is some shampoo and a comb for her hair that I got from our supply closet," I heard the nurse say.

"You're a saint. Thank you so much," Warren replied.

"Are you sure she shouldn't get herself checked out?" the nurse asked. "She looks really banged up, and I'm afraid she could have some internal injuries."

"She says she's fine. But thank you again. I know she's anxious to get back to our friend."

"I'll check back in a little while and see how she's doing," she said.

Warren handed me the shampoo, and it burned the back of my head as I lathered it. I looked down and watched the suds swirling with blood down the drain. When I finally finished, I stepped out and let Warren wrap me in a towel. I put on the blue scrubs and shoved my clothes into the trashcan. They were irreparable. My torn scalp felt like it was ripping as I brushed the tangles out of my hair. I briefly considered using Warren's knife to just cut my hair off, but I realized if I did, Adrianne would probably kill me when I got home.

Nathan was in radiology when I finished up in the bathroom. The nurse took us to the stall in the emergency room where they would bring him back, and we waited in two chairs. I rested my head against Warren's shoulder and tried to release all the stress that had built up throughout the day. It was hopeless. Even after fifteen minutes, my hands were still trembling.

An unfamiliar ringtone came from Warren's chest pocket. He pulled it out and looked at it. "This is Nathan's," he said. "It's a Texas number. Should we answer it?"

"Yeah, it's probably the FBI." I took the phone from him and hit the answer button as I put it to my ear. "Nathan McNamara's phone," I said.

"Hi, is this Sloan?" a woman asked.

"Yes, is this Agent Silvers?"

"It is," she said. "I wanted you to know that we've searched Abigail Smith's home and office and found very substantial evidence to support your statement. We didn't find Ms. Smith, however. It seems that either Rex Parker or Tito Juarez may have tipped her off. I thought you should be warned in case she suspects you might have spoken with us."

I actually laughed. "Thanks for the warning, Agent Silvers."

"Is something funny?" she asked.

"No, ma'am," I said. "I just really don't think this day could get any worse. We are at the hospital after a very serious accident."

"Oh, I'm sorry to hear that. Is there anything I can do for you?" she asked.

"Just find the girls Abigail has taken. And please get Larry Mendez off the streets."

"I'm doing everything I can on both fronts. Please let

me know as soon as possible if you hear anything at all from Abigail," she said.

"I will." I kept my laughter to myself that time.

Warren looked at me. "Mendez is still out there?"

I stared at the phone in my hands. "Guess so."

He was quiet for a moment before turning toward me. "Will you be all right here by yourself for a while?"

I almost asked why, but the fiery look in his eye answered the question.

Nodding, I touched his cheek. "Go find him."

* * *

I was busy losing a game of Solitaire on Nathan's phone when two nurses pushed his rolling hospital bed back into the room. He was sitting up at a slight incline, and he looked groggy. They had cleaned most of the blood off his face, and had changed him into a clean hospital gown. His arm was tethered to an IV pole.

I stood up, walked to his bedside, and took his hand. "Hey, how are you feeling?"

"Like I've been raised from the dead," he said with a hint of a painful smile.

I leaned over and pressed a kiss to his forehead.

"Where's Warren?"

"He went out to run some errands. What did the doctors say?"

He shook his head. "Not much. They took some x-rays and did a CT scan to check for broken bones and internal injuries. I wonder if they'll find anything."

"I wonder the same thing," I said.

Nathan's fingers squeezed mine. "What happened back there?"

Carefully, I eased down onto the edge of his bed. I looked around to see if there was anyone else within earshot of us. I lowered my voice. "The black guy, Samael, is another angel we had met before. Abigail can summon people like I can, except she's much better at it. She had summoned Warren to where she was waiting."

Nathan cracked a smile. "Did he tell you that to justify his awful driving?"

I laughed. At least he still had his sense of humor.

His smile quickly faded. "What happened while I was dead?"

My face twisted into a frown. "Well, Warren used his power to kill her body, and Samael did something—I don't know what—with her spirit."

"Warren used what power?"

I scrunched up my nose. "You don't want to know."

He pressed his eyes closed. "No, I probably don't. How did she kill me?"

I shrugged my shoulders. "I'm really not sure. I don't know if she choked you to death, sucked the life out of you, or if her slamming you into the brick and concrete was what did it."

He grimaced. "How did you bring me back?"

I dropped my head. "I have absolutely no idea." A nurse stopped in to check a machine he was attached to. When she was gone, I leaned closer to him. "Do you remember anything about it? Being dead, I mean."

He shook his head. "Nothing."

His answer was disappointing. I had hoped for a full report about what it was like on the other side.

Just then, a doctor appeared around the curtain. "Nathan McNamara?" He was holding a metal clipboard in his hand.

"Yes," Nathan answered.

I stood up and stepped back over to my chair.

The doctor looked down at his sheet. "You're a lucky man, Nathan," he said. "Somehow, you don't have any broken bones. Any new ones anyway. The CT scan showed quite a bit of scar tissue and inflammation around two different spots on your spine, a few places on your rib cage, and your right shoulder, but those appear to be previous injuries.

Nathan's mouth fell open. I'm sure his expression matched mine. Neither of us spoke.

The doctor looked down at him. "I would like to hold you here overnight, just to be on the safe side. And you're going to be very sore for a few days, I'm afraid."

"I can handle sore," Nathan replied.

The doctor smiled. "Once we get some paperwork done on our end down here, someone will come and move you to a room upstairs. I'm going to get you some pain medicine and have the nurse come and clean you up a bit more."

"Thank you, Doctor," Nathan said.

The doctor shook his head. "Don't thank me." He pointed up toward the ceiling with his index finger. "You need to be thanking someone a lot higher up."

Sometime later, they moved Nathan to a regular room. It had a chair that converted into a bed, and I was half-asleep on it when Nathan turned the volume all the way up on the television. "Sloan, check it out!"

I pushed myself up. "What is it?"

He pointed to the television.

It was a news broadcast with a brunette anchor woman, and behind her was a picture of Larry Mendez. She spoke directly into the camera. "Panic broke out at a local Wal-Mart shopping center this evening in downtown San Antonio when there was what witnesses described as a loud explosion that left one man dead and many shoppers terrified. Alec Ortega is live on the scene. Alec, can you tell us what happened down there tonight?"

The screen switched to a scene in the parking lot with the Wal-Mart sign lit up in the background. "No one is really sure what happened tonight at this popular shopping center downtown. Numerous calls were made to police from customers who said an explosion happened inside the store." He held his hands out in confusion. "However, investigators have found no sign of explosives or any damage that could have been caused by one. What they did uncover was a man's body near the center of the store, but they say there is no sign of foul play. We spoke with Police Chief Albert Bechard and this is what he had to say."

The camera cut to an interview with a man in a police uniform. "At this time, we have found nothing that indicates there was any kind of explosion here at this store despite the testimony of countless shoppers and employees." The man looked genuinely puzzled. "We did recover a deceased person, but there is no sign the two events were related. The victim is forty-two-year-old Larry Mendez of Bexar County, and at this time, it appears as though he died of natural causes. We have found no evidence to suggest otherwise."

Nathan's jaw was dropped when he turned to look at me.

I pinched my lips together.

"Do you know something about this?" he asked.

My eyes widened, and I slowly shrugged my shoulders.

"Where is Warren?"

I shrugged again. "I don't know. I don't have a phone, remember?"

Just then, the door slowly opened and Warren's head peeked through the crack. "Is this the right room?"

"Yeah, come in," I said, sitting up on the edge of my makeshift bed.

He walked into the room. "Sorry, it took me forever to find out what room you guys were in. The nurse at the desk —" He stopped talking when he saw the horrified look on Nathan's face. "Uh, hey, Nate. How are you feeling?"

Nathan didn't answer.

I caught Warren's eyes and discreetly pointed toward the television.

"Larry Mendez is dead," Nathan said.

Warren blinked with surprise, but it wasn't very convincing. "Really?"

I almost laughed.

"How'd that happen?" Warren asked, walking over and sitting down next to me.

Nathan's expression was caught at the crossroads of confusion, anger, and fear. "I thought you might tell me. Where've you been?"

"Oh." Warren looked at me. "I've been out just tying up some loose ends."

"Warren." Nathan's tone was scolding.

Warren smiled. "I almost forgot." He reached inside his jacket and pulled out a white plastic bag. "I got you a get well gift." He tossed the bag onto Nathan's lap.

Nathan unrolled it.

It was a pack of Skittles, inside a shopping bag…from Wal-Mart.

23.

Nathan was discharged the next morning, and we were able to book a flight back to Asheville that afternoon. When we got back to North Carolina, I instructed Warren to drive us all back to my house. Nathan attempted a weak protest, but he was still in a lot of pain and didn't have his normal amount of arguing power.

He was still complaining as he leaned on me for support going up my front steps. "I'm fine, Sloan."

"That argument would be a lot more effective if you weren't using me as a crutch right now. You died two days ago. That's kind of a big deal. I don't want you staying in that apartment all by yourself, so you're going to stay here with us. You can sleep in the armory."

He looked down at me. "The armory?"

"You'll see." I fumbled with my keys till I got the correct one in the front door.

I helped him up the stairs inside till we reached the guest room. "Holy mother," he said, looking around in astonishment at the arsenal.

I rolled my eyes and helped him over to the bed. "I know. I feel like I live at Fort Knox without all the gold."

He winced in pain as he lay down on top of the comforter. I pulled his pain pills out of my coat pocket and put them on the nightstand. "You should take something and try to rest. We're going to run check on my dad, but we won't be gone for too long."

He nodded. "OK."

"I'll go get you some water." I scampered downstairs and retrieved a bottle of water from the refrigerator as Warren carried the load of suitcases in the front door. "Here, let me help." I took Nathan's backpack from him.

"Thanks," he said as he followed me up the steps.

I walked back in the guest room and put the water on the nightstand and the pack beside the bed. "Call Warren's phone if you need anything. We'll bring you back some dinner."

"Sounds good."

"Are you sure you'll be OK?" I asked.

He nodded. "Positive." As I turned to leave, he called out to me. "Sloan, wait."

I walked back over to the side of his bed. "Yeah?"

He reached his hand toward me. "I never said thank you."

I laughed. "Nathan, I've almost gotten you killed once, and I actually got you killed a second time. You really don't need to thank me."

He nodded and pulled me down next to him. "Yeah, I do. You didn't give up. You saved my life."

Tears tickled the corners of my puffy eyes. There was so much I wanted to say to him, but I knew it wouldn't be fair to anyone. I leaned over and gently touched my lips to his forehead. I lingered there for a second to hopefully convey a message I could never say out loud.

"I love you," he whispered.

A tear slid down my cheek and dripped onto his. When I pulled back, his eyes were closed and he was smiling.

I stood up. "We'll be back in a little while."

When I walked out of the room, I pulled the door closed gently behind me. Warren was waiting with his hands in his pockets. If he had been watching from the doorway, he didn't say anything.

"You ready?" he asked.

I nodded. "Yep."

We drove to my dad's house, and he was sitting on the front porch when we pulled in the driveway. I couldn't help but jog up the front path toward him and fall into his arms.

He sighed and kissed the side of my head. "Welcome home, sweetheart."

"You have no idea how glad I am to be back," I told him as Warren caught up to us.

Dad put his hand under my chin and examined the bruising on my face. "What happened to you?"

I shook my head. "I'm fine. It looks worse than it really is."

Warren smiled as he walked up onto the porch. "I promise I didn't do it."

He laughed and put his arm around my shoulders. "Come on. Let's go in. It's chilly out here." We turned and walked inside. "I expected a phone call when you met Sarah to tell me if she was actually your birth mom."

"Well, I broke my phone even worse when we were in Texas, and we had a lot going on. And yes, Sarah—her name is actually Kasyade—is the one who left me at the hospital."

We sat down on the sofa in the den. Take-out food containers littered the room. "What else did she have to say?" he asked. "Did she tell you who your father is?"

I shook my head. "No. She refused to tell me,

actually."

He cocked his head to the side. "Really? Why?"

I blew out a sigh. "Oh, Dad, I don't even know where to start." I leaned forward on my elbows. "For starters, she's not a good angel. She almost ended up killing all of us."

His eyes widened. "Really?"

"Yeah."

He looked confused. "She was so nice when I knew her."

"Warren and another angel we met ended up destroying her. At least for the time being," I said. "I know one thing. I'm not going back to Texas anytime soon."

He shook his head. "I would assume not. Is that how you got the bruises?" He pointed to my face.

"Yeah. It could have been a lot worse than it was," I said.

He rubbed my back. "I'm sorry your visit with her wasn't the reunion you had hoped for."

I smiled at him. "I got all I needed from her. I know a little bit more about where I came from and what I am."

He nodded. "That's good."

"Dad, we're going to stay at my house right now if that's OK. Warren leaves in a few days, and Nathan is staying with us because he caught the worst of the violence down in Texas. He really needs to be looked after for a while."

"Of course, sweetheart. I'm getting along pretty well here," he said. "I've cooked twice this weekend and haven't even had to call the fire department once."

I laughed. "That's awesome."

"Are you going back to work?" he asked.

"Yeah. I don't want to, but I need to go in tomorrow to do some catching up," I told him.

He nodded. "I think it would be good for you. I went back to the office yesterday and saw some patients. Getting back into a routine will be good for us both."

My shoulders slumped as I looked from him to Warren. I wondered if anything about my life would ever be *routine* again.

* * *

When Warren and I left about an hour later, the sun was starting to set behind the mountains. Streaks of orange, pink, and purple swirled through the sky. A few bright stars twinkled against the dying light of the sun.

Warren wrapped his arms around me from behind. "You OK?"

I took a deep breath. "This is just the beginning, Warren. We haven't seen anything yet."

"Are you afraid?"

I nodded. "Did you hear Samael? He said the whole spirit world can sense me now. I can't hide from them." I shuddered in his arms. "They're coming after me to kill me."

He pressed a kiss to the bend of my neck. "Something tells me you're not that easy to kill."

"Is that supposed to make me feel better?"

He tightened his arms around me. "Think about it. If the evil spirits can see you, so can the good ones. You won't be alone. And don't forget what else Samael said. He said you would have protection, even if you can't see it."

"I'm afraid."

"I know."

A faint ripple against the sky caught my attention. It was a very delicate shimmering wave against the colors of the horizon. I squinted and tried to focus on it, but couldn't make the figure any clearer. I pointed up to it. "Do you see that?"

His eyes followed my finger and carefully searched the sky. "See what?"

I knew exactly what it was and remembered Samael's words, *protection unseen*. For the first time, I knew I was seeing an angel. It seemed so obvious to me, splayed against the horizon, that I wasn't sure how I had missed seeing them before. I admired the silvery rippling figure again and felt a calm rush over me.

Finally, I smiled and hugged Warren's arms that were around my waist. "Nothing. Let's go. I want to stop by Adrianne's on the way home and heal her leg."

He smiled as he reached down and wrapped his hand around mine. "Do you think you can really do it?"

I nodded and glanced toward the sky. "I know I can."

24.

By some miracle, we all made it three full days without any catastrophes, supernatural uprisings, or criminal disasters. But Thursday morning came, and it was more difficult to get out of bed than usual. I had been awake for a while, listening to the sound of the shower and then the hair dryer, but somehow I had convinced myself that if I didn't get up, the day couldn't really begin. After a while, the door opened and Warren leaned in the bathroom doorway wearing only a pair of jeans. His black hair was hanging around his shoulders.

He smiled at me. "It's time. I need your help."

"No. Come back to bed."

"Sloan." His tone was even but cautionary.

Groaning, I pushed myself up off the bed. It was almost ten in the morning.

I walked into the bathroom, and Warren pulled out the vanity stool and sat down. He brushed his hair back and tied it with an elastic band. He looked at me in the mirror. "You ready?"

I ran my fingers through the end of his ponytail. "I

can't do it," I whined.

He watched me in the mirror. "Am I going to have to do it myself?"

I sighed and shook my head. "No."

With trembling hands, I gripped his hair and took the pair of scissors he was holding over his shoulder. "It will grow back," he said as I stared at it. "Cut."

Cringing, I brought the scissors close to his head. The doorbell rang. I jumped when I heard it, slamming the scissors down on the counter.

"Damn it, woman," Warren grumbled as I ran out of the room.

When I reached the front door, I swung the door open to see Adrianne standing there holding an overnight bag and a cup of coffee. Her hair was cropped short in a pixie style, and she had on a pair of bright red, four-inch high heels that almost brought tears to my eyes. She stepped effortlessly over the threshold of my front door like she had never been injured at all.

"I'm so glad you're here. I need you." I was panting.

"Well, hold up because Nathan is coming in right after me." She nodded back outside to where Nathan was climbing out of his truck.

"Nate, the door's open!" I called to him and grabbed Adrianne by the hand.

She looked down at me. "Maybe you should at least put on a bra before he gets in here, and have you even brushed your hair?"

"No. I just got out of bed." I dragged her up the stairs.

"What's so important?" she asked.

We walked into my bedroom. "Hair emergency."

Warren was still sitting in the vanity chair with his arms folded over his bare chest. She froze in the doorway and looked down at the scissors. "What's going on?"

"He wants me to cut it. I can't do it." I pushed her forward into the bathroom.

She stepped over behind him and put her hands on his shoulders. She leaned down close to his ear. "Trust me. You don't want her to do it. She cut her own bangs one time in junior high and wound up with a haircut like mine," she said, pointing to her own short hair. She leaned over him and picked up the scissors. "All of it?"

He nodded. "All of it."

I felt like I was going to throw up as the scissors sliced through his ponytail. I stumbled back a couple of steps into my room.

"Where is everyone?" I heard Nathan call downstairs.

"My room," I shouted back. "Come on up!"

Warren looked over at me. His hair fell just to his ears. "Please put on some damn clothes, Sloan."

"Whoops!" I yanked open a dresser drawer and grabbed the first thick material my fingers found. I slipped a black sweatshirt over my head.

Adrianne handed me the end of the ponytail. "Here you go."

My bottom lip popped out. "Will you guys laugh at me if I cry right now?"

"Yes," they said in unison.

Nathan walked into my room holding a travel mug and a file folder. "What's going on?"

I nodded toward the bathroom where more black hair was falling to the floor.

He looked around the doorway. "Oh, that sucks," Nathan said. "Do you feel your superpowers fading right now?"

"I can still whip you in a fight if necessary," Warren said over his shoulder.

Nathan laughed. "Well, don't whip me till you've seen

this." He handed Warren the paper. "It was in my email this morning."

"What is it?" I asked, stepping over next to Adrianne so I could peek over his shoulder.

Warren was shaking his head. "I don't believe it."

I read aloud the lines marked with a highlighter. "Department of Children and Family Services. Rachel A. Smith. 1992, 1997-2000."

Warren looked back up at me. "In 1992, I was eight."

Both my hands shot up over my mouth. "Oh my god."

Adrianne looked at me with alarm. "What is it?"

No one answered her.

It wasn't by chance that Abigail was working there when Warren and Alice were placed in the home of a child molester. He crumpled the paper slowly in his fist.

Nathan crossed his arms. "But if she was there, why didn't you feel it when she left?"

Warren shook his head. "I don't know, but right now I'm more concerned about what she was doing there in the first place."

I put my hand on his rigid shoulder and caught his eye in the reflection of the glass. "This isn't over."

The muscles working in his jaw. "No, it isn't."

After a long, awkward, and tense moment in the bathroom, Adrianne pointed to her watch and looked at us all with wide and cautious eyes. "I hate to interrupt all the mysterious brooding in here, but we need to get a move on, Warren, if you want to keep to your schedule."

He cleared his throat and straightened in the chair. "You're right. Proceed."

Adrianne ran her fingers through what remained of his hair. "Do you want it all buzzed off, or do you want it within military regs and as long as possible?"

"You can do that?" he asked, blinking with surprise.

She nodded. "Of course I can," she said. "Aren't you glad I came over? Please don't ever let Sloan near your head with a pair of scissors or clippers."

I swatted my hand at her, but she ducked out of the way. "Let me get rid of that," I said, taking the ball of paper from Warren. I bent to throw it in the wastebasket under the bathroom counter.

Nathan started laughing.

"What?" I asked, looking back at him. Then I noticed Warren shaking his head with his eyes rolled up at the ceiling. My voice jumped up an octave. "What is it?"

Warren pointed toward the mirror. "Look at your back."

Craning my neck over my shoulder, I saw the reflection of the letters S.W.A.T. across my shoulders. I groaned. Nathan was doubled over, practically howling.

"What did I miss?" Adrianne asked.

My arms flopped to my sides in defeat. "It's Nathan's shirt," I said. "It's a long story."

She sighed and went back to cutting. "I can only imagine."

Nathan dabbed at his eyes with his sleeve as his cackles subsided. "Not that I'm complaining about your outfit, Sloan, but why aren't you dressed?"

"She's not packed either," Warren said.

Nathan shook his head.

I pouted again. "It's too hard."

Adrianne jerked her thumb toward the bedroom. "Go get your shit together, right now."

Dropping my head, I shuffled back to my bedroom, grabbing an overnight bag out of my closet as I went. I shoved some pajamas, clean underwear, and an outfit for the next day into the bag. My migraine medicine and my Xanax were on my nightstand. I dropped them in the top of the bag and zipped it shut. The sound of the clippers buzzing in the bathroom made me cringe.

When Adrianne was finished, my boyfriend looked like a giant GI Joe action figure. As he stood, she brushed the hair off his shoulders with a hand towel.

"You did a good job, Adrianne," he said, running his hand over the top. He turned around and looked at me. "Do you like it?"

I sighed. "You don't have the ability to look bad, babe."

It wasn't the haircut I hated. It was the reason behind it. He leaned over and kissed me. "It will grow back, and then I'll never have to do this again," he said. "Are you about ready to go?"

I nodded, but dropped my shoulders in defeat.

After I had dressed, and Warren finished gathering everything he needed, the four of us walked out onto the front porch. I locked the front door behind us.

"What are we driving?" Adrianne asked.

"Not my truck," Nathan said. "Sloan's going to be puking all the way home with one of her migraines, and I just had the carpets cleaned from the last time."

I frowned. "Shut up."

"We're not taking the Challenger either." Warren looked down at me with eyes that dared me to argue.

"We'll take my car." I sighed and rolled my eyes. "You guys suck."

"Do you have your migraine medicine?" Warren asked, taking my keys from me.

I nodded. "In my bag."

Next door, a flag in the shape of a turkey fluttered on the breeze. Thanksgiving was just around the corner, but I didn't have a thankful bone in my body. Warren was leaving, my mother was gone, demons wanted me dead...the list went on and on. As we walked to my car, I was already fighting back tears. It was going to be a rotten day.

Warren drove, and Nathan and Adrianne got in the back seat. I was glad they had both offered to make the trip to Charlotte with us. I knew that between Warren leaving and the migraine that would follow, I would be in no shape to drive myself home. Maybe the efforts of the two of them combined could keep me from completely going to pieces.

As we merged onto the interstate, Adrianne leaned between the front seats and looked at me. "So, have you heard anymore from the FBI?"

I put my feet up on the dash and hugged my knees to my chest. "Yeah, they called yesterday to say that they've tracked down Abigail's establishments in Los Angeles, Chicago, and New York City. It's probably going to be one of the largest operations ever taken down before," I said.

Adrianne sighed and shook her head. "Wow. That's crazy."

Warren looked back at her in the rearview mirror. "Did Sloan tell you how she was laundering the money?"

"Huh-uh." Adrianne shook her head. "How?"

"They think she was counting the payments as *donations* to Morning Star Ministries," Warren said.

Nathan sipped his coffee. "She was sending out end-of-the-year receipts and everything."

Adrianne's mouth fell open. "You've got to be kidding me."

I looked back at her. "What's worse is the ministry reported over ten million dollars in income last year."

She covered her mouth with her hand. "That's sick. What's going to happen to those girls?"

I sighed. "I hope someone legitimate will actually try and help them recover."

Adrianne sat back in her seat. "It's hard to believe this stuff happens here in America."

Nathan was nodding. "They say sex trafficking generated more than nine billion dollars in just the United States alone last year."

"God help us," she said. "Are they still looking for Abigail?"

"Of course. She's on the Most Wanted list now," Nathan said. "There's a reward for $500,000 from the FBI for information that will lead to her arrest."

She tapped her fingernail on my leather seat back. "But they won't ever find her, will they? She won't come back looking the same, right?"

"I highly doubt it," I said. "We watched her body turn to dust."

She sat back in her seat. "But she will still come back?"

I nodded. "Samael said she would have to procure another body."

"Do you know how it's done?" Nathan asked.

"Demons possess people, right?" Adrianne said.

I shrugged. "I really have no idea, but I'm hoping it's a lengthy process."

Nathan leaned forward. "Hey, Warren, have you thought anymore about what you're going to do to Rex?" he asked. "You threatened him pretty good."

"Oh, I think about it every day," Warren said, looking at him in the mirror. "I'm going to let him sweat about it till I get back. Then I plan on paying him a little visit in prison."

"To do what?" Nathan asked.

Warren and I both looked back at him.

He held up his hand. "Let me guess. I don't want to know."

Warren looked at me and winked as he smiled. I reached over and meshed my fingers with his.

* * *

We pulled up to the front entrance of the Ramada Inn

near the Military Entrance Processing Command Station in Charlotte. Warren put the car in park. "Nate, you wanna grab the bags while I go check in?"

"Sure," Nathan said, wrenching his door open.

Adrianne opened her door. "Come on. Let's go help Nate."

I was clutching my overnight bag when Warren came out and took it from my hands. He handed keys to both Nathan and Adrianne. "Thanks, guys," he said and dropped my bag back into the trunk.

Confused, I spun around toward him. "What are you doing?"

Adrianne nudged me with her arm. "Get back in the car. We'll see you tomorrow."

I looked up at Warren. "What's going on?"

He smiled at me. "It's my last night with you, and as much as I like these two"—he nodded toward Adrianne and Nathan—"I'd really like to have you all to myself for just a little while."

I felt my cheeks flush red. "All right."

I hugged Adrianne and Nathan goodbye, and Warren opened my car door for me. "Where are you taking me?" I asked.

He laughed as I got in. "You don't have to be in control of absolutely everything, Sloan. Stop asking so many questions."

When he got in and started the engine, I laughed. "Is this date going to end in chasing bad guys or fighting demons like all the other ones do?"

He chuckled and fastened his seatbelt. "God, I hope not."

Thirty minutes later, far outside the city limits, he turned onto a two-lane highway. We passed a billboard and two smaller signs on the road advertising the North Carolina

State Gun Show. I turned in my seat and pointed at him. "If your idea of a romantic last night together has anything to do with a gun show, we might as well just end this relationship right now."

He chuckled and reached for my hand. "I'm a little smarter than that." He nodded toward my window. "Look."

I followed the direction of his gaze and saw another sign that read *Willow Mountain Inn and Botanical Gardens*. My mind floated back to our date night in San Antonio when he so adamantly shot down my idea of visiting the gardens there.

I covered my mouth and laughed. Then I leaned over and kissed his cheek. "Well played, sir," I said. "Well played."

The inn was a beautifully restored Victorian, Queen Anne-style house, surrounded by lush greenery and flowers that were still blooming in the fall. The brochure in our room said it mostly functioned as an event place for weddings and parties, but there were six private villas which were rented out to overnight guests. Warren confessed he had help in planning the evening, but I already knew it the second we walked through the door. The place had Adrianne's name written all over it.

We enjoyed a private dinner in the heated outdoor gazebo, shared a bottle of wine, and talked about anything and everything except for deployments or demons. I almost felt like we were a completely normal couple.

He finished off what was left in my glass and offered me his hand. "Let's go for a walk."

A little dizzy from the wine and his intoxicating presence, I rested my cheek against his strong arm as we wandered along the stone pathways that wound around elaborate flowers and plants. We crossed over a quiet creek on a storybook stone bridge, and the faint scent of lemon balm and dill floated along the cool breeze.

I stopped walking and took a deep, refreshing breath. "Is this heaven?"

When I looked up at him, he was smiling. "If it isn't, I don't want to be there."

Turning to face him, I stretched up on my tiptoes and looped my arms around his neck. As we embraced, I closed my eyes to sear the moment into my memory.

After a minute, he reached up and took my wrists in his hands, pulling them gently down between us. "Do you remember when we were in San Antonio and I told you I wasn't going to propose to you?"

I laughed. "Yeah. I don't think I can forget about that conversation."

"Well..." He held up his hand. On the tip of his pinky finger was a large, circular diamond with a halo of smaller diamonds around it. It was glistening in the pink and orange glow of the last rays of sunlight.

My mouth fell open. "What is this?"

His eyes were wide, but his mouth was tipped up around the corners. "This still isn't a proposal," he cautioned.

"Then. What. Is. It?" I asked, carefully articulating my words.

He took a deep breath. "I know our life together is very complicated, and I'm sure it always will be. In fact, I'm pretty damn sure it's only going to get worse from this point on." He paused to laugh. "Angels and demons be damned because I don't want anything else in this world more than I want you and all of the mess that comes with us being together."

I raised a skeptical eyebrow. "This sounds like a proposal."

He reached into his pocket and pulled out a ring box. He opened it, placed the ring in the cushioned velvet center, and snapped the box shut. I cocked my head to the side and glared at him as he tucked the box back into the inside chest pocket of his jacket.

I put my hands on my hips. "Are you just trying to be an ass or what?"

He put his hands on the sides of my face. "No. I'm not trying to be an ass. I just want you to know how serious I am about us." He took a step closer to me. "I don't ever want to wonder if you might have any regrets."

I opened my mouth to spew my objection, as well as a few more obscenities, but he covered my lips with his finger.

"I know you love me, but you love him too." He bent slightly to look me directly in the eye. "While I'm gone, I want you to really consider it and decide, with absolute certainty, what you want for the rest of your life."

My brow crumpled. "Are you breaking up with me?"

He shook his head. "No. But I am giving you the next few months to really get honest with yourself and with me and Nathan." He put his hand over the pocket where he had stashed the box. "I want you to be sure because when I put this ring on your hand, it's going to be for forever."

I dropped my gaze to our feet, and a tear dripped from my eye and splashed onto the toe of his boot. Warren was right. I knew he was. Knowing it was the right thing to do didn't make it any easier though. I didn't deserve Warren. Hell, I didn't deserve either of them.

He tipped my chin up and brought his lips down to meet mine. "I love you," he said again when he pulled away.

"I love you, too."

* * *

Adrianne had a loaded smile splashed across her face the next morning when Warren and I met her and Nathan in the lobby of the Ramada Inn. "Well? Did you two have fun last night?"

I smiled and looped my arm through Warren's. "It was

a beautifully spectacular evening."

She clapped her hands with glee. "Yeah? Did anything *exciting* happen?"

Heat rose in my cheeks. Lots of exciting things happened, but none of them would I share with Adrianne…at least not in Warren's presence—or Nathan's. I recognized her tone though, and I held up my bare left hand. "We're not engaged, if that's what you're wondering."

Nathan looked at Adrianne. "You owe me twenty bucks."

She rolled her eyes.

Warren laughed and looked down at his watch, then at me. "We've got to get going. Are you ready?"

I pouted. "No."

He sighed and tugged on my arm. "Come on."

Nathan drove my car down Whitehall Park street till we reached a large four story, white building. I was riding in the back seat practically sitting in Warren's lap. When he parked in the lot near the front, we all got out. Warren pulled his duffle bag out of the trunk and dropped it on the curb.

Adrianne wrapped her arms around his neck. "Be safe. I'll pray for you," she said.

He smiled. "Thanks, Adrianne."

Next, he turned to Nathan. "Come home safe, brother," Nathan said.

Warren pulled him into a tight hug. It was odd seeing the two of them embrace. Odd, and perfect. "Take care of her for me," Warren said when he stepped back. "Keep your damn hands to yourself, but take care of her."

Nathan laughed. "I will."

Warren gave me a warning glare. "Don't let her run off and get herself into a shit-load of trouble while I'm gone."

I held up my hands. "I don't do that!"

"Right," all three of them said at the same time.

Nathan and Adrianne got back into the car. Warren took a slow step toward me and reached for my hand. He rested his forehead against mine and closed his eyes. "In all seriousness, please be careful."

"I will be. I promise."

He tucked my hair behind my ears. "The Glock you shot when we were in Texas is in your nightstand by the bed. It's loaded, just in case. Get Nathan to take you to the range again. You need to practice."

I groaned. "I don't wanna."

He put his arms around me and pulled me close. "I don't care."

Tears began to well up in my eyes. "Please come home to me."

He pressed his lips against my forehead. "Always."

Tilting my chin up with his finger, he kissed me long and slow. The magnetic energy surged through us, and I enjoyed its intoxicating tingle one last time. My knees felt weak when he finally pulled back. He lifted my left hand up and kissed the spot where I should have been wearing that sparkling diamond.

He cut his eyes at me. "Just out of curiosity, if I had asked, what would you have said?"

"You know what I would have said." I sniffed and rubbed my eyes, smearing mascara across the back of my knuckles.

He cupped my face in his hands and wiped under my eyes with his thumbs. Staring into his eyes, I let the sensation of his kind soul burn itself into my memory. He kissed me one more time. "I love you," he said.

"I love you."

Stepping away, he picked up his black bag, slinging the strap over his shoulder. He headed toward the front door and paused at the entrance to look back and wave one last time. I still hated his short hair.

Then he was gone.

* * *

The car was silent till we got out of Charlotte's city limits. Adrianne finally reached back and touched my arm. Her makeup was smudged from crying a little too. "Are you OK?" she asked.

My cheeks were still wet with silent tears. I nodded and squeezed her fingers. "Yeah. I'm OK."

"You wanna talk about what happened last night? I thought for sure you were going to show up engaged this morning." She pointed from Nathan to herself. "We placed bets on whether or not he was going to propose to you."

I folded my arms over my chest. "And I want to know why Nathan was so sure he wouldn't."

Nathan kept his eyes on the road. "Because he told me."

My head snapped back in surprise. "He told you?"

"Yeah. He said he wanted to, but he needed to give you some time to make up your mind without him being in the picture."

Adrianne split a glance between both of us. "Make up your mind about what?"

Nathan and I both stared at her.

"Ohhhhh." She turned back around and slouched down in her seat. "Well, this is awkward."

Nathan seemed as desperate to change the subject as I was. He looked over his shoulder at me. "How's your head? Is it starting to hurt yet?"

I looked up with surprise. "Not at all, actually."

He looked down at the odometer. "That's weird. I figured it would have started about ten miles ago."

A surprising thought exploded in my mind, and the puzzle pieces swirled and snapped together.

My new instant ability to heal.

Being able to see Warren's soul.

Detecting angels even though they weren't visible.

The reason why the spirit world was suddenly so interested in me.

The absence of my migraines…

Warren hadn't completely left me at all.

"Oh my God."

Adrianne turned around in her seat again at the sound of alarm in my voice. "What is it?" she asked.

I clamped my hand over my mouth to prevent myself from blurting it out.

I'm pregnant.

THANK YOU FOR READING!

⭐⭐⭐⭐⭐

Please consider leaving a review on Amazon!
Reviews help indie authors like me find new readers
and get advertising. If you enjoyed this book, please tell
your friends!

The third novel in
The Soul Summoner Series
is coming soon!

In the meantime, there's a FREE Book waiting for you at
www.thesoulsummoner.com/detective

THE DETECTIVE
A Nathan McNamara Story

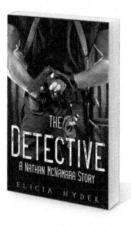

Book 1 - The Soul Summoner
Book 2 - The Siren

Standalone Novella - The Detective
FREE at www.EliciaHyder.com

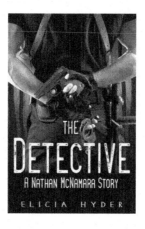

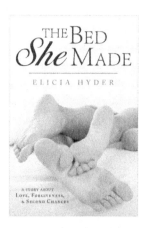

The Bed She Made

2015 Watty Award Winner for Best New Adult Romance

To Be Her First

The Young Adult Prequel to The Bed She Made

CPSIA information can be obtained
at www.ICGtesting.com
Printed in the USA
LVOW13s2329120417

530645LV00007B/88/P

9 780996 448383